❦ CRITICAL PRAISE FOR TAFFY CANNON ❦

"Taffy Cannon, I predict, shortly will be recognized as one of the genre's heavy hitters.... Cannon is a gifted writer, adept at plot and people, making her debut an event that readers everywhere should cheer.... A gifted entertainer with a unique vision."

—San Diego *Union–Tribune*

"Cannon's first Nan Robinson thriller [*A Pocketful of Karma*] will leave readers eager for a sequel.... Cannon's skeptical heroine and her elusive villain stake out the wilds of L.A. in an auspiciously flavorsome foray."

—*Publishers Weekly*

"This very good first mystery is definitely worth acquiring.... A well-told, compassionate tale with an underlying theme of accepting responsibility."

—The Poisoned Pen *Booknews*

"*Tangled Roots* is tense, entertaining, and satisfyingly thorough."

—*Library Journal*

"Cannon excels at capturing the flavor of her Southern California settings, as well as at creating complex, fascinating characters and intriguing stories.... Her smooth, clear prose, wry sense of humor and keen insight make her a new mystery writer to watch."

—Grounds for Murder *Newsletter*

ALSO BY TAFFY CANNON

Convictions: A Novel of the Sixties

Mississippi Treasure Hunt (for young adults)

THE NAN ROBINSON MYSTERY SERIES

A Pocketful of Karma

Tangled Roots

Class Reunions Are Murder

GUNS AND ROSES.

GUNS

AND

ROSES.

AN IRISH EYES TRAVEL MYSTERY
SET IN COLONIAL
WILLIAMSBURG.

by Taffy Cannon.

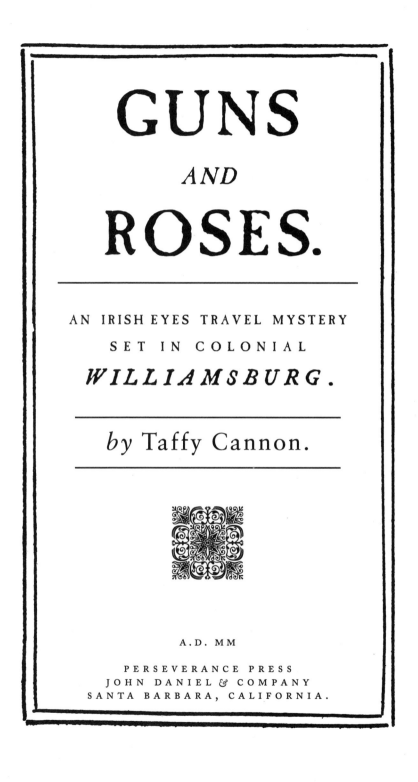

A.D. MM

PERSEVERANCE PRESS
JOHN DANIEL & COMPANY
SANTA BARBARA, CALIFORNIA.

A Perseverance Press Book
Published by John Daniel & Company
A division of Daniel & Daniel, Publishers, Inc.
Post Office Box 21922
Santa Barbara, California 93121
www.danielpublishing.com/perseverance

Book design by Eric Larson
Cover photo courtesy of the Colonial Williamsburg Foundation

LIBRARY OF CONGRESS CATALOGING-IN-PUBLICATION DATA
Cannon, Taffy.
    Guns and rose : and Irish eyes travel mystery set in colonial Williamsburg / by Taffy Cannon.
        p. cm.
    ISBN 1-880284-34-0 (alk. paper)
    PS3553.A5295G8 2000
    813'.54—dc21   99-042053

This book is for Melissa,
who brought me back to Williamsburg,

and for Bill,
who shares his gift for travel.

ACKNOWLEDGMENTS

IN a general sense, I am grateful to Thomas Jefferson who set so much in motion, to the Frenchman who drew the map, and to John D. Rockefeller, Jr., who was smart enough to listen to Rev. W.A.R. Goodwin and rich enough to make a difference in restoring Colonial Williamsburg.

More specifically, the guides and docents who know so much and share it so joyously seem to spring in limitless supply from the rich soil of Virginia. Thanks to all of you.

And very specifically, both Major James M. Yost of the Williamsburg Police Department and Danny L. McDaniel, Director of Security, Safety and Transportation Services for the Colonial Williamsburg Foundation, would like me to point out that the sorts of things depicted in this book solely happen in fiction. Botsforth Tavern exists only in my imagination.

Finally, I am indebted once again to Bill Kamenjarin.

GUNS AND ROSES.

❦ PROLOGUE ❦

IT WAS all over very quickly.

The figure on the bed lay still now, wonderfully still.

But wait, was that a finger twitching there? No, just a trick of the light. It was dimly lit here, but of course, that was part of the point.

Everything had not gone precisely according to plan, but things rarely do. What was important was the result, and this result was perfect.

Flexibility. That had been the key, even more than planning. Knowing when to move forward, when to draw back, when to change course.

And of course, when to kill.

❦ CHAPTER ONE ❦

BLANCHE WEDDINGTON went down with a shriek, a resounding thud, and a clattering crash that left the party in stunned silence.

Across the patio, Roxanne Prescott reacted instinctively. She spun toward the sound, evaluated the situation in a horrified moment, then sprinted past the startled men and women who stood frozen, holding champagne glasses and canapé plates. Roxanne knelt at the side of the fallen woman, now wailing loudly in pain.

"My ankle," Mrs. Weddington moaned. She had landed half-sitting and was supporting herself with her left hand, braced on the tile beside her. Her right leg, extending from beneath the hem of a long floral-printed skirt, showed no obvious signs of injury. The ankle in question was almost certainly her left, twisted beneath her ample body. The fallen tray of abandoned canapé plates and glasses that had caused the dreadful crash lay nearby, a single half-eaten cucumber sandwich resting unnoticed on Mrs. Weddington's lap. Roxanne picked up the sandwich, deposited it on the tray, and used both hands to help support the woman's weight.

"Oh my God!" Ralph Weddington, the injured woman's husband, squatted nearby, rubbing his hands ineffectually. He was a slight man with thick glasses and almost no hair. "Blanche, are you all right?"

Clearly not. Shifting her own weight slightly to continue supporting the woman, Roxanne lifted the torn skirt enough to see Mrs. Weddington's left ankle twisted at an appalling angle.

"Help me get off it," she sobbed softly.

Roxanne considered briefly, then provided enough support to allow the lady to move her rump off her ankle. Mrs. Weddington was now resting on her right hip.

A young waiter who'd been circling with an open champagne bottle stood gaping.

"Call the paramedics and get the manager," Roxanne ordered the waiter, who hesitated briefly, then fled. She turned to the injured woman. "What happened, Mrs. Weddington?"

Blanche Weddington shook her head. "I don't know," she wailed. "I slipped...."

As Roxanne patted the woman's hand, Ralph Weddington trembled helplessly. Roxanne looked around at the assembled members of her tour group. Some had only arrived within the hour and all wore expressions of shock and dismay.

"Did anybody see what happened?" Roxanne asked quietly. Keep things calm. Another instinctive reaction.

A dozen men and women murmured, but only Harriet Greene, a sprightly little senior from Chillicothe, Ohio, spoke. "She started to slip," Harriet announced, frowning, "and then she seemed to overbalance. I saw her grab for that little table, but by then she was halfway down." Harriet shook her head solemnly. "There was no way to reach her in time."

The hotel's owner-manager, an intense woman in her early forties, arrived moments before Roxanne heard the distant whine of an ambulance siren. Without moving, Roxanne explained what had happened.

"My husband will go to the hospital with her," the manager declared quickly, with a nod toward the graying but youthful man who had just materialized beside her. He smiled convivially, as if he'd hoped for an evening at the Emergency Room. The innkeepers were former D.C. corporate attorneys who had jettisoned legal practice to refurbish and run the Potomac Arms, a charmingly genteel small hotel dating from the early nineteenth century.

Once the paramedics bustled onto the patio, Roxanne felt a

strange sense of déjà vu as she filled them in and watched them load the injured woman onto a gurney. The essentials were the same as ever; only the location and the style of her uniform differed. It was eight months since Roxanne had last gone on patrol with the Austin Police Department, eight months since the night she called in the horrific "Officer down" and watched her partner die on the weather-beaten back porch of a run-down frame shack in south Austin.

She deliberately banished those memories, concentrating on the situation at hand. She debated going to the hospital, wondered briefly what Maureen would do, decided that so early in the tour her own responsibility probably lay with the majority still on their feet.

Once the ambulance left, the hotel manager briskly set about restoring gaiety to the Irish Eyes Travel group. She apologized in a vague and general way—there'd be no admissions of liability from anyone who'd ever practiced law—then began replenishing glasses from a fresh champagne bottle. Where Mrs. Weddington had fallen, the young waiter scooped up broken glasses and the other detritus of the toppled tray.

Roxanne knelt to investigate the accident site. A clear, viscous slick on the ground smelled like soapy violets. She pointed out the substance to the manager, who gamely knelt for her own examination, grimly recalculating liability.

Roxanne returned to her group. Conversation had resumed around the patio and most of the folks were now seated at small tables. They chattered excitedly about the upcoming trip, seventeen—now fifteen—strangers united to share a week of sight-seeing.

At six-thirty on a late April Saturday, the outdoor patio was still warm and balmy. They would spend tonight here in Alexandria, Virginia, jumping-off point for the "History and Gardens of Virginia Tour," which Roxanne had privately renamed "Guns and Roses." She had been looking forward to the trip for two months, though she'd never dreamed she'd be leading it solo. She was supposed to accompany and assist her Aunt Maureen, owner of Irish Eyes Travel, a Del Mar,

California, agency that specialized in "educational" tours for the well-heeled. Roxanne had envisioned her role strictly as backup: chatting up the guests, schlepping luggage, studying Maureen's techniques, absorbing the wonders of life as a tour guide.

Then, three days before Guns and Roses was slated to blast off, Maureen O'Malley awakened itching all over, with strange little bitelike bumps sprinkled around her body. An emergency visit to the dermatologist had produced a flabbergasting diagnosis that threw the future of the tour into doubt.

Chicken pox!

Roxanne had assured her itching aunt that she could manage the tour alone with no trouble whatsoever. "I've been chasing down bad guys for years," she had told Maureen breezily, "so how hard can it possibly be to chaperon a bunch of well-behaved adults?"

Famous last words.

At least, she thought, as she sat down to make the acquaintance of the Flanagan family, it was the kind of accident that could have happened no matter who was in charge.

"I understand you won the lottery," Roxanne said to the Flanagans, with a tinge of unconcealed envy. She herself had won a couple of Quick Picks over the years, and had known a juvenile officer who won ten grand, but the Flanagans were big-time.

"Seventeen million dollars," Patrick Flanagan announced expansively. Patrick was a good-looking, thirtyish Irishman with freckles and a glossy mop of thick black hair that gleamed in the fading light.

"Plus change," Merrily Flanagan added. She was in her late twenties, wearing a striped hot-pink shorts outfit and a lot of gold jewelry. Roxanne counted six rings, including a headlight diamond that had clearly been added later to the plain gold wedding band on Merrily's left hand. The rings looked like the sort of stuff you'd get with a handful of quarters from a gumball machine, except that the settings were expensive and—given the lottery—it was entirely possible that the stones were real.

"I told them I'd be happy to take the change," Bridget Flanagan said, with a self-conscious shake of her head. Patrick's mother seemed less comfortable in this setting than her son and his wife. Her hair was also black and had been sculpted into an upswept lacquered 'do that could probably deflect bullets. When she tossed her head, not a single hair moved independently. "But Patrick said he'd take me traveling instead."

"Merrily, we roll along," Merrily sang, slightly off-key. "That's where I got this new spelling for my name." This was, indeed, something Roxanne had wondered about, albeit fleetingly. "Used to be spelled M-e-r-i-l-e-e, but that didn't seem cheerful enough for our new life." She smiled merrily.

"Is this your first trip?" Roxanne asked. This small talk came more easily than she'd expected. Hard to realize she was actually being *paid* for this, and a good sight more than she'd ever made as a cop.

"Oh, no!" Merrily answered, with a slightly affected chortle and a wave of one beringed hand. "We've done Vegas twice, and Mom Flanagan wanted to do the old country, so we did Christmas in Ireland." She rolled her eyes skyward. "I guess it was pretty enough, but even with my furs I could never quite get warm."

Roxanne could just imagine what Merrily Flanagan's taste in furs might run to. She allowed herself a brief flash of Cruella De Vil. "Well, I know *that* wasn't an Irish Eyes trip, because my Aunt Maureen said this is the first time you've traveled with us."

"It was the agency's name that did it," Merrily confided, inserting a long, slender cigarette into a shiny holder and lighting it. It looked as if she were preparing to conduct an orchestra. "Mom always wanted to do historic Virginia, and when the travel agent told us about this tour and your place being named Irish Eyes, well, that was that."

"Well, we certain hope you all will enjoy yourselves," Roxanne told them expansively. "So. Did y'all quit your jobs when you found out you'd won?"

"You bet your sweet ass we did," Merrily answered.

Harriet Greene and Edna Stanton, the two elderly Ohioans, were quietly eavesdropping nearby. Harriet dropped a fork, startled.

Patrick Flanagan grinned. "I was working at this repair shop, for a guy who was, like, the world's worst boss. Marty Conner his name was, and everybody called him Genghis Khan-er." When he paused expectantly, Roxanne rewarded him with an insincere chuckle. "Anyways, me and Merrily, we find out we've won one night and we're out partying all night long. Comes morning, the two of us go dancing into the shop with the boom box blasting 'Take This Job and Shove It.' Old Genghis just could not *believe* it!"

"And then we went straight to the mall where *I* was working," Merrily went on. They'd clearly told this story often and never tired of it. "I was in Plus Sizes at Sears. Same thing, only we went in the main door of the store and played the song all the way back through to my department. All around us, people were asking what was happening and screaming and carrying on once they found out. It was like leading a parade."

They were joined now by Larry and Josie Vanguard, the tour's honeymooners. Josie was a longtime Irish Eyes client whose late husband had suffered a fatal coronary arguing with a construction boss at a development site in Temecula a year earlier. Irish Eyes Travel had booked Josie on the Caribbean gambling cruise where she had met Larry Vanguard.

"Aren't there people coming out of the woodwork from all over, with their hands out?" Josie asked the Flanagans. Josie had been a very wealthy widow, and there was enough empathy in her question to make Roxanne wonder a bit about Josie's new bridegroom.

"You bet," Patrick Flanagan told her, with a captivating grin. "But you know what? Folks've been saying no to me my whole life and I know *just* how to say it myself."

The hotel manager caught Roxanne's eye from the doorway and she excused herself. "My husband just called from the hospital," the manager told her. She did not look happy. "The ankle is definitely broken, and apparently she has a blood pressure problem as well. They're going to set the fracture and they want to keep her overnight."

Roxanne put on what an old boyfriend had called her cop face and thanked the manager. Her watch showed a far later time than she felt. Her body was still on west coast time, three hours earlier, but the time difference would allow her to visit the hospital before calling Maureen with the bad news.

When the Irish Eyes group moved to a restaurant across the street for some Colonial chow, Roxanne watched her charges settle into fairly predictable groups.

Three generations of a bicoastal family sat apart from the others. Barbara and Monica Dunwoody, a mother and daughter from La Jolla, had been in the small group who'd flown out from San Diego with Roxanne this morning. Monica was in her early twenties and her mother somewhere in her forties, one of those impossibly buffed California women who augment strenuous daily workouts with substantial investments in a plastic surgeon's Keogh plan. Roxanne suspected that people sometimes mistook Barbara and Monica for sisters, which would mortify the daughter as much as please her mom.

Barbara Dunwoody's aunt, however, would never be mistaken for anything but an old lady. Mignon Chesterton was from Birmingham, Alabama. Her accent was thick and her manner regal. In the brief period since Mrs. Chesterton had joined her younger relations, she had unblinkingly assumed command. It would be interesting to see how their group dynamic changed once Barbara's husband, Dave, joined the group in Richmond on Tuesday.

The Flanagans and Vanguards had stayed together, and when Roxanne heard the lottery story beginning again, she joined a more loosely structured group that had pushed together two tables and was already chattering eagerly away about the coming day's itinerary. This group included the Ohio ladies, Harriet Greene and Edna Stanton, and a recently retired couple from Grand Rapids, Dick and Olive Forrester. It also included the tour group's only child, Heather Tichener, a precocious ten-year-old traveling with her grandmother, Evelyn. The Ticheners had provided a wonderfully infectious enthusiasm on the plane ride across the country.

Already the hapless Blanche Weddington was practically forgotten.

❦

Maureen O'Malley was naked in her bedroom, grimly applying calamine lotion, when the phone rang.

She had hoped the worst of it was behind her, but no such luck. Today was the most horrendous of all, an agonizing over-all itching that seemed to emanate from her very bones. The doctor had warned her that adults with chicken pox suffered more than children, but this was an appalling understatement. She kept hopping in and out of cool, gloppy baths full of colloidal oatmeal powder, finding scant comfort, wondering each time why she couldn't just dump a five-pound canister of Quaker Oats into the tub and be done with it.

Chicken pox was a ridiculous experience for a sixty-two-year-old woman.

She was still running a fever, and had been mentally reviewing news stories from recent years about children who had died or undergone multiple amputations as a result of chicken pox complications. She pictured her own obituary: LOCAL TRAVEL AGENT ITCHES TO DEATH.

Somehow Maureen had avoided childhood infection, and she'd never had children of her own. She had finally traced her exposure to a barbecue with friends whose grandchildren were visiting. The kids, her friends had assured her cheerily two days ago, were all better now. The wretched little brats.

So Roxanne's report of Blanche Weddington's accident came as an almost welcome diversion, and Maureen felt herself slipping automatically into business mode. "They have trip insurance, so if they want to go home, they're covered for their costs and we don't need to worry about reimbursing them."

"I don't think they *want* to," Roxanne replied, "or at least *he* doesn't. He seems kind of wistful, but henpecked, and I don't think she's one to suffer in silence. But the ankle is broken in three places and there's no way she can go tromping around with the rest of us."

"Then let's spring her from the hospital and get them back to wherever they want to go," Maureen decided. "She told me they live half the year in Naples, Florida, and go back for summers in Detroit. He's a retired auto executive. Either place, they'll be out of your hair and the insurance should pay up without any problems."

"I don't think she can travel right away. And we're scheduled to pull out of here first thing in the morning."

Maureen shrugged, which set a particularly bothersome pock on her right shoulder to itching again. She twitched in irritation, trying to ignore her absurd reflection in the mirrored wardrobe doors of her bedroom. She looked like some kind of scrawny plucked bird basted haphazardly with Pepto-Bismol.

"We'll get the hotel to comp his room for however long it takes, and I'll set up their plane tickets," Maureen told her niece. "Now, I know the Weddingtons weren't traveling with any of our other people, so we don't have to worry about that. Had they had a chance to bond with anybody yet?"

"Not really," Roxanne answered without hesitation. "They were talking to the Forresters, the other folks from Michigan. But it couldn't have been more than superficial getting-to-know-yous. The Weddingtons hadn't even been here an hour when she fell."

"Sheesh. They'll be mad as hell once it hits them. Dammit anyway!" Maureen took a deep breath, which hurt. Was she getting pocks in her lungs?

"It'll be fine," Roxanne reassured, "and I'm sorry to bother you."

"I may have a kiddie disease, but I'm still running this business," Maureen retorted irritably. "Your job now is to get a good night's sleep and keep smiling."

"I'm so cheerful my cheek muscles hurt," Roxanne told her. "But relax, Maureen. Something was bound to go wrong sometime on this trip and now it's over with."

Maureen swallowed a snappy comeback as a cluster of

pocks in the center of her back began acting up. She'd *never* be able to reach them. She wished she could remember what she'd done with the ivory back-scratcher she had brought home from an early trip to Africa, back when ivory was an interesting natural material and not a political issue.

She got the necessary phone numbers from Roxanne and began running another oatmeal bath. It provided little comfort to realize that nobody would know that the efficient businesswoman on the other end of the line was almost totally immersed in gruel.

❦

Roxanne decided to wash her hair before going to bed so she could slip out to the hospital again first thing in the morning. She stepped into the shower and just let the warm water pour over her for a few wonderfully relieving moments. Then she opened the little bottle of complimentary shampoo and stopped cold.

It smelled like soapy violets.

Exactly like the slippery patch where Blanche Weddington had fallen on the patio.

❦ CHAPTER TWO ❦

"GEORGE WASHINGTON *never* had false teeth made out of wood."

The docent's voice was patient, her Virginia accent soft and cultured. She wore a crisp khaki skirt, an elegant floral scarf, and a mildly pained expression. This was obviously a question she'd tired of years ago.

"His teeth were made of ivory, for the most part," she went on, "occasionally using animal teeth and even incorporating a few of his own teeth that had fallen out."

Now *there* was an appealing image. Roxanne shifted her weight, half-consciously rubbing the tip of her tongue along the inside of her own teeth. This was a whole lot more than she'd ever wanted to know about George Washington's dental problems.

"Are they in the museum here?" The question came from Ohio septuagenarian Edna Stanton, whose own pearly choppers were secured by modern technology's finest adhesives.

"No, ma'am. They're in the DAR Museum in Washington," the docent answered firmly. "Around the grounds here at Mount Vernon, you'll notice quite a lot of walnut trees. President Washington was *very* fond of walnuts and we believe he used to crack them open with his teeth. Which would help explain *why* he needed dentures in the first place."

She smiled and ushered them indoors, where another docent explained that the decidedly garish green on the walls of Mount Vernon's largest room was actually George Washington's favorite color. Roxanne wondered idly if he'd been color-blind. He'd definitely been upwardly mobile. The pine woodwork inside was painted to resemble mahogany in a process called "graining" that wouldn't fool a cross-eyed beaver.

"Health department wouldn't like *that!*" Dick Forrester noted jovially, as the docent explained that the Washingtons—who fed and housed some four hundred–odd guests a year at Mount Vernon—served meals on boards laid over sawhorses. As the retired owner of a chain of steak houses across northern Michigan, Forrester was probably no stranger to health code violations. His wife, Olive, plump and cheerful, nodded agreeably.

They had left the hotel only slightly behind schedule after breakfast this morning, giving the Irish Eyes tourists a chance for a brief walk through Alexandria's Old Town while Roxanne visited the hospital. Blanche Weddington was in reasonably good spirits, resigned to canceling the trip. Maureen had already booked the Weddingtons on an afternoon flight to Detroit, where their main set of doctors was located. Until this morning, it hadn't occurred to Roxanne that the wealthy elderly with multiple residences also maintained multiple medical teams.

As they left the mansion and walked toward the kitchen outbuildings, Roxanne joined Josie and Larry Vanguard, the honeymooners. The Vanguards were clearly two people who had been around, and yet they exhibited a sweet, dewy-eyed quality normally associated with those a third their age. Roxanne found their hand-holding and nuzzling rather charming. Their interests on the tour were evenly divided: he was guns, she was roses. As Josie Vanguard described an intense passion for tulips, Roxanne smiled genially. That cop smile was right useful in this new business.

🌱

Spread yourself around, Maureen had counseled. So when the group headed down toward Washington's tomb, Roxanne made a point of walking with Mignon Chesterton, the Alabama dowager.

"How are you doing this morning, Mrs. Chesterton?" Roxanne asked carefully. The idea of calling this Southern matriarch by her first name seemed an unconscionable breach of manners. She was so unabashedly Southern that Roxanne half expected her to start trilling "Dixie."

"Quite nicely, thank you." Mrs. Chesterton's tone was mildly patronizing, and a bit dismissive. If she felt annoyed that her niece and grandniece had sprinted on ahead, she certainly wasn't going to share her concerns with the help. She was wildly overdressed in a flowery, lace-collared dress with matching shoes, hat, and handbag. She even wore pristine white gloves. Her makeup looked as if it might crack and crumble if she smiled too suddenly, and her lavender-rinsed silver hair was styled in precise little ringlets.

"I think it's really terrific that you and your relatives are able to take this trip together," Roxanne said. *Be enthusiastic*, Maureen had told her. *Let them open up.* Roxanne matched her pace to Mrs. Chesterton's slow, deliberate stride.

Mrs. Chesterton shot a steely glance at Roxanne. "Family gatherings are always interesting, aren't they?"

Yes indeedy. Also interesting was the obsequious way her relentlessly sophisticated niece and grandniece fawned over her. Roxanne was not at all clear why Monica Dunwoody, in her early twenties, wasn't living on her own, working and/or going to school. So far, her moods seemed to vacillate between mild indifference and extreme ennui. She showed zero interest in either guns or roses.

"My aunt told me that your—is it nephew-in-law?" Mignon nodded curtly and Roxanne continued, "—that he's in the textile business." Maureen O'Malley made it her business to know the salient particulars of her clients' lives. On the west coast, Dave Dunwoody dealt mainly in Asian imports, but in the South he brokered specialty fabrics from America's own dwindling textile mills.

Mrs. Chesterton merely nodded again, and they made the rest of the trek in silence.

After some Ye Olde Colonial Lunche at the Mount Vernon

Inn, the group boarded the bus, and Irish Eyes Travel headed down the road toward Fredericksburg and the tour's maiden battlefield. Roxanne had been apprehensive about this stop, military history outside Texas not being one of her strong suits.

"Fredericksburg was a pretty little town that had the terrible misfortune to be located midway between Richmond and Washington, D.C., during the Civil War," Roxanne began cautiously as the bus pulled into the National Park Service Visitor Center. There were folks on this bus who had forgotten more about any single Civil War battle than she knew about the entire war. And sure enough, once they headed into the battlefields themselves, Dick Forrester took command of the guide chores.

With a jocular reference to himself as the "rooster in the hen house," Dick first made sure everybody understood he was a World War II vet, and interrupted Larry Vanguard—busily chewing on his bride's ear—long enough to determine that the younger man had been in Korea. Patrick Flanagan, the lottery winner, had never served at all, but Dick was forgiving. These days, he implied, there weren't nearly enough wars.

The group went first to Chatham Hall, which had been commandeered, then used and abused by the Yankee army. The place had an abandoned, half-neglected feel to it.

Inside, ten-year-old Heather Tichener searched for traces of Clara Barton, who had labored long and hard over the endless stream of battlefield casualties brought to the mansion. At one point, she and Walt Whitman had simultaneously performed surgery in a room where George Washington had once slept and Abraham Lincoln had twice been entertained, an astonishing collection of experiences for a single set of walls.

From Chatham, the bus drove through the town of Fredericksburg, past the crowded Confederate cemetery and a life-sized painted replica of Robert E. Lee—reduced in one final and definitive humiliation to holding the lunch specials board at a local restaurant—and then headed into the woods.

Here, in actual battlefield territory, a routine was quickly established: Dick Forrester would explain strategic maneuvers as everybody repeatedly exited the bus to tromp around. The woods were a bright and vivid April green, wonderfully still except for the sounds of woodland creatures and the whispers of Yankee and Confederate ghosts. All along the way, they passed grassed-over trenches, part of the five remaining miles of breastworks dug by slaves and soldiers under the direction of General Lee.

But by the final stops on the Fredericksburg segment of the Guns and Roses tour, not everybody even bothered to get off. The Flanagans, for instance, found seats at the far back of the bus and appeared to be passing around a flask.

What on earth, Roxanne wondered, were they doing on this tour?

❧

From Fredericksburg, the Irish Eyes bus headed on to Charlottesville and the second night's lodgings. Fifteen passengers had spread out on a bus with seats for thirty, and Roxanne sat up by the driver, watching in amazement as the verdant Virginia countryside whizzed past.

This was gorgeous territory, far more lush than any place Roxanne had ever lived. Her beloved Texas Hill Country had its glorious moments in spring, but browned out quickly once summer settled in. And southern California—well, for all the water they pumped into it, the place was still basically a desert.

The bus driver was an easygoing fellow in his late thirties who'd be with the tour until they reached Williamsburg. Maureen had used Jerry MacKinnon before and swore that he'd make Roxanne's work effortless, but she hadn't mentioned that he was an insufferable flirt. Maybe he wasn't with Maureen, twice Roxanne's age.

"Seems like a pretty good group," Jerry MacKinnon pronounced with an authoritative nod, careful to keep his voice pitched low. "No wheelchairs, no walkers, everybody seems healthy enough. Heck, you've even got Mr. Rotary there doing the guide chores. Several guys, too—that's not always the case. The kid helps, too."

"How?"

Jerry shrugged as he pulled into the passing lane and hit the gas. "Spreads out the demographics. Sometimes when you get a group of just older women, it gets—I don't know, kind of fussy. Like being at the sorority's fiftieth reunion or something. But this group, it's more a stew." He turned his head and grinned. "An Irish stew, eh? Irish Eyes?"

"Uh-huh," Roxanne replied diffidently. "You're speeding, you know. Nine miles over the limit."

Jerry shrugged again. "Don't see any cops."

"There's one right here," she told him flatly. "On leave. I've written a lot of tickets for speeding buses, too. I was first on the scene once when a school bus took an exit ramp too fast and rolled. It was…well, let's just say it was pretty bad." The stuff of nightmares, actually, four children dead in the wreck and dozens more seriously injured. For months afterward, Roxanne's dreams were filled with high-pitched screaming and oceans of bright young blood. "So let's keep it to the limit, okay?"

"Sure thing, Officer." Jerry MacKinnon lifted his foot off the accelerator and carefully signaled his return to the slow lane. He shook his head. "Wouldn't have taken you for a cop. How'd you end up *here?*"

"The luck of the Irish," she told him with a crooked grin.

❦

Nicholson Plantation literally took Roxanne's breath away.

As the bus drove up the long, curved driveway in the country outside of Charlottesville, the plantation spread out before them like a color plate from one of Maureen's coffee-table travel books: a white mansion with graceful two-story white pillars, pale yellow shutters, a full-length front gallery, and vast emerald lawns.

The grounds were ablaze with flowers. Flowers were something that Roxanne had been frantically cramming about this past month, an area where she was hopelessly ignorant. Maureen had assured her that travelers on a trip like this one tended to be amateur experts who fully expected to know more than the guide and would cheerfully flaunt their horticultural knowledge to each other.

But Roxanne did know enough to recognize azaleas and rhododendrons blooming profusely across the front of the plantation home, edged by beds of tulips and daffodils. Other flower beds were replete with gazebos, trellises, and arbors—structures she would not have been able to differentiate a month ago—and beyond the garden lay a cluster of small white cottages. The entire place was surrounded by dense woods, a forest painted in varying shades of pale springtime green, accented by tall dark pines. Lacy dogwood and redbud decorated the forest's edge. Behind her in the bus, Roxanne could hear her charges oohing and aahing.

A lively woman on the sunset side of sixty bounced down the front path to greet them, accompanied by a big shaggy white dog who might have been fashioned from industrial mops. Roxanne stepped down to meet her.

"I'm Laura Freeman," she announced, offering a delicate hand, "and you must be Roxanne. Welcome to Charlottesville, my dear, and to Nicholson Plantation."

As Roxanne accepted the ladylike finger press, the dog enthusiastically buried his nose in her crotch.

"Snowball!" Laura chided gently. "Naughty, naughty!" The dog backed away, tail between his legs, looking utterly chagrined. "Go lie down, now." There was nothing resembling command in her tone, but Snowball backed off a dozen paces and lay down compliantly. Even the damn dogs were genteel here.

"Now," the plantation hostess continued, "let's get all of you settled into your rooms, and then I *do* hope y'all'll join me in the garden for some lemonade or sherry. Dinner will be at six-thirty. Cornish hens with our special home-grown herb dressing." She tucked her hand proudly—and proprietarily—through the crooked elbow of a silver-haired man in khaki pants and navy blazer who had followed her down from the house. "This is my husband, John. He's a professor of history at the University of Virginia."

As the tour group descended from the bus, Roxanne introduced them one by one to the Freemans. Everyone wore name tags, but she'd had no trouble keeping her charges straight from the very beginning, a job skill that transferred neatly from police work. All too often on the force it had been necessary to wade into an unfamiliar situation and sort out the players quickly. Matching fifteen memorized names to fairly obvious faces was almost too easy.

Laura Freeman consulted a clipboard as she announced room assignments. Irish Eyes Travel had booked the entire plantation for the following two nights, breakfasts and dinners included. Ground-floor bedrooms in the mansion would be occupied by the Ohio ladies, Edna Stanton and Harriet Greene, and by Mignon Chesterton. The four second-story guest bedrooms were assigned to Dick and Olive Forrester, Barbara and Monica Dunwoody, Josie and Larry Vanguard, and Evelyn and Heather Tichener.

The Flanagan trio were in one of the outlying cottages, as were Roxanne, and Jerry MacKinnon, the bus driver. The Flanagans required accommodations that could always be locked, presumably to guard the royal jewels. Merrily had changed a couple of her rings today and was wearing such outrageous earrings that if the stones were real, the jeweler who made them had probably wept at the abuse.

It rather pleased Roxanne to have a little distance from the rest of her group. She was starting to realize that time alone on this trip would be a rare and precious commodity. Jerry MacKinnon might be a chaser, but he probably had a wife and kids somewhere, and like so many men Roxanne had met, he'd cooled considerably once she showed her badge, even figuratively.

As Roxanne and Jerry unloaded the group's ridiculous array of luggage, a middle-aged black man in work clothes helped distribute it. He shook his head in wordless wonder at the seven—count 'em—pieces used by Patrick and Merrily Flanagan. Merrily's original design featured shiny white patent leather covered with hot-pink lightning bolts.

By the time the last bags were delivered and Roxanne had dumped her own suitcase—which suddenly seemed light enough to juggle—in her cottage, the group had already begun reassembling in the gazebo, guzzling sherry with giddy abandon.

The Dunwoody-Chesterton party appeared sans Monica. Barbara Dunwoody had changed into cream-colored slacks and a lightweight cotton sweater, probably hand-knit by natives on some oppressed island. Barbara's aunt, though not the sort who ever slipped into something more comfortable, *had* removed her hat and gloves and brought out a black filigree fan.

"An Irish toast for the Irish Eyes group," Professor Freeman suggested, holding his glass aloft. "May you be forty years in heaven before the devil knows you've died."

"To the health of your enemies' enemies," Patrick Flanagan toasted, raising his own glass. An interesting concept.

"May there be a generation of children on the children of your children," Bridget Flanagan added with a coy smirk.

"Mom!" Merrily Flanagan flushed angrily.

Enough already. Roxanne began clinking glasses with a neighbor and everyone gratefully joined in.

Dick Forrester, jazzed by his success as Fredericksburg battlefield guide, immediately plunged into the extensive details of his D-day experiences, and his return to Normandy for the fiftieth-anniversary commemoration. His wife, Olive, who'd probably heard the D-day stories a thousand times, wore a long-suffering half smile and kept her hand cupped tightly around her wineglass.

"How interesting," Harriet Greene commented acidly, when Dick stopped for air and a sherry refill. "My late husband was a paratrooper in the invasion. He could never bear to discuss the experience." Her tone might have shamed a more sensitive man into silence, but Dick blustered on until Evelyn Tichener bustled down the walk from the house, all aflutter.

Evelyn had changed into a puce silk warmup suit and fluffed up her hair. "I do hope you won't mind," she apologized hastily, "but Heather simply couldn't wait a moment longer to begin her little role-playing."

Moments later, Heather made a grand and timeless entrance, striking a pose beneath an arbor dripping pale lavender wisteria. Snowball, the dog, was at her heels.

"How kind of you to invite Felicity and myself to tea." Heather curtsied, holding up a large and lovely doll. Heather and the doll wore identical long pink Colonial dresses with dainty flower-sprigged aprons and lacy white caps. The effect in the late-afternoon garden was absolutely charming. Even the dog fit.

"Oh, you have Felicity!" Laura Freeman exclaimed, delighted. "May I see her?"

"Certainly. This is Mrs. Freeman," Heather told the doll with studied formality. It should have been too precious for words, but somehow it worked. "We're staying at her plantation tonight. Just a few more days till we get you back home to Williamsburg."

Even as unregenerate a tomboy as Roxanne had to admit that the doll was beautiful: delicate features, creamy complexion, cool green eyes, and thick, lustrous russet hair. Heather had explained the story of Felicity on the airplane from San Diego, that she was a character from 1774 Williamsburg, from the American Girls series of books for young readers. "This is the first time she's seen Williamsburg in two hundred years," Heather had announced very seriously, cradling the doll protectively in her arms. "She was quite afraid of the airplane, but I told her it was simply like riding in a carriage with wings."

Now Harriet Greene gave a little chuckle, her irritation with Dick Forrester forgotten. "She looks just like you, Roxanne."

"Except that my hair's never been that long. Also, I'm fresh out of lace bonnets," Roxanne answered lightly. There *was* a resemblance, at least in coloring, though Roxanne's hair was several shades darker, cut in short and casual curls with a tendency to frizz. The doll's nearly waist-length mane gleamed perfectly straight, tied at the nape of her neck.

"I have one you could borrow," Evelyn Tichener offered with a wry shake of her head. She was probably close to seventy, with a simple silver pageboy and an almost-trim figure. "Heather insisted that I make myself a Colonial costume, too, so we can skulk around Williamsburg together with absolute authenticity." The indulgent granny rolled her eyes.

"Did you make Heather's dress?" Roxanne wondered. Her own sewing was limited to the occasional emergency button.

"Not this one," Evelyn answered, "but I *did* make Heather her first Colonial dress, and I've done a few of Felicity's things, too."

Heather spoke again to her hostess, Laura Freeman. "I don't suppose there'll be any horses I can ride in Williamsburg," the girl said wistfully, "but I'm sure we can act out the Gunpowder Incident. Felicity discovered that Governor Dunmore was planning to remove the rebel colonists' gunpowder from the Magazine, and she spread the alarm. It's a very famous historical incident."

"Didn't you say this was a fictional character, dear?" Edna Stanton asked, frowning. Edna was a no-nonsense lady with a stout figure and a regrettably horsey face.

"Well, yes," Heather admitted, "but nobody knows who really sounded the alarm that night."

"Quite true, young lady," Professor Freeman agreed with a chipper grin. He seemed to have taken a head start on the sherry. "So why *shouldn't* it have been Felicity?"

And that, Roxanne decided, was sufficient blurring of fantasy and reality for just now. If a UVA history professor was willing to concede that a doll might have played an important role in the American Revolution, this conversation was clearly beyond *her* humble control. She quietly excused herself and went to call Maureen, noticing that the Vanguards had never shown up in the garden at all. At a guess, they were road-testing their four-poster up in the mansion.

It would have been nice to call California sprawled on her bed with a stiff belt of bourbon in hand, but the guest rooms had no phones. Authenticity came at a price, it seemed, though Maureen guaranteed ample modern plumbing at all locations. Roxanne headed toward the main house, where Laura had earlier pointed out a pay phone in a tiny glass-doored closet off the basement dining room.

The booth was occupied by Monica Dunwoody, who'd changed into skimpy white shorts and sat braced in what looked like a parody of a yoga posture, with one long, tanned leg propped high on the wall. Monica, who looked more cheerful and animated than she'd been since arrival, smiled, held up a finger to signal she'd be out shortly, and then turned her head away, laughing gaily into the phone.

Somehow it didn't look like a conversation likely to end quickly.

Roxanne wandered upstairs, admiring the mahogany furniture in the sumptuously renovated parlor. Scarlett O'Hara would have been proud to rip down these royal blue satin curtains and stitch up a new dress, and she could have used the lace sheers for some mighty provocative undergarments.

She paused for a moment to look at her reflection in the full-length gilt-edged mirror that hung at the base of the wide curved stairway. Her Irish Eyes Travel uniform was a distant cousin to her Austin Police Department one, but decidedly more flattering: tailored tan slacks, white blouse, forest-green jacket. Her gold-and-green metal Irish Eyes name tag was emblazoned with shamrocks. She ran her fingers through her hair, which was indeed starting to frizz in the afternoon humidity. With her red hair and dark blue eyes, she *looked* like somebody who ought to be working for an operation called Irish Eyes, a selling point she had used on Maureen O'Malley last Christmas when she had first approached her aunt for a job.

Roxanne crossed into a library filled with leather chairs and glass-encased bookshelves. The library was a curious hybrid, one part Dumas Malone to one part Danielle Steel. She checked her watch again, but just when she was about to give up and go back to her cottage, she saw Monica Dunwoody outside the open library window, meandering toward the group in the gazebo. Roxanne turned to go downstairs and make her call. Then she heard Barbara Dunwoody's voice and turned to see her looming before her daughter, white with fury.

"And just what have you been doing?" Barbara demanded.

Monica glared defiantly. "I'm sure that's no business of yours, Mother Dear."

"You've been talking to Nick Winfield."

"And what if I have?"

Roxanne couldn't help smiling. She'd been in this conversation herself as a girl. Probably every female in America had at one time or another. She considered leaving, then decided that knowing the hidden tensions in her group could only make her job easier.

"Believe it or not, Monica, your father and I have your best interests at heart."

Monica raised her eyes skyward and gave a shuddering sigh. "You have no *idea* what's best for me. And I'm sick and tired of hearing the two of you trash Nick. You haven't taken the time to know him, you *or* Dad."

Barbara's eyes narrowed and she placed her hands on her hips. "I know he has a criminal record, Monica. The boy is a convicted *thief.* He's been to *prison.* Let's not forget that you met him in *rehab*, for God's sake!"

"I was there myself, Mother Dear. As a patient, though you don't want to admit it."

"You made a few mistakes, darling, that's all." Mother Dear had evidently decided to go for appeasement. Roxanne could have told her it wouldn't work. "And your father and I simply want to protect you from making any further mistakes."

"Nick is *not* a mistake!" Monica looked like she wanted more than anything to slug her mother. Instead, she stepped back and smirked. "If his mother weren't Mexican, you wouldn't care."

Racism. Now *that* was an interesting interjection. Roxanne felt an unexpected twist in her gut, thought briefly of Frank Rodriguez and the innuendos after his death.

"If his mother were a United States senator I *still* wouldn't want you involved with him," Barbara shot back. "The boy has a criminal record and he's a drug addict."

"He's clean now."

"You have no way of knowing that."

"And you have no way of knowing that *I'm* clean, either. Do you, Mother Dear?" Monica taunted.

To her credit, Barbara opted for patience. "Monica, darling, you must believe we want what's best for you. That boy will only cause you heartbreak later."

Monica stamped her foot. "The *hell* with later. And the hell with you and with Dad and with old pruneface Aunt Mignon. You're ruining my life and I don't have to stand for it. As soon as I get back I'm opening my shop with Nick as my partner."

"Your father and I would love to help you start your boutique. But not if Nick Winfield is going to be involved. And that's that."

"It's prejudice, pure and simple," Monica shot back. "I know *just* how you feel about Mexicans. You can stop patronizing me. I'm not a child, Mother Dear. I'm twenty-three years old."

Barbara Dunwoody gave a silent, mirthless laugh. "You may be legally of age, but frankly, I haven't seen much evidence of maturity."

"Well, *fuck* maturity!" Monica hollered, definitively losing this mother-daughter round of Chicken. She turned on her heel and stalked off.

Barbara Dunwoody watched her daughter go, sighed deeply, and started up the steps of the mansion. With no time to escape, Roxanne ducked to the very back of the library and began flipping through a history book full of depressing photographs of manacled slaves. Upstairs somebody crossed a creaky floor and a shower began running. The Vanguards coming up for air, at a guess.

Not until she heard Barbara's bedroom door close upstairs did Roxanne go down to the basement and call Maureen to debrief her aunt on the events of the day. Afterward, she took the long way around the still-occupied gazebo to her cottage for a shower and a snort of bourbon before dinner.

Nicholson Plantation, she decided, as she sat on the tiny back deck of the cottage and watched a cardinal disappear into the almost impenetrable woods, might not be Monica

Dunwoody's idea of a perfect vacation spot. And when she herself had more experience with Irish Eyes Travel, it might not be her own.

No way around it, though, it was a mighty fine place for sipping whiskey near the end of a very long day.

❦

Patrick Flanagan lay naked in the steamy, rumpled sheets of the four-poster bed and ran the remote control through the TV channels twice. Merrily had been *hot* just now, even more than usual, and she was a girl of vigorous appetites. Patrick figured that as long as he had Merrily, he'd never need an exercise program.

Merrily was singing snippets from *Cabaret* in the shower, her soprano voice enthusiastic, if slightly off-key. Patrick found "Star Trek" and watched until she finished her shower and returned to the bedroom wearing wisps of black lace and a garter belt with black fishnet stockings. Merrily loved sexy lingerie and had a well-honed sense for what turned Patrick on.

She strutted across the room several times, tossing around clothes from various open bags, considering possible jewelry selections against her creamy breasts in the mirror at the foot of the bed. After a few minutes, she made a point of coming over to look for something on the bedside table and Patrick caught a blast of Opium. He languidly reached out and snared her around the waist, pulling her onto the bed.

"We'll miss dinner," Merrily murmured, tracing little circles on his chest with her perfect long nails. Today they were magenta.

"They'll feed us when we get there," Patrick assured her, carefully peeling away a wisp of black lace. Merrily arched her back happily and Patrick reached for the remote control to kill the TV.

As he did, he saw his wife's diamond-studded watch on the bedside table, noticed the time, and swiftly played Wherewould-I-be? Back in St. Louis on a gray afternoon, he'd be at the shop, looking at another hour, easy, of listening to old Genghis Khan-er bellow and whine.

He turned his attention back to the provocative lady in his bed, the one part of his life unchanged in any obvious ways by the lottery, except that Merrily now had an *incredibly* extensive collection of sexy lingerie.

Life, thought Patrick Flanagan, was good.

❦

Heather Tichener had never felt this happy in her entire life. She was so keyed up, she thought surely she would burst. They'd done so much already, all jumbled together in her mind. And with every passing hour, things just got better.

In two more days, she'd be in *Williamsburg!*

Don't expect too much, Mom had cautioned before she left, frowning the way she did when she thought Heather was getting a little too dramatic. *You don't want to create unreasonable expectations and disappoint yourself.*

As if anything could ever be less than perfect in this enchanted wonderland, this astonishing state, which had already overwhelmed her with its plantations and battlefields and thick green forests. Well, all right, maybe the battlefields *were* a little boring. Still, this morning she'd seen a piece of hardtack that was a hundred and forty years old (and still looked pretty untasty), and this afternoon she'd been in a room where *Clara Barton* had nursed wounded soldiers.

Despite her exhaustion, sleep didn't come immediately. But finally she did fall into slumber, secure in her bed beside Grandma, with Felicity tucked under a coverlet by the window, wearing her lace-trimmed night shift and lappet cap.

❦ CHAPTER THREE ❦

THE THING about clichés, Josie Vanguard thought blissfully, as she sipped orange juice in the Nicholson Plantation dining room, was that they so often were dead-on accurate.

Like the one about marrying first for love, then for money, and finally for fun.

Joe Bob Quinn had been for love, back in El Cajon when they were wild and passionate kids indulging a lust that had given Josie three children and endless heartache. She might have been able to live with his constant womanizing, had Joe Bob not knocked up his boss's daughter, and with typical survivalist instincts, left Josie to marry her.

Later, after more years of scrabbling than she cared to think about now, she had been secretary to Ronald McArthur, head of McArthur Construction, when his wife lost her prolonged and painful struggle with cancer. Josie had been poor long enough by then. Quite deliberately, she maneuvered her boss's dependency, emerging as Mrs. Ronald McArthur, to the horror of Ron's Rancho Santa Fe relatives. Seven years later, Ron had left her a wealthy, lonely, and sexually unfulfilled widow.

Larry Vanguard had turned that lonely widow into a playful girl again. Josie was wonderfully, deliciously in love with the man she had married three weeks ago in Las Vegas. She looked at him now across the table and marveled at her incredible luck. Larry was not particularly handsome, not a guy you'd notice right away in a group. His hair was thinning and his eyesight was so awful that he wore his glasses everywhere but in bed, where he maintained—quite correctly, quite *fantastically*—that he could operate solely by touch. So all right, he had a bit of a tummy, but he wasn't really fat, not any more than she herself was.

And my God, the sex! It had seemed, during the long years of assuring Ron that his impotence didn't matter in the slightest, that she might never get laid again. She had pretty well convinced herself that what she had enjoyed back with Joe Bob was some kind of fluke, that she honestly didn't care.

She had been wrong.

Josie knew she was richer than she had ever dreamed of being. And a tiny voice in the back of her mind never quite let her forget that Larry was not. But he made no attempt to present himself as other than what he was: a sometime salesman, easygoing business promoter, and happy-go-lucky gambler. And as far as she was concerned, that was quite enough. He had even offered to sign a prenuptial agreement, though she had ultimately decided not to bother. She didn't want to demean him.

Across from her Larry finished stirring cream and sugar into his coffee and winked as he lifted the cup to his lips. "An hour ago," he murmured softly, just for Josie. That was something else she loved about Larry, that he carried the pleasures of their bedroom across the threshold into their everyday life, reminding her at unexpected moments just how luscious this midlife love could be.

Larry sipped his coffee, then suddenly screwed up his face and spit the coffee back into the cup. "Arghh!"

Josie jumped, then leaned forward anxiously. "Honey, what on earth?"

Larry wiped his chin. "Salt," he announced grimly. "In the sugar bowl."

❦

Roxanne looked up, startled, from where she sat with Harriet Greene and Edna Stanton, plainspoken midwesterners she'd already grown fond of. To allow for an early start on a busy day of sight-seeing, breakfast was being served promptly at eight, and everyone but the Flanagans and Monica Dunwoody was already seated. Monica claimed she never ate breakfast, and the Flanagans had requested only coffee, delivered to their cottage on a silver tray.

Now Roxanne leapt to her feet, uncertain just what was required but instinctively aware that the tour guide had to Do Something. At the table where the Vanguards and Forresters sat, Josie had also jumped up, removing her husband's cup to the sideboard.

Scanning the scene, Roxanne noticed Olive Forrester emit a tiny gasp and draw her fingers to her mouth, then lean toward her husband, frowning, and touch his arm. Dick Forrester pulled back, expanded his already considerable bulk like some grumpy old bullfrog, and glowered at her. The cheerful restaurateur briefly vanished, then returned as Dick chuckled. "Like being back at the frat house," he said. Olive cringed, eyes downcast.

Roxanne gently took Larry's coffee cup from Josie and hastily sampled the sugar bowl. By cracky, it *was* filled with salt. "Just some silly mistake, I'm sure," she reassured the Vanguards lightly, removing the offending sugar bowl. On the sideboard sat the coffee pot and additional cups. She quickly poured Larry a new one.

By now everyone in the room knew what had happened, and salt was quickly discovered in three other sugar bowls: the Dunwoody-Chesterton table, the Flanagans' table from last night, and ironically, Roxanne's own.

It seemed pure chance that Larry had discovered it first. Mignon Chesterton had already stirred salt into her coffee but hadn't yet tasted it—perhaps there *was* a God—and her niece Barbara was waiting for herbal tea, very California. At Roxanne's table nobody'd noticed because Harriet and Edna's tea—plain old Lipton's, thank you very much—had not yet arrived. Roxanne herself added only the occasional ice cube to her own coffee.

Instinctively sensing trouble, Laura Freeman hustled out of the kitchen just in time to swoop away Mignon Chesterton's cup and replace it. "I simply can't *imagine* how such a thing could happen," Laura fussed. "Why, I filled those bowls myself just yesterday afternoon."

"There was sugar in this bowl last night." Josie Vanguard spoke up suddenly. "I had some decaf after dinner."

Larry took Josie's hand and gave a forgiving laugh. "Must be ghosts in the night. No harm done, in any case." He leaned toward the table where Heather Tichener clutched her orange juice, agog at the excitement. "Might I borrow a cup of sugar, young lady?"

"Why certainly, sir," Heather answered in her best Colonial-girl tones. She rose, handed him the sugar bowl, and curtsied with a giggle, an effect somewhat diminished by today's jeans and T-shirt.

And breakfast continued without further disruption.

❧

"My late husband would have really appreciated this place," Harriet Greene told Roxanne as they waited for the Garden Tour after visiting Monticello. Harriet was surprised by her own nostalgia. Bert was gone eleven years now and she missed him far less than she would ever have expected. "The way Thomas Jefferson never quite got it finished. My Bert was a real Mr. Fix-it and our house was always a work in progress." She had a sudden fleeting memory of the rec room back in Chillicothe thirty years earlier.

"And since he died, I don't think you've changed so much as a towel rack," Edna noted dryly. "Just imagine what Bert might have accomplished if he'd had a hundred slaves under his direction. Of course, it might have been awkward. Folks are just *so* peckish about slavery these days."

Roxanne chuckled appreciatively. She'd been waiting all day for a chance to talk to Olive Forrester alone. Now Dick Forrester was catnapping, propped against a tree trunk, his mouth hanging open like a cartoon character about to swallow a bumblebee. And their guide for the Garden Tour had arrived. Roxanne was delighted to see Olive briefly consider staying with Dick, then leave him napping. She matched her pace to

]34[

Olive's and made a noncommittal remark about the impromptu nap.

"Oh, Dick can fall asleep anywhere," Olive replied. "Just like Thomas Edison, he always says."

"I've never been much of a napper myself," Roxanne admitted. The guide was pointing out *Jeffersonia diphylla*, a thoroughly unremarkable plant in one of the extensive flower beds bordering the serpentine walk around the west lawn. Which hadn't, apparently, been a lawn at all during Jefferson's time, just a collection of tall grasses scythed once or twice each summer.

"You know," Roxanne went on, "I was wondering about something. This morning, when there was that business of the salt in the sugar bowls, I happened to notice...." She let her voice trail off discreetly.

Olive Forrester's plump face flushed and she clasped her hand tightly on her sturdy Coach shoulder bag. "Why, I, uh..." she stammered helplessly.

"I wondered if perhaps..." Once again Roxanne let the silence speak for her.

And this time Olive Forrester turned beet-red. "Dick likes his little practical jokes, that's all."

Terrific. Just what the group needed, a half-assed practical joker. It made sense, though, in a fourth-grade sort of way. "And you thought perhaps—"

"Only for a second," Olive answered hurriedly. "And of course I was mistaken. Dick would never dream of doing such a thing." She looked imploringly at Roxanne. "You won't say anything to Dick, surely. *Please* don't upset him, this trip is so very important to me." She gulped. "To us."

"Of course not," Roxanne agreed, far from happy to learn that Dick Forrester was the group's own Mr. Whoopee Cushion. And there was something else going on here, no question about it. Olive Forrester's protests were too frantic.

Was Mr. Hand Buzzer perhaps a batterer?

"He wouldn't have done it," Olive went on. Protesting too much again.

"Of course not," Roxanne agreed cheerfully, as the group

continued down into Jefferson's Grove, a forest area called
Elysium, or Paradise. Here Jefferson had cleared out—or
maybe just *planned* to clear out, the Monticello landscape re-
constructionists weren't entirely sure—the underbrush and low
branches. The effect was a natural cathedral.

But somehow she didn't feel soothed.

❦

Just what was she doing here, anyway?

The question lodged in Roxanne's mind as she drifted to
sleep on Monday night and was still stuck there when she
awoke at 6:30 Tuesday morning in her cottage at Nicholson
Plantation. Birds sang outside and sunlight glowed softly behind her drawn shades and lace curtains.

She stretched in the queen-sized bed, pulled the pink ruffled
sheet up to her chin, and swept her gaze aimlessly around the
well-furnished cottage. It was strange how the humble bed-
and-breakfast—once the mainstay of the adventurous but cost-
conscious traveler—had evolved. Today's B&B, according to
Maureen, was often an end destination, where two-career
couples with oodles of money and little free time could sneak
off and pretend to be on vacation. And God knows there was
nothing cheap about the modern B&B, which offered none of
the agreeable anonymity of a hotel; you had to be willing to
break bread with strangers and chat up the hosts.

Today the Irish Eyes group was headed for Richmond, their
last day and night before settling into Williamsburg for three
nights and four days of full-scale Colonial immersion.

Roxanne knew she would feel more secure once they were
off the road. She was exhausted by keeping track of these
wealthy tourists and their extravagant expectations, their pas-
sions for camellias and parrot tulips and rhododendrons, their
obsessions with specific periods of American military history—
and by constantly worrying that one of them would wander off
somewhere and get lost.

This was a far cry from the blend of freedom and regimen-
tation that constituted police work.

Fourth and final child, only daughter, in a family where law enforcement stretched back for three generations, Roxanne Prescott had grown up secure and loved in the Texas Hill Country town of Mecklenburg, twenty miles outside Austin. Her daddy, Sandy Prescott, had been the Mecklenburg chief of police for some fifteen years now, and Granddaddy Prescott had been a Texas Ranger like his father before him. Roxanne remembered how magical Granddaddy's badge and white dress Stetson had appeared to her impressionable young eyes, recalled the deep, sonorous twang with which Granddaddy told his amazing yarns. Like her older brothers, Roxanne could never get enough of those adventure tales, which came to assume almost mythic proportions.

Not so very far from the truth, it turned out, that part about "mythic." As a college criminology major, Roxanne had tracked down many of Granddaddy's tales. She learned that some were part of general Ranger lore, further discovered that Granddaddy hadn't even been *alive* for some of the adventures he claimed. Somehow the inconsistencies never seemed to matter much. Roxanne could never bring herself to ask him about it. He was too imposing and too special to her; it would have seemed like a personal attack. She had chosen instead to have him elaborate on the stories that weren't in the books, the ones that seemed genuinely to be part of his own Ranger experience. She would ask later about the other stories.

But now it was too late. Granddaddy Prescott was in a nursing home outside Mecklenburg, his memory gone. Two years ago, he had started getting fuzzy in the spring, around Easter. By Memorial Day he was forgetting people's names. By July Fourth he was getting into his car and driving, finding himself in places like Ozona and Lufkin and once even Hereford, up in Deaf Smith County in the Panhandle. Uncertain how he'd gotten there, he'd go to the sheriff's station, like an old fire horse, and call his son. The first couple of times, at close range, Granddaddy got home on his own. Then he started home from Lubbock and wound up in Las Vegas, and after that, Sandy Prescott flew out and drove him back. That brief but scary period culminated in a call from the Texas Ranger Hall of Fame in Waco.

Then, finally, reluctantly, police chief Sandy Prescott confiscated his father's car and keys, and a week later Granddaddy was in the locked wing of the nursing home outside Mecklenburg. There he sat vacant-eyed and docile, a heartbreaking husk of his former grandeur.

Granddaddy Prescott was one of the reasons that Roxanne had always wanted to be a cop.

She could not remember a time when she hadn't assumed it would happen, had never for a moment considered that being female might present a problem. Even Granddaddy, though he chuckled sometimes, hadn't come right out and said anything overtly discouraging. Girls *could* be cops by the time Roxanne was old enough to go on the force. They *were* cops. And if there wasn't always a red carpet rolled out for her, the challenges were manageable for someone who had grown up with brothers, unafraid of spiders or snakes, a crack shot from childhood.

Two of Roxanne's three older brothers were also cops, Ben a juvenile officer in Houston, Tom a detective in Austin. Both seemed to remain genuinely happy with their work. Roxanne, however, had grown increasingly discontented.

She wanted something else, something more, something different. Long before that awful day when Frank Rodriguez got shot, she had started thinking seriously about leaving. She knew she'd never make any decent money as a cop, at least not as an honest one. She was tired of working odd shifts that changed as soon as she got used to them.

She wanted out, without knowing where or what that meant.

In the aftermath of Frank's shooting, all the doubts had crystallized in a chain reaction so rapid that she found herself all but paralyzed.

Frank had been shot point-blank by a shotgun-wielding escapee from a small-town Oklahoma jail where he'd been tossed to sober up after being picked up blowing a .23 on Saturday night. What the Oklahomans didn't realize was that Jimmy Ray Otis was speeding and drinking to get away in both body and spirit from a bloodbath he had left behind in the Tennessee trailer park where his estranged wife had taken up residence with another man.

Nobody was likely ever to know how Jimmy Ray Otis got from Oklahoma to his sister's house in Austin. Neighbors hearing screams dialed 911, sending Roxanne and Frank Rodriguez at 8:30 on an August evening on what would be Frank's last call. Jimmy Ray himself could not explain. He died an hour after Frank did, by his own hand, cornered scarcely a mile away.

It would have been awful enough to lose a partner, to worry forever at the instinct that had led Frank to say he'd go around back after nobody answered their initial knock. Frank was senior to Roxanne, could just as easily have sent her instead. And she would have gone without hesitation. It was just part of the job.

What she hadn't expected was the backlash.

Suggestions that a woman and a minority man had somehow brought less to the situation than a couple of white guys would have. Implications of inadequacy. Grumblings about affirmative action. It was a whispering campaign for the most part, promulgated by a local right-wing radio talk show host who always referred to Frank as Francisco. It didn't help to hear friends reassure her that the radio bozo had a pea-sized brain barely as big as his pecker. Here she was, in the middle of a nightmare, beset by her own guilt, and some dimwit was using Frank's death to forward his own moronic agenda.

She hadn't wanted to give anyone the satisfaction of seeing her quit. And yet, as time passed, she began to wonder why she *shouldn't* just chuck it all, or at least take an extended leave. She had been a fine cop, after all.

It began to seem downright silly to stay just to prove she wasn't a quitter.

Then Maureen O'Malley swept through town in late December on one of her periodic grand tours, and things suddenly fell into place. Roxanne took her aunt to an Austin beer garden on an unseasonably warm winter afternoon and shamelessly pitched her for a job.

Rather to her surprise, Maureen immediately liked the idea of hiring her only niece.

"Great timing, Rox," Maureen responded enthusiastically. "Lois has been wanting to leave for months." Maureen had squinted and examined Roxanne from the tips of her red curls to the toes of her battered boots. "Lose the Western look, girl, and I can put your picture on the Irish Eyes brochure."

Once in Del Mar on the job, Roxanne quickly discovered that certain skills transferred easily from police work: organizational ability, thoroughness, attention to detail. As on the force, she dealt a lot with people through much of her work day.

The travel business had decided advantages over law enforcement. The people she encountered in the course of the average day were mostly cheerful and anticipatory, seeing Roxanne because they wanted to, and not because of some hideous trauma in their lives. Nobody was bleeding. Nobody was visibly armed. Folks on drugs mostly used Valium and Prozac, and they all had permanent addresses.

Best of all, nobody was hauling ass over some seven-foot fence that she'd have to scale in hot pursuit.

She had set about learning the business: mastering the computer, making reservations, issuing airline tickets. Meanwhile, all around her she felt a new kind of freedom. Southern California, it seemed, would take anyone at face value, and she deliberately didn't speak of her police background. She no longer felt any need to prove how tough she was.

Still, there were moments of occasional panic. Like right now. It was dawn again and she had fourteen people depending on her to get them to their next meal and their next souvenir shop and their next hotel and their next infusion of historical/botanical trivia.

And her primary backup was twenty-five hundred miles away, suffering from chicken pox.

❦ CHAPTER FOUR ❦

RAIN IS definitely a four-letter word in the travel industry.

When Roxanne finally opened her curtains at 7:00 on Tuesday morning, the earlier sunshine had already been obliterated by fast-moving gray clouds. When she got out of the shower at 7:20, it was drizzling outside, and by the time she reached the mansion's basement breakfast table at 7:55, a soft warm rain was falling steadily.

Damn!

Only sugar in the sugar bowls today, thank you Jesus. And the weather was supposed to be clearing in the east. Maybe today would be an easy one?

Or maybe not. Roxanne had barely cut into her cream cheese–stuffed French toast when bus driver Jerry MacKinnon beckoned to her from the outside doorway, looking highly peeved. The bus, he informed her grimly, had a flat tire.

Damn again!

Taking care of the problem held things up nearly two hours, what with the rain and Nicholson Plantation's remote location. While Jerry MacKinnon—assisted by former auto mechanic Patrick Flanagan, to the chagrin of his social-climbing female kin—dealt with the tire, their hostess Laura Freeman rose to the occasion beautifully and offered an impromptu talk on the Sally Hemings controversy.

Did Thomas Jefferson have a long-term affair with Sally Hemings, the comely teenaged slave girl who sailed for Paris as attendant to the daughters of the minister to France in 1784 and returned just a touch *enceinte?* Did she bear Jefferson several children, in fact, house servants like the other members of the Hemings slave family? Did he set those fair-skinned mulatto children free, as promised, by letting them quietly slip away into the night once they reached adulthood?

Or—was the whole business trumped up by a political opponent/journalist seeking scandal during the off-year election in 1802? And if that was the case, then why *did* Jefferson set Sally free when he died? But not sooner?

Roxanne listened to the discussion bemused, having regarded this particular question as definitively answered by DNA testing of numerous Jefferson and Hemings descendants. But the argument raged on.

Dick Forrester, speaking on behalf of scientific technology, offered a bewildering analysis of Y chromosome mutations, probability theory, and the various interrelationships among Monticello's residents. Josie Vanguard, for romantics everywhere, seized on the undisputed fact that Sally Hemings had been Martha Jefferson's half-sister, noting that the same qualities which attracted Jefferson to his wife might logically have also drawn him to her sibling.

Laura Freeman, however, came down firmly against the notion of Sally-as-slave-wife, and would not be budged. She argued that unless Jefferson himself were to be exhumed and tested—a most unlikely prospect—the results of any testing remained speculative, since Jefferson had left no legitimate male descendants.

In the end, nobody agreed on much of anything, but the discussion provided a wonderful distraction, rife with innuendo and titillating to the max. The Irish Eyes gang lapped it up.

Inquiring minds, after all, can never really rest.

❦

The Museum of the Confederacy had a definite point of view, and it was one that Mignon Chesterton felt wonderfully at home with.

Mignon's first visit to the museum had been a childhood train trip with her maternal grandparents. The Depression was in full swing then, and the exhibits in the Alabama Room, where they lingered longest, had seemed to almost shimmer in the glow of yesterday's dreams. Mignon's Grandmama had been born after the end of the conflict, but Grandpapa was older. He had never known his own daddy, killed at Gettysburg, but he vividly remembered the end of the war and the return of the survivors.

Now, nobody did.

People looked at history differently these days, it seemed. They lost sight of the real issues in their scurry to make everything multicultural, a term Mignon found appalling. You couldn't discuss history, after all, without dealing in conflict, and most conflicts produced at least one winner and at least one loser. Once you started mushing up the details to appease vocal minorities, it was far too easy to lose sight of the big picture altogether. Besides which, the folks doing the loudest squawking often seemed to be the most poorly informed.

Mignon hoped that nobody would spoil the Museum of the Confederacy visit by being argumentative or attempting to interject current racial issues. She firmly believed any museum should be taken on its own terms, and if one would be offended by those terms, one should stay home.

"Where do they *find* all this neat stuff?" Heather Tichener asked. The girl was thoroughly modern, yet seemed genuinely enthralled by history, in a way that none of Mignon's young relatives ever had.

"Donations, my dear." Mignon gestured at displays painstakingly arranged in glass cases. "These items have been handed down for generations, but you can see the ravages of time on many of them. Those moth holes in that lovely uniform jacket, for instance. Donating such items to this museum assures that they'll be properly cared for." And the museum's collection was probably growing at a rapid clip these days, with donations pouring in from contemporary families with no sense of their value.

"*Gross,*" Heather announced with a grimace, after reading the small print around the surgery kit used to amputate Stonewall Jackson's arm up at Fredericksburg.

Mignon tended to concur. She felt similarly queasy about the moth-eaten uniform neatly sliced mid-thigh where a Gettysburg battle surgeon had cut away the fabric from a Confederate general's fatal wound. But bloodshed was a part of war.

Wishing to avoid unpleasantness, Mignon elected to visit the flag collection in the basement while the others went through the slavery exhibits upstairs. And then, all too quickly, the visit was over. Barbara and Monica didn't mind, of course; they'd been restless throughout most of it. Mignon was increasingly concerned about them both. Monica, always flighty, seemed edgy and apprehensive about the impending reunion with her father. And Barbara—well, Barbara was trying too hard to be perky.

Mignon wondered again about what Barbara had told her— and about what her niece had only hinted at—after dinner last night. How much *veritas* had there been in the vino?

❦

It was 5:30 by the time they reached the historic Harrison Hotel in downtown Richmond. Roxanne swiftly assigned rooms and then headed for the sanctuary of her own. Tonight's dinner was open. Maureen promised that the group would split into amiable segments and head out on their own. For her part, Roxanne intended to soak in the tub for at least an hour, then find a good steak house and have a pound or two of prime beef.

Of course, it wasn't quite that simple.

❦

Bridget Flanagan was not about to admit to anyone that taking this trip was one of the more colossal mistakes of her life.

Her sole comfort was in knowing that she didn't have to worry about having wasted the money. Money was something she would never have to worry about again so long as Patrick took proper care of her, and she fully intended to see that he did.

It was all that snotty Edith Mason Wainwright's fault that Bridget was on this stupid trip in the first place. Old Edith had been one of Bridget's clients way back when the Flanagans first came to St. Louis so Mike—rest his soul—could join two cousins in a fledgling heating business. Bridget, a demon housekeeper, was to temporarily clean houses to help support the family during the transition. Nobody realized then that the cousins were such lousy businessmen that it would take a decade to get the fool business into the black.

A decade during which Bridget went to Mrs. Wainwright's enormous home three times a week, scrubbing floors and polishing silver and listening to her employer's endless reminiscences about Tidewater Virginia. "You really *must* visit the Tidewater, Bridget," Mrs. Wainwright would drawl in that molasses-thick accent. "It's God's country." As if a Southern vacation was an option for a family surviving on bologna and potatoes.

Mrs. Wainwright, a childless widow, was agoraphobic, a term Bridget learned years later from television. At the time she had seemed merely to be a very rich fruitcake who had everything delivered and was deathly afraid of stepping out of the big double doors of her seven-bedroom mansion. Twice a year, Mrs. Wainwright went by chauffeur-driven limousine to visit her family in Virginia. One of Bridget's favorite images was of this hideously proper old lady peeing into a bucket, or perhaps a chamber pot, in the back of the limo. It was impossible to imagine her relieving herself in some grimy gas station rest room.

Always, through those years, Bridget had told herself that one day she *would* visit Tidewater Virginia. She would pull up the circular drive leading to the Mason family homestead in a limo of her own, would alight and announce haughtily that she had come at the behest of her dear friend Edith Mason Wainwright. "The *Virginia* Masons," Mrs. Wainwright had always said, and Bridget bit her tongue to avoid countering with an observation about the St. Louis Flanagans. Mrs. Wainwright paid very well indeed.

Now Mrs. Wainwright was long dead, and Bridget had no idea whatsoever where to find her surviving relatives. The dream remained, however, and this tour had seemed to offer a means of fulfilling it.

She had never stopped to consider that the state of Virginia might be every bit as boring as old Mrs. Wainwright.

Patrick and Merrily hadn't said a single critical word, though it was obvious they were no more interested than Bridget in these run-down old buildings and dusty monuments to people and events she knew nothing about. None of them were even kept properly *clean*.

Still, Bridget had experienced worse. She would stick it out.

❦

Mignon Chesterton was terrifically annoyed with herself.

She'd intended to bring along the new issue of *Southern Living*, which arrived just before she flew to Washington, but she'd left the silly magazine on her kitchen table. Now she had at least two hours to wait for dinner, and nothing to read except *Pride and Prejudice* or *Sense and Sensibility*. Mignon always packed serious literary works when she traveled, and was invariably surprised to discover that she really wanted light escape.

Maybe the gift shop in the lobby would have something. She slipped back into her walking shoes and rode the elevator downstairs. The gift shop selection was limited, though, and as she examined the possible choices, she happened to glance out through the window into the lobby.

Why, what on earth was *he* up to? And who could that be with him?

She shook her head and turned back to the magazines. Undoubtedly it was none of her business.

❦

Evelyn Tichener's feet hurt.

Evelyn took regular walks around her neighborhood back home in Solana Beach, but she simply wasn't prepared for the extensive hoofing they'd been doing the past several days. What's more, ten-year-old Heather was apparently inexhaustible. Evelyn was looking forward to an evening of doing absolutely nothing.

She carried her train case into the bathroom and set it on the toilet seat. These old hotels were charming in their own way, but the bathrooms were certainly cramped. With a sigh, she unclicked the locks and lifted the lid.

The smell hit her just as she saw the bag. Lying atop her cosmetic case was a Monticello gift shop bag, the size they put postcards in.

But it wasn't flat.

It bulged.

And it bulged in a manner that corresponded precisely to the disgusting odor of dog doo-doo that came wafting out of the train case. The bag was folded neatly at the end. Evelyn watched her own hand reach out and carefully undo the folds, just long enough to see that her nose had not misled her.

This was simply too much. Evelyn slammed down the lid of the case and rushed back into the bedroom, where Heather was unpacking her own bags. "Please go get Roxanne," Evelyn ordered crisply. No need to get Heather worked up, too. "Her room is five-forty-two, just down the hall. Tell her that I need to see her immediately."

"Why?" Heather continued unpacking. She insisted on removing every item from every suitcase at every stop.

"Because I just had an unpleasant experience."

"What?"

Evelyn stuck out her lower lip and blew strongly enough to riffle her silver bangs. "I found a bag of dog poop in my train case. Now *go!*"

Heather, for once, was stunned into silence.

❦

Roxanne donned her cop face before following Heather back down the hall. The door to the Ticheners' room was ajar, and Evelyn was struggling to open a window that had been painted shut sometime around the Appomattox surrender. Various suitcases, garment bags, and carryalls were open around the room, showing evidence of hasty examination.

Evelyn was mildly hysterical.

"In there!" she told Roxanne, pointing toward the bathroom, waving her fingers frantically around her nostrils. "How on *earth* could such a thing *happen*...?"

But Roxanne was already in the bathroom, gingerly lifting the lid of Evelyn's sturdy molded train case, observing the odiferous Monticello gift bag atop a welter of bottles and tubes and containers. She used a tissue to lift the bag, determining that, by golly, it *did* seem to contain turds from a fairly large dog. She then shook the turds into the toilet and flushed. The odor lingered. She located a switch for the bathroom exhaust fan and checked the window well enough to determine that it was no more likely to open than the one in the bedroom.

Evelyn was sitting by the bedroom window looking woozy when Roxanne came out. Heather stood beside her, anxiously rubbing her grandmother's shoulder.

Roxanne scooped a handful of change out of her pocket. "Heather, why don't you run down to the soda machine at the end of the hall and get your grandma something to drink? Seven-Up maybe? Get something for yourself, too." She handed the girl an ice bucket off the dresser. "And you know what? We could use some ice, too."

"But I—"

"Let's don't argue," Roxanne told her mildly. Heather departed with no further fuss. "Now, Evelyn, maybe you ought to put your head between your knees for a moment."

Evelyn shook her head. "I'm all right," she said. "It was just such a *shock!*" Her color had improved markedly, so Roxanne didn't force the issue.

Heather, setting a land speed record, returned with two sodas and a half-full ice bucket. Roxanne poured the 7-Up over ice and handed it to Evelyn.

"When was the last time you had your train case open?" Roxanne asked.

"Oh goodness, let me think." Evelyn took a sip and furrowed her brow. "Before breakfast this morning. I put it outside our room with the rest of our bags."

Standard Irish Eyes procedure.

Then bus driver Jerry MacKinnon had collected it and brought it down to the front hall, also SOP. Because of the flat tire, Roxanne realized, all of the group's luggage had sat unattended for hours while everyone wandered about. Plenty of time to.... She had a grim thought. Plenty of time to plant lots of turds if one were so inclined and had access. Snowball, the plantation mutt, was of a size to produce plenty. She thought of her own suitcase, as yet unopened.

Appeasement first.

"This is absolutely appalling and I can't imagine how it happened," Roxanne began. "I am outraged, flabbergasted, distressed beyond belief...." She continued in the same vein for a good long while, a technique she'd learned from her mother. Overapologize sufficiently, and the aggrieved party will eventually feel compelled to reassure you that whatever happened wasn't really so awful after all. "I have a feeling," she concluded, "that perhaps there's some kind of problem going on among the staff at Nicholson Plantation...."

"You mean like a labor dispute?" Heather interjected.

Roxanne looked at the girl with heightened interest. Where did she get this stuff? It was clear from Evelyn's surprised expression that her grandmother had no idea.

"Perhaps," Roxanne said. She didn't want to think about the possibility that somebody in the Irish Eyes group might be responsible. Though she was willing to bet that practical joker Dick Forrester didn't have any dog dung in *his* bags. "Nothing in your train case seems to have been, um, dirtied. The bag looks to have been folded closed."

"It was," Evelyn said with a shudder. "I opened it myself."

Roxanne thought quickly. This news would sweep through her group even if nobody else had shit in their suitcases. But she wanted to keep the incident as low-key as possible.

"If you'd like," she offered, "I'll be happy to go through your train case and wash everything. Not that anything has anything actually *on* it, though, as I already mentioned."

"I couldn't ask you to do that," Evelyn said, in a tone that suggested Roxanne better hustle her butt into the bathroom and start scrubbing.

"Don't be silly," Roxanne told her, taking off her jacket, rolling up her sleeves, and moving back into the bathroom.

Should she go check on the others? If they came to her room, she wouldn't be there. Better to deal with the crisis she already knew about, she decided. She devoted the next fifteen minutes to lovingly bathing and patting dry every item in Evelyn Tichener's train case.

"Done," she announced finally, after wrapping the Monticello gift bag in the small plastic sack which had lined the bathroom trash can. She tucked the parcel in her jacket pocket.

In the bedroom, Heather was dressing her Felicity doll in a white nightgown.

"She's *very* tired," Heather announced. "This has been a difficult day for her. She doesn't care much for traveling."

Smart doll. "And how about you?" Roxanne asked. "Do you like traveling?"

Heather's whole face lit up. "Oh, *yes!* I absolutely adore it!"

"That's what we like to hear," Roxanne told her, on behalf of the entire travel industry. "Evelyn, how would you and Heather like to join me for dinner as my guests tonight?" With luck, they'd decline.

Evelyn slowly shook her head. "I don't know, I was thinking of just having a bowl of soup sent up, but maybe Heather…"

Not at all what Roxanne had anticipated, but she had offered. "Heather? What do you say we go out for dinner and let your grandma rest up a bit?"

"I'd absolutely love it," Heather told her, blue eyes glittering in anticipation. "Shall I dress up?"

Yipes. "Well, you could probably skip the Colonial costume. Casual should be fine. School clothes, say?"

"My school has uniforms," Heather responded wearily, "but I get the idea."

❦ CHAPTER FIVE ❦

DAVE DUNWOODY turned his key in the door, stuck his head inside the hotel room, and called out softly, "Honey, I'm home!" Barbara's suitcases were open, but the bedroom was empty.

"Dave!" Barbara rushed out of the bathroom, squealing in delight, and ran across the room to hug him. "I was afraid we wouldn't see you till after dinner!"

He took his wife in his arms and kissed her lightly. "Would I miss being with my best girls for some silly business dinner?" As Barbara started to answer he pressed one finger across her lips. "Now darling, don't answer too quickly. Not *did* I, but *would* I? My golly, girl, you've been *missed.*"

"So I see," she murmured, pressing herself into him.

"It's been a long time," he responded, gently pulling her blouse out of the waistband of her skirt. She responded by moving her lips into the hollow of his throat, nuzzling, brushing flutter-kisses up along his neck.

It was ten days since Dave had left home in La Jolla on this current trip, a journey that had taken him to San Francisco, New York, Paris, and finally back to Richmond, one of his three offices in the U.S. He'd been putting together a complicated import deal with some people he didn't trust entirely, and they had insisted on an unexpected meeting in Paris. Posturing, he considered it to be. Their fabrics all came out of the Middle East and their offices were in New York. But Dave could posture, too.

Barbara had been mighty annoyed when he called to tell her he'd be late meeting them for this trip because he had to go to France. But it wasn't, as he'd pointed out, as if she would be by herself. She'd probably have a better time with her Aunt Mignon if it were just the two of them for a while, anyway. Barbara had taken her mother's sudden death two years ago very hard, and she was just now starting to get over it. Mignon Chesterton was the last real tie to her Avondale girlhood in Birmingham, memories Dave knew were important and nourishing to his wife.

"And how much have you missed me?" she whispered now, rubbing her body gently into his, sliding a hand inside his jacket, around his back. Her fingers were strong and supple. Barbara had begun and abandoned a hundred different activities and hobbies in the twenty-four years of their marriage, but the only one Dave really cared about was the Oriental massage class she'd taken when they lived in San Francisco.

He nodded toward the connecting door, felt her shiver as he ran his fingers along the smooth flesh of her back. Damn, he'd been gone a long time. "Who's in there? Your aunt? And is the door locked from our side?"

"Monica," Barbara whispered back, unbuckling his belt with one hand, loosening his tie and unbuttoning his shirt with the other. Her breath was hot and heavy on his chest. "She's sulking. The door's locked on both sides." She moved her fingers slowly south from his waist and he felt the same incredible desire for her that had enticed him a quarter of a century ago. It really said something when you could go that long and still get the same pleasure out of making love to your wife.

"Aiiiiiieeee!"

The scream came from behind the connecting door.

Barbara and Dave broke apart in confusion, looked at each other.

"Monica?" he asked, startled, pulling himself together.

Barbara was already at the door, unbolting it, banging, calling out. "Monica, are you all right? Monica?"

She was leaning on the door when it flew open, throwing her

off-balance into the room. Monica managed to step out of her way, barely seemed to notice Dave.

"The most...dis*gust*ing...eeeyyuuuu..." Then Monica burst into tears and crumpled onto the floor.

A moment later, Dave noticed the smell.

❦

As Roxanne stepped out into the hall from the Ticheners' room, a loud male voice accosted her. "Hey! Are you Roxanne Prescott?"

No sanctuary here. "Yes?"

The man striding purposefully in her direction was fiftyish, fit, focused, and a little forbidding. Roxanne realized who he had to be just as he stepped forward with his hand extended. He did not look happy.

"Dave Dunwoody," the man announced. He wore the New South standard executive male uniform: navy blazer, gray slacks, white shirt, subdued tie, steel-framed glasses. But the tie was askew and one of his shirt buttons half-undone.

"Pleased to meet you," Roxanne told him easily, shaking his hand, noticing a distinct scent of Brut. With luck it would mask whatever odor the package in her jacket pocket was carrying. "I've been looking forward to meeting you."

Dave Dunwoody nodded briefly. People apparently were always looking forward to meeting him. "We have a problem," he declared ominously. "Is there somewhere we can talk?"

"My room's over here," Roxanne told him, pointing down the hall. He followed her without speaking until they were inside.

"My daughter has been subjected to an extremely unpleasant experience," Dunwoody announced. "Animal feces was put into her suitcase sometime today. What in-God's-name kind of tour are you people running here?"

The Dog Shit Special.

"Mr. Dunwoody, I'm terribly sorry to hear that," Roxanne assured him. "Please have a seat." Dave Dunwoody looked around briefly, then pulled out a wooden chair at the desk and sat. Roxanne remained standing, the bag in her pocket feeling almost radioactive. "There seems to have been some kind of problem at the bed-and-breakfast where we were staying, and I haven't had an opportunity yet to check back with the proprietors."

"You mean this happened to everybody?" he barked, captain of industry dressing down an errant deckhand.

"I don't know," Roxanne answered. "There was another similar incident that I'm aware of and I haven't yet spoken with the others."

She'd *have* to now, though, and the sooner the better.

"This is intolerable," Dave Dunwoody informed her.

"I couldn't agree more," Roxanne told him. Agreeably. "Where were the feces found?"

"In one of Monica's smaller bags."

"How did she happen to find it?"

He narrowed his eyes. "She opened the bag and was overwhelmed by a disgusting odor. All the clothing in that bag will have to be discarded."

The rich, being different from thee and me, apparently hadn't heard of laundering. And him in the textile business, too. "We'll certainly take care of any problems, Mr. Dunwoody. Believe me, I'm just as upset as you are about this incident, and I assure you that it is totally aberrant as far as Irish Eyes Travel is concerned. We'll find out what happened and appropriate steps will be taken, I guarantee it."

Like what? Cutting off Snowball's Alpo?

But he seemed satisfied. "I told my wife this had to be some kind of dreadful joke gone wrong."

"I don't find it funny, Mr. Dunwoody. Might I see the, um, evidence?"

"You'd have to enter the sewage system to do that, young lady. My wife disposed of it immediately."

Oh well. "Were the feces loose in Monica's bag?"

He shook his head. "In some kind of little paper sack."

"Were there any markings on the sack?"

"You'd have to ask my wife or daughter," he admitted.

"So you didn't actually see it yourself?"

Dave Dunwoody stood and glared. "Are you suggesting that the incident didn't occur? You know, we've paid quite a lot of money for this tour and for what's supposed to be intensive personalized attention. The security of my daughter's luggage —and, it sounds like, that of others as well—was violated. I want to know just exactly what kind of operation you people are running, and if I don't get some satisfactory responses, you'll be dealing with my attorney."

Who was certain to be long on personal charm.

Roxanne moved between the man and the door. Pompous windbag. She smiled ingratiatingly. "Mr. Dunwoody, I can assure you that nobody associated with Irish Eyes Travel had any involvement whatsoever in this appalling prank. Furthermore, we *will* investigate and do our very best to determine how such a thing could have happened. Now. Is Monica in her room? I'd like to speak with her."

"Monica is resting comfortably." He made it sound as if she'd survived a jumbo jet crash, or at least childbirth. "She has nothing further to add."

At that he walked around Roxanne, opened the door, and left her standing, mouth agape.

Once he was gone, Roxanne pulled the bagged sack from Evelyn Tichener's train case out of her pocket and stashed it on her closet shelf. Then she made a quick reconnaissance of her own mercifully unbothered suitcase and set off to visit the other tour members.

It didn't take long. She skipped the Dunwoody-Chesterton party, spread out over three rooms now that Big Daddy was on the scene. If there were additional surprises in their luggage, she'd hear about it soon enough.

She found Harriet Greene and Edna Stanton in their room. Harriet sat at the desk nibbling on a pen and writing postcards, while Edna paced around, reading aloud about restaurants from a guide to downtown Richmond. The two women had already opened all their bags uneventfully, but were intrigued to learn about the Snowball Special. Edna saw nothing sinister in the event, though Harriet had her doubts. Harriet, Roxanne suspected, would always have doubts. She was a crusty little thing.

Roxanne took several deep breaths before knocking at the Flanagan suite, where Bridget was napping in one room and Patrick and Merrily watching "Star Trek" in the other.

Merrily squealed in horror at the mere thought of having that icky stuff in her bags. But there was nothing amiss with any of the jillions of pieces of white patent leather luggage. Probably, Roxanne realized glumly, only because each and every one of them was locked. Still, it was interesting to get a fast glimpse into each bag as Merrily tentatively opened it. Clothing. More clothing. The kind of shoe wardrobe Imelda Marcos might have had if she shopped at Target. Tons of electric beauty accessories—hair curlers and face steamers and even a foot massage tank for Bridget's aching tootsies.

But no dog shit.

Only the Forresters and the Vanguards were left now, and nobody answered when Roxanne knocked at their respective doors. She trudged downstairs and located the two couples in a back booth of the bar. They were cheerful and expansive, with at least one round under their belts already. Roxanne envied them that.

Neither couple had totally unpacked, but so far they'd found no canine surprises. The men yukked it up, sending their wives upstairs with Roxanne to check the unopened bags.

"I guess they figure women have some special expertise in dealing with excretory affairs," Olive Forrester noted dryly. "And I suppose they're right at that. We go from diapers to pooper scoopers to incontinent pads, and these days sometimes all three at one time in the same family."

Josie Vanguard laughed. "The other day, I saw a woman in the supermarket who had both Ensure and Similac in her cart. The poor thing."

"Well, just 'cause I've changed plenty of diapers in my day doesn't mean I want to find some dog's business in my bags," Olive groused.

But she didn't, and Josie, who had expressed a preference for checking her bags privately, quickly returned to announce the Vanguard bags had been spared.

Now for the follow-up.

❦

Dick Forrester watched the women leave the bar and signaled the waitress for another round for himself and Larry Vanguard. Damn, this was turning into a fine trip, dog shit or no. It had been an incredible thrill to take over when they went through the Fredericksburg battlefield, and if everybody wasn't as interested as he might have liked—that Flanagan pup sprang immediately to mind—well, it was their own loss.

Dick loved history, always had.

He was fascinated by the history of his own home turf, northern Michigan, where lumber had influenced everything. Logging, paper, furniture. The family furniture business had petered out in Grand Rapids a generation ago, but Dick had quickly cottoned that folks would always want to eat. And in his neck of the woods, that meant meat and potatoes. Which he still thought would make a fine name for a restaurant, no matter what Olive said. "Meat and Potatoes." Nothing equivocal about that. And it would play well in northern Michigan, for sure. None of this salad bar crap.

Being retired was a challenge, but now Dick had the time and flexibility to do the kinds of travel he'd always dreamed of. Like Normandy for the fiftieth anniversary of D-day, an enormously moving experience. The bloodstained beaches where he had once felt so astonished to be alive had carried him back through time and brought him overwhelming sadness. The same sensation he had on any battlefield, but intensified a thousand times because this one was his own. Dick had not survived through bravery, he knew. It had been sheer and simple luck.

Beside him now, Larry Vanguard was strangely silent. Dick shook himself out of Normandy melancholy and turned to his drinking buddy. Not a guy he'd necessarily select out of a crowd, but okay. Also a bit slippery about just what it was he did, other than marry Josie. Olive was quite certain Larry Vanguard was a gold digger, and Dick had a feeling she might just be right.

"So tell me more about these 900-line phone calls," Dick suggested now. What was keeping the girls, anyway? "I always thought those things were just talking dirty."

"Much, much more," Vanguard assured him smoothly. "We can do all kinds of marketing through 900-lines, and the beauty of it is the simplicity. We offer gardening tips, nutrition, investment ideas. Even some popular culture. For instance, I've got some lines featuring Lancelot. Maybe you've heard of him?"

Dick had absolutely no idea what Vanguard was talking about. Lancelot had been one of King Arthur's knights, and not a very loyal one at that. "Doesn't ring a bell."

Vanguard shook his head. "No reason why you would know, actually. It's a generational thing. Lancelot's a rock star, a major, *major* star, only he got into a bit of trouble a while back and he's in jail right now."

"The murderer!" Now Dick remembered. Something about drugs and a dead thirteen-year-old girl in a Fort Worth hotel room.

Larry Vanguard gave a sad shake of the head. "Yes, that was unfortunate, that poor child dying. Although in fairness to Lancelot, there was a great deal of evidence that she looked at least eighteen and had already been in trouble with the authorities for a couple of years. Regardless, Lancelot is paying his debt to society."

"He get the death penalty?" Dick was trying to remember. One of his grandchildren had been upset about the Lancelot conviction, a sad commentary on contemporary morals.

"Life in prison," Vanguard answered, "which was a lucky break, frankly. In Texas they'd as soon fry you as say howdy. In any event, Lancelot is doing some powerful talks on our 900-lines—the horror of the tragedy, his abused childhood, what life was like as a megastar on the road, how he misses his music, et cetera. And of course his profits are all going to the girl's family."

Maybe so. Dick figured it was a safe assumption that Lancelot's generosity was dictated by some Son-of-Sam law. That before the dead girl's relatives saw any booty, Larry Vanguard would take a hefty slice off the top for operating expenses. And he'd be willing to bet his flagship restaurant that Vanguard had some dirty talking lines going, too.

❦

Roxanne returned to her own room, poured herself a bourbon, and called Nicholson Plantation. Laura Freeman, who'd probably danced a Virginia Reel when the Irish Eyes bus finally pulled out that morning, answered the phone with a sob in her voice. Dave Dunwoody had given her a jingle and a piece of his mind.

"He was rather…abusive," Laura sniffled. She was adamant that the Nicholson Plantation staff were falsely accused. "*Nobody* here would do such a thing. Why, the very idea! It is absolutely out of the question, Roxanne, and I'm stunned speechless that you might accuse me."

"No accusations, Laura, certainly not from me." In a way, Dave Dunwoody had greased the skids by playing bad cop. Not that it appeared to be much of an act in his case. Roxanne spoke soothingly. "What I'm trying to do is figure out why these two relatively harmless—but nonetheless extremely upsetting—things happened to our guests during our stay with you. Even if this was somehow aimed at you, that doesn't make it your fault. Maybe somebody's trying to get back at you for something. One of your current employees, or somebody who used to work for you, or an angry student of your husband's, whatever…" She wanted to keep the parameters broad enough so Laura would feel she could come clean, if there really were a problem at Nicholson Plantation.

Which Roxanne fervently hoped was the case, because otherwise there was a problem with the people on her tour and she did *not* want to have to deal with that possibility. Other people's problems were no longer her business.

But Laura couldn't come up with any explanation, and she sounded sincere, almost frantic. Roxanne decided to shower before calling Maureen in Del Mar, but she'd barely gotten wet when her own phone rang. Laura had wasted no time phoning in *her* side of the story.

Maureen read her the riot act. It would not do, her aunt pointed out sharply, to get a reputation among wealthy clients as a travel agency that packed poop surprises in the guests' luggage.

❦

Much as she loved her grandmother, Heather was *really* excited about going to dinner with Roxanne.

She wore her purple denim skirt and long-sleeved pink-and-lavender striped blouse, with her brown hair brushed till it gleamed and tied back in a purple satin ribbon. Roxanne took her to a steak house near the hotel and told her to order anything she wanted. After studying the menu for a long time, she decided on Surf 'n' Turf, which her parents would never let her order. For that matter, Heather had never been to a steak house at all because Mom didn't eat red meat. Roxanne didn't seem to worry about red meat, though; she ordered the Cattleman's porterhouse steak, very rare. Actually, it didn't even look *cooked.*

Roxanne told her she had nieces and nephews about Heather's age, and she asked lots of questions. She really seemed to pay attention, too, as Heather told her about soccer and softball, Girl Scouts, dance lessons, her fourth-grade studies, her favorite TV shows, her parents, and of course, Felicity and Williamsburg.

"Grandma gave me books about all the different American Girls characters," she explained, "but from the very beginning, Felicity was my favorite. I've read all the Felicity books three or four times."

"When did you get the doll?"

"For Christmas a year ago. Grandma actually *made* some of her clothes. She's a really good sewer. And since then, they've been giving me the other things that go with her. I have a corner of my room with just the Felicity furniture and stuff."

Dinner arrived then, and Heather worked her way enthusiastically through the entire meal, even though the broccoli was *way* overcooked. She even managed to make room for a slice of lemon meringue pie. They had three lemon trees at home in

Solana Beach. Maybe she could get Grandma to teach her how to make lemon meringue pie.

The dog poop had been disgusting, but this night was an unexpected treat. When they got back to the room, she loaned Roxanne her copy of *Meet Felicity* and the most recent American Girls catalogue.

Tomorrow, Williamsburg!

❦

Alone in her own room at last, Roxanne pulled on the old Big Bend T-shirt she slept in, double-locked her door, and propped herself up in bed briefly to flip through Heather's catalogue.

It was beautiful stuff, and incredibly pricey. Roxanne felt unaccountably homesick for her own barefoot Texas childhood, spent climbing trees and building forts with her brothers and the neighborhood boys. She fell asleep wondering what it would be like to have enough money to be able to pick up the phone and offhandedly order the complete Felicity ensemble for a cool grand.

❦

Shortly after 3:00 A.M., Roxanne's telephone rang. She answered, groggy and disoriented, after several rings.

And then she heard a gutteral voice give what could only be described as a fiendish chuckle.

❦ CHAPTER SIX ❦

THE CALLER laughed again.

"Hey!" Roxanne interrupted, sitting up abruptly, groping on her bedside table for the light switch, knocking the doll catalogue onto the floor in the process. "I think you've got the wrong number, partner."

But she was talking to a dial tone.

There'd be no getting back to sleep right away, however. The call had both startled and energized her. A downtown hotel in Richmond, Virginia, seemed an odd spot for folks to be making crank calls in the middle of the night. Had the caller really been trying to reach Roxanne Prescott? And why in the devil had the hotel operator put the call through at such an hour, anyway?

She angrily punched "0" to find out, sat through seven rings, and was then stunned to be put on hold. It was 3:07 according to the digital bedside clock. 3:08. 3:09. She fumed, wondering irritably if the operator was too busy to talk to Roxanne because she was putting through some other crank call.

The reason for the delay, however, turned out to be even worse. The hotel operator, who sounded extremely upset, had just been on the line with Dick Forrester. Immediately after fielding an irate call from Dave Dunwoody.

Somebody had been systematically calling all the members of the Irish Eyes group in the middle of the night—and laughing.

Laughing? This was decidedly weird, though certainly better than explicit sexual suggestions. But *laughing?*

Roxanne found out the operator's name was Estelle, apologized for Dave Dunwoody, got directions to the switchboard office, and told the woman that when she arrived in five minutes, she expected the night manager to be waiting for her. Stating such a definite plan provided a certain amount of momentum. Next she turned on all her lights and hastily dressed. A uniformed authority figure could quell all sorts of disturbances, she knew, and her Irish Eyes outfit was decidedly more appropriate than the Big Bend T-shirt.

It would help if she could bypass Dave Dunwoody, who might already be bearing down on her room like an out-of-control heat-seeking missile. She cautiously peeked into the hall before leaving her room, then raced down five flights of stairs. On the ground floor, she followed directions to the tucked-away Harrison Hotel switchboard.

Estelle was the only operator on duty at the moment, though the small room had space and equipment for at least two others. Roxanne introduced herself and focused on the young man in the ill-fitting brown sport coat who seemed, despite near-emaciation, to completely fill the tiny room. Surely no more than twenty-three, he was still slightly troubled by acne. He was a full-bore wreck—wringing his hands, pacing anxiously, giving off a sharp odor of nervous sweat.

"Ned Davenport," he announced, extending a sweaty palm. "I'm the night manager, ma'am, and I can assure you that this is *not* the way we run our hotel!" On he blathered, making it quite clear that nothing in such poor taste had ever happened at the Harrison Hotel before, although there *had* been some unpleasantness during a brief period of Yankee occupation in the 1860s.

"Well, regardless of past history, this has happened *now*," Roxanne told him, swallowing her irritation. "And according to what Estelle told me earlier, the only people affected are with my group. I don't like the idea that somebody is targeting my people and annoying them."

No need to tell this wet-eared dolt about the salt or the flat tire or the dog shit. Or Blanche Weddington's fall back in

Alexandria, which was starting to look more sinister with each passing hour.

Roxanne smiled conspiratorially at Estelle. "Now. First things first. Is there a procedure that allows you to block calls from going to a particular room?"

Estelle nodded helpfully. She was about the same age as several of the Irish Eyes travelers, minus the benefits of cosmetic surgery and unlimited funds. She looked old and tired, in a shapeless, faded blue floral print dress. "All they have to do is ask us to hold their calls. We'll set them up so that even any calls direct-dialed from outside will be routed right here instead."

Finally some good news.

"Then let's do that right this minute for my entire group," Roxanne told her. "At least we can assure that nobody will be bothered again before we leave in the morning. And maybe you could also do it for my room, at least until I leave this office."

"We were just about to do that very thing," Ned Davenport broke in, though it seemed clear that the thought had never occurred to him. "Estelle, here's a list of the rooms registered to Ms. Prescott's group." He seemed relieved to have something to do with the piece of paper he'd been awkwardly shifting from one hand to the other.

"I'll get right on it," Estelle told him perkily, punching numbers into her console. After just a few moments she looked up. "All done."

It was a start.

"Now *any* calls will automatically come down here?" Roxanne asked. "From inside *or* outside?"

Ned, who obviously didn't know, looked at Estelle, who nodded.

"Then please keep a record of any attempts to reach any of the members of my group," Roxanne told Estelle, "starting immediately and running until we check out after breakfast. Get as much information as you possibly can from each caller and make sure you reach *me* with the messages first."

"What should I do about the wake-up calls?" Estelle asked,

a tinge of concern in her voice. She seemed to take it personally that people had been abusing her phone system.

"You'd better make them for any of my people who asked," Roxanne decided. "Was anybody in our group already having their calls blocked?"

Estelle looked down the list. "This one, Stanton and Greene. They left a six A.M. call and said to turn off their phone till then. That was the only one, though. Not all these people called to complain just now, either."

More good news. Unless the recipients of the calls had suffered fatal coronaries and wouldn't be missed till they failed to show for breakfast.

No, Roxanne would have heard about that by now. Everybody except Bridget, Mignon, and Monica had roommates, and Dave had accounted for the latter two in his earlier tirade to Estelle. Hard to believe he'd barely been with the group for twelve hours.

"Who *did* you hear from?" Roxanne asked.

"This Mr. Dunwoody," Estelle reported with a definite shudder, "and Mr. Forrester. Just a minute, hon." A light was flashing on her machine and she pushed a button. "Operator," she said, rather tentatively. "Oh, just a moment, please, she's right here." Estelle pushed a button and pointed to a phone on the table. "Miz Prescott, it's a lady for you and she sounds upset."

Roxanne crossed her fingers and prayed it wasn't Bridget Flanagan.

It was Evelyn Tichener instead, reporting an experience similar to Roxanne's. She had been trying to direct-dial Roxanne's room, when her call was transferred down. Which showed, at least, that Estelle's re-routing machination had worked.

"I didn't want to make a fuss," Evelyn apologized, "and I don't want to wake up Heather, either." Evelyn spoke softly. "I feel rather silly because all the fellow did was giggle. But I simply *cannot* get back to sleep, and I felt you should know."

Roxanne apologized profusely, something she was getting altogether too good at. She decided not to suggest the tranquilizers she'd noticed in Evelyn's train case; the woman was probably already verging on overdose. "You said your caller giggled? Was it a man or a woman?"

"Why a man, I think. Isn't it always men who do this sort of thing?"

And teenagers of various sexes. "The voice was low?"

"Well, I guess so. I mean, I was *asleep* when the phone rang and just a little groggy."

Vivan los barbitúricos! "Did you happen to notice the time of the call?" Roxanne asked.

"Oh, I don't know, dear, maybe twenty minutes ago. I never thought to look at the clock, silly me. I was so *surprised*."

"Would you like me to bring you some tea?" Roxanne asked. It would give Ned Davenport something useful to do, assuming the guy knew how to boil water.

"Oh, no, dear, that's very sweet of you but I'm sure I'll be all right now. It's just been such a *difficult* day." Yup. "I've half a mind to just go right on home," Evelyn went on, "but Heather has her heart set on Williamsburg, and after all, that's why we made the trip in the first place. I simply couldn't bear to disappoint her."

"And you won't," Roxanne reassured. "You know, I wanted to tell you again just how much I enjoyed my dinner with Heather. She's truly a lovely child, Evelyn, and so very bright." It couldn't hurt to throw in a little unctuous praise, and it was true anyway. The girl was remarkably unspoiled despite her privileged background and occasional lapses into precocious world-weariness.

"Why, thank you, dear. We'll see you in the morning, then."

Roxanne hung up, feeling suddenly drained. She turned to Ned and Estelle.

"I know you can dial from room to room by using 'seven' first," Roxanne said, "and those calls won't go through any kind of central system. And you said there's also a way people can dial in directly from outside and reach guest rooms?"

"Certainly," Ned agreed eagerly. Better it be an Outside Force than some internal screwup on his watch. "The hotel's number, hit the pound button, then the room number."

"Is there any way to tell if a call is coming in that way?"

"No," Estelle answered sorrowfully. "It wouldn't even *get* to me if they hit the pound button right away. It would just sail right on by in the wires somewhere." Estelle shook her head, mystified by the technology. She'd probably been routing phone calls since PBX wallboards with plug-in cords.

"So the calls could as easily have come from outside the hotel as from inside," Roxanne summarized. Though the odds against an Outside Force seemed astronomical. For one thing, only the Irish Eyes group had reported being bothered, and the caller had known everybody's room numbers. Three possibilities, then: somebody from the hotel, somebody from the Irish Eyes group who'd paid close attention during check-in, or an outsider standing nearby at the same time. Roxanne had no particular memories of odd strangers lurking about during check-in, but she hadn't really been looking, either. She'd been racing through the procedure, thinking only of the blessed solitude that lay ahead. From now on, it seemed, she'd need to be on constant full alert.

"Undoubtedly," Ned told her, looking relieved. It had probably occurred to him by now that he'd have to explain all this to some superior in the morning, and an Outside Force sounded like just the ticket. Roxanne doubted that he had much future in hotel management. He'd probably be over his head inserting Lunch Special sheets into the restaurant menus.

She thought of something else. If anyone had tried to reach Harriet Greene and Edna Stanton by dialing their room, the call should have been rerouted to Estelle. "Did you get any hang-ups or wrong numbers around three o'clock?"

"Why yes, now that you mention it," Estelle answered. "I had a wrong number."

"Male or female?"

"Male, definitely."

"And what did he say?"

Estelle furrowed her brow. "I said, 'Good evening, Harrison Hotel,' and he just said, 'Oh, I must have the wrong number,' and hung up." She shrugged. "It happens all the time. Our number is close to the number for a pizzeria that the college students use a lot."

At 3:00 A.M.?

"This sounded like a college student?"

"Youngish, yes." Estelle considered. "Not Southern, though."

"Did he have some other kind of accent?"

The operator shook her head. "Not really."

A young male with no accent. Now *that* was a hot lead. Roxanne sighed. "Have you called the police yet?"

Ned Davenport blanched. "Why, no, I didn't see the point until after I'd spoken at greater length with you." He looked like he'd rather scrub toilets than call the cops. "They weren't exactly *obscene* calls, after all. More like somebody having a little joke?"

"I don't find it funny," Roxanne answered grimly. "This needs to be reported." *Needs* was probably an overstatement, but the cops might know of a pattern of similar harassment with other groups in transit. And it had to be against *some* local ordinance to harass people by phone, even if the offense was merely misdemeanor snickering.

Plus, it would simplify dealings with her various distressed charges if she could assure them that Richmond's Finest were on the case. "I'll stay here until they arrive, but I really think that the report should be filed by hotel management, Mr. Davenport. Also, I'd like for you to see to it that my group has some kind of private room for breakfast in the morning. My people are likely to still be rather upset."

"You betcha," Ned Davenport assured her with a sudden and entirely inappropriate grin. "I'll have the Jefferson Davis room made up special for y'all."

He seemed palpably relieved to have a request he *knew* he could fill.

❦

Maureen O'Malley paced and fumed.

And itched, of course. Itched and itched and itched and itched.

At first she had thought Roxanne was joking in this latest call, but she'd realized almost immediately that was too much to hope for. Roxanne could be plenty irreverent, but she wasn't the kind of person who woke you up at dawn and told outrageous stories just to raise your blood pressure.

"On the plus side," Roxanne went on, with that distinctive Texan twang, "they came up with a real doozy of a breakfast buffet. Enough food for a football fraternity, all set out in this little room with heavy red velvet curtains and a crystal chandelier the size of my car."

"The Jefferson Davis Room," Maureen replied automatically. She'd stayed with half a dozen groups at the Harrison Hotel over the years, a couple of times with group dinners in that very room. She could picture the opulent breakfast, too: one of those massive Southern meals with five kinds of meat that has everybody napping on the bus half an hour later. "How are the clients taking all this?"

"They're pretty skittish," Roxanne admitted reluctantly. Maureen could tell that it just killed her not to be in control. She got that from her daddy, the police chief. "And they're starting to get a little anxious about being around each other. I can't say that I really blame them much."

"Damn!" Maureen paused a moment. "And nothing like this has happened in Richmond hotels before?"

"Not that the night cops knew about," Roxanne told her, "but it's the kind of thing that hotels would want to keep quiet and the guys on patrol wouldn't necessarily know about anyway. That kind of incident would be handled by a different unit."

"Were you able to figure out the order the calls came in?"

"I tried to make a time line, but it was pretty much impossible. For one thing, most of the room clocks are off by a few minutes in one direction or another, and even though I keep telling everybody to synchronize their watches, those aren't necessarily accurate either. Plus, some people corrected their room clocks afterward. Dick Forrester claims to have actually called the time number to do it. And since they all say they were awakened by the ringing phone—just like I was, as far as that goes—nobody has anything external to pin it to. No Miracle Knife commercial on the late show or passing fire truck, nothing like that."

"The calls all came close together?" Maureen asked. She desperately wanted a cup of coffee, but she'd still been lying in bed suffering when the call came from Richmond.

"Uh-huh. About all I know for certain is that my call came after the ones to the Dunwoodys and the Forresters, because they were already complaining when I tried to call the switchboard. And I wasn't last, but I was close to the end."

"So you couldn't do anything to stop it," Maureen noted.

Roxanne gave a short, derisive *hmph*. "What could I do? Bang on doors? Take it from a cop, that's even scarier than the phone ringing in the middle of the night. I wouldn't even have called *you* this early, Maureen, except we leave for Williamsburg in ten minutes and God knows what'll happen next. Maybe the bus will blow up."

"It'll be fine, I'm sure," Maureen told her niece. Not that she expected Roxanne to believe the insincere reassurance. She didn't even sound convincing to herself.

Or to Roxanne, apparently. "I tell you, Maureen, this tour is just too strange for me. I thought I was *done* with police reports in the middle of the night."

"You're doing fine," Maureen soothed again, not entirely sure she meant it. Surely this nonsense would not be occurring if Maureen herself were escorting the tour.

Or would it? Was this something aimed at her, and at Irish Eyes Travel?

Maureen sometimes had to fight to keep her big mouth shut, but she generally managed to avoid offending people too badly, and she'd learned to be quick with an apology. She had never thought of herself as a person with enemies, though there were undoubtedly people who didn't like her much. That was fine, though, since there were people *she* didn't like much, either.

"The laughter part is what seems so odd to me," Roxanne went on. "Whoever made the calls never said a word. It was just all different kinds of laughter. Larry Vanguard heard somebody going, 'Hyuck, hyuck, hyuck.' Dick Forrester's caller said, 'Tee-hee-hee-hee.' So did Bridget Flanagan's. Patrick and Merrily had a giggler. Mignon Chesterton's caller 'Ho-ho-ho-ed' like a department store Santa. Monica Dunwoody's went, '*Ah-ha-ha-ha-ha.*' And Dave Dunwoody said he didn't really know, the caller just laughed, and what the hell difference did it make and what the fuck was the matter with this tour?" Roxanne sighed. "He had me there."

"You told me yesterday—was it just yesterday? Damn, it *was*—you thought maybe Dick Forrester put the salt in the sugar bowls. Does he seem like the kind of fellow who'd get his jollies from laughing at folks in the middle of the night?"

"Who knows? Work long enough as a cop, you find out everybody's got a kinky side. However, his wife swears that when the phone rang, *she* woke up first and had to nudge Dick—who was snoring, as she put it, to beat the band—awake to answer the call."

"A perfect alibi for a prankster," Maureen said, grimly. The odor of coffee-on-a-timer began to waft upstairs. Reason to live. Maybe.

"Maureen, this feels really *specific* to me," Roxanne said firmly. She was sounding more like a cop with every passing minute. "Like maybe it's aimed at you. Is there somebody who has it in for you? Or for Irish Eyes?"

"Kiddo, I'm not interesting enough to have enemies. Just a medium-boring California triple-divorcée with a mortgage and a business that I hadn't thought of as struggling until just this week."

"It might not be directed at you. But I'm having a hard time finding another reason for anybody to go to so much trouble. Fairly pointless trouble, at that."

"I hope you realize this can't go on."

"*I'm* the one who feels unable to go on," Roxanne snapped back. "I got three hours' sleep last night before the phone rang, and maybe another hour after I finished with the cops. Take this seriously, Maureen."

"I *am* taking it seriously, dammit!" Maureen looked at the calamine-encrusted sores on her arms and felt like sobbing. "I've had this business twenty-seven years, Roxanne. I'm sure I've made plenty of people plenty mad at one time or another. But not so they'd want retaliation. Now. Practical matters. How are you handling the luggage when you go to Williamsburg?"

"I've got that all set up. Only bellmen will handle our bags when we check out. Under my supervision at the hotel room end—which I need to get out and do right now—and under Jerry MacKinnon's supervision on the bus-loading end."

"Well, go tend my clients, then," Maureen told her. "I'd thank you for calling, but somehow I just can't get my heart into it."

She hung up the phone, wondering if she could just will herself to stop worrying about what was going on in Virginia. Of course she couldn't.

But neither could she think of anyone who would want to harm Irish Eyes Travel.

What in the devil was happening?

❦ CHAPTER SEVEN ❦

"FORWARD INTO the past!" Edna Stanton announced giddily as the bus pulled away from the Harrison Hotel.

"Williamsburg or bust!" Harriet Greene answered with an uncharacteristic twinkle.

Their cheeriness was not quite enough to lift an atmosphere that was becoming increasingly paranoid.

Roxanne desperately wanted to get this tour back on track. Through no doing of her own, it had shifted focus and direction into a perplexing pattern of harassment.

Richmond was only fifty-odd miles away from Williamsburg, an easy hour's drive along interstate so densely wooded that even the median was forested. Behind her in the bus, Roxanne could hear the tour members talking quietly among themselves, but the camaraderie of the first few days was rapidly deteriorating. The bus seemed oddly empty, too, with the Dunwoody-Chesterton party traveling separately in Dave's car. Which was probably just as well. Dave Dunwoody on the tour bus would make the vehicle feel like one of those Volkswagens crammed with circus clowns. Only not funny.

Roxanne deliberately deflected any attempts that driver Jerry MacKinnon made at conversation and tried unsuccessfully to catch a brief nap. MacKinnon had dismissed the crank calls as nonsense, which was easy enough for him to do since he hadn't received one.

Which raised another interesting question. Just what did they know about Jerry MacKinnon? Of everyone, he had the easiest access for tampering with luggage, and he'd definitely been around during room assignments at the Harrison Hotel. Hauling luggage into the lobby, he'd been perfectly situated to overhear room numbers.

Still, he seemed genuinely surprised to learn of the night calls. And surely he would claim to have received one, if he were responsible for the others.

❧

The Dunwoody-Chesterton party was waiting for them on the patio beyond the lobby of the Williamsburg Inn when the bus pulled in. Mignon Chesterton and Monica Dunwoody sat slightly removed, pointedly ignoring each other like strangers in the waiting room of a specialist in venereal diseases. The older woman watched folks dressed all in pristine white, lawn bowling on an impossibly manicured green, while her great-niece flipped desultorily through a fashion magazine. Neither of them seemed overly excited about rejoining the group, but Barbara and Dave were in good spirits, laughing and talking over what looked very much like Bloody Marys. Barbara was full of excited plans and Dave seemed exceptionally amiable.

The Irish Eyes accommodations at Botsforth Tavern in the restored historical section would be ready after lunch. Meanwhile they were all issued Patriot Passes and a guide for a brief introductory tour. Jerry MacKinnon was left to guard the bus in the parking lot of the Williamsburg Inn, assured that he'd never again work for Irish Eyes Travel if he so much as left to take a leak. Roxanne could only hope he'd regard this as a threat and not a blessing.

❧

Olive Forrester found Colonial Williamsburg absolutely enchanting. They hadn't even *gotten* to the restored area yet, and already she felt as if time had stopped two hundred years earlier. The hotel doormen were in colonial breeches, for goodness sakes!

Their guide was slim and fiftyish with a cultured drawl and a calm, unhurried approach. Where did they *find* all those docents, anyway? They seemed to spring in limitless supply from the rich Virginia soil.

Olive tucked her hand through Dick's arm and gave him a little squeeze. He smiled down at her, then turned his attention back to the camcorder he was operating single-handedly on the other side of his large body. She couldn't help wishing now and then that Dick would spend a little less time shooting videotape and a little more paying attention to her. He could learn a lot on that score from Larry Vanguard, whose lavish attentions to Josie—the soft-spoken murmurs and double-entendres, the smoldering glances, the touchy-feely interplay in public, and most of all the numerous hasty adjournments to their various bedrooms—were truly awe-inspiring.

Even if, as Dick claimed, Larry was a con artist who probably peddled everything from miracle diet pills to Krugerrands.

"Right now we're in America's largest living history museum," the guide explained, as she led them into the heart of the restored area.

This place was magical, and Olive found it particularly gratifying to watch young Heather. Olive's own children had been bored by history, a subject Olive had taught for several years long ago before her first pregnancy. She'd had a couple of students like Heather, girls she still remembered fondly and with great clarity. One of them had become a history teacher at the local high school, named District Teacher of the Year.

"Eighty-eight original buildings have been restored and you'll have the opportunity to see Colonial trades and crafts as they were actually practiced in the late eighteenth century," the guide went on. "Throughout the restored area, period characters will be happy to talk about their lives, as they remain in character. We make every effort to be historically accurate. If they didn't have it in 1780, we don't have it here now. Which is why you won't see any azalea bushes or tomato plants in the restored area."

Now the guide led them into a charming back garden full of geometric tulip beds. Dick broke away and began moving back and forth, taping.

"This is a typical tripartite yard," the guide explained. "The first yard included the house and various dependencies, which is what we call the outbuildings such as kitchens, laundries, and privies, known as 'necessaries' back then. Daylilies were often planted around the necessaries, and were sometimes called 'privy plants.'"

The group members who'd revealed themselves to be gardeners laughed at that. Olive had been stunned to discover the extraordinary differences in how they gardened, too, depending on where they lived. She was particularly jealous of Josie, who had flowers blooming *year-round* in her San Diego garden, where it never ever froze.

"The middle yard would have the vegetable garden, as the home in the next yard over there does today. This area is an interesting mix, the farthest north that many plants will grow and the farthest south that others can survive." Olive noted with some jealousy that the peas were already nearly three feet tall, and it wasn't even May yet!

"And the very back part of the yard held stables," the guide concluded, opening the first of a series of gates in the low white picket fences.

"Oh, look how the gates close automatically!" Barbara Dunwoody exclaimed. "What a clever idea!" She swung the white picket-fence gate back and forth, watching it close time after time on its own, apparently by gravity.

Dick recorded the motion as Olive stopped to examine the gate. It was a relatively unobtrusive and delightfully efficient system. A hefty-looking five-inch-diameter iron ball hung on a six-foot iron-link chain connected to the gate and also to a thick pole anchored in the ground nearby. The whole business was painted white to match the fence.

"We could have used something like this when the kids were small," Olive agreed. "They were *always* leaving the gate open and letting the dog out."

But the others had moved on by now, and the three hurried to catch up as the group suddenly emerged onto Duke of Gloucester Street, the mile-long main drag connecting the old Virginia Capitol at one end and the College of William and Mary at the other. The street bustled with activity, and their guide stopped in the shade of a tree, giving the Irish Eyes group a moment to acclimate themselves. An elaborately gilded horse-drawn carriage containing five obvious tourists passed briskly. There were no cars in sight.

"Duke of Gloucester Street has been fully restored, and we don't allow any vehicular traffic in here during the day. Still, in some ways it looked very different in Colonial times," the guide told them with a smile. "None of these trees were here, for example."

"I thought this area was heavily forested," Olive put in. Forestry was something she knew a fair amount about, as befit a northern Michigan native.

"It was," the guide agreed, "but they didn't hesitate to *use* any available trees for furniture and building and fuel. Wood was essential and the trees here were *needed*. Also, people in the eighteenth century believed the trees interfered with their air. If you ever visit here in the summer, when it's rather humid, you'll understand why they'd do everything possible to encourage breezes!"

"Did they have these brick sidewalks then?" Edna Stanton was always interested in practical matters.

"No," the guide answered, smiling, "and the street wasn't paved either. As you can well imagine, everything was *very* dusty. Or muddy, depending on the weather. One derogatory report at the time said the street was 'ninety-nine feet wide, one mile long, and one foot deep.' There were also five deep ravines along its length. If you stood watching a carriage travel from one end to the other, it would disappear entirely from sight each time it entered a ravine."

"Cool!" Heather opined, squatting and then jumping high in an apparent re-creation. She repeated the jump several times, then stopped in mild embarrassment when she noticed several kids in a school group watching from across the street. They looked to be about fourth graders, and Olive did not envy their harried-looking young teacher. Still, it would be great fun to teach history in Virginia. Think of the field trips!

"How do you know where things actually were?" Harriet

Greene asked skeptically. Harriet was annoyingly keen on facts and getting every teeny-weeny detail just right. Olive suspected she was one of those super-organized women who sneaks out to the garage to dust her hubby's workbench. There would be no catch-all drawers in Harriet's kitchen, no mishmash of magazines beneath her glistening coffee table. She probably ironed her underwear and hemmed her rags. "Surely all these buildings aren't original."

"No, they aren't," the guide agreed. "Many have been reconstructed to eighteenth-century specifications. But any open spaces you see now were open spaces back then. In some cases, buildings from later periods were removed from those lots. But in answer to your specific question, we were fortunate in having what's known as the Frenchman's Map to guide us. We believe it was drawn by a French officer who was looking for places to house troops after the siege at Yorktown. His map showed the precise locations of streets and buildings, even the various outbuildings, all in wonderful detail."

Around them, the streets were filled with tourists wearing photo ID badges, natural fibers, and expensive cameras. Except for some of the school groups, the overall atmosphere was tranquil and relaxed, partly because of a significant number of people standing in doorways and moving serenely among the twentieth-century tourists in full Colonial garb, rich in individualized detail.

For the most part the women wore functional dresses and had realistic bodies that were soft and pillowy, not unlike Olive's own. It was rather nice, in fact, to see that there was somewhere left in the country where the female standard of beauty didn't require intimacy with some massive chrome exercise machine.

The men wore dark trousers that stopped just below the knee, with light, calf-hugging stockings and black buckled shoes. Their shirts were white, their jackets and dark vests cut along eighteenth-century lines. Nowhere was there evidence of makeup, contemporary hairstyling, or anachronistic jewelry. Nearly everyone wore some sort of head covering—ruffled mobcaps for the ladies, tricornered black felt for the gents—and some of their shoes were even authentically single-lasted.

Olive might have missed this footwear technicality, had not Heather previously discussed it in connection with Felicity's wardrobe. Single-lasted shoes, Olive had learned, were identical left and right, and it was up to your own foot to make them fit.

Which was fine if you were a plastic doll, but probably darned uncomfortable for a human, she thought, remembering her own podiatric surgery with a shudder.

❦

Monica Dunwoody was bored silly.

Tedious, that's what all this history junk was. Tedious. It was one of Monica's favorite words lately, and it described all too much of this miserable trip.

It was a ridiculous idea to begin with, all of them hopping off to Virginia together like some fifties TV show replayed on Nickelodeon. This wasn't Daddy's kind of vacation, even if he *did* do a lot of business in Virginia, and Mom mostly was just doing it to please Aunt Mignon. Since Grandma's death, Mom had stopped talking about what a pain Aunt Mignon was and had begun to be downright nostalgic about her, a position Monica could not understand for one single minute.

Aunt Mignon was just too gruesome for words. She wore weird makeup and dressed like one of those stuffy statues in the museums she was so nuts about. Proper like you wouldn't believe. *Etiquette*, that was a big thing with Aunt Mignon. The *proper* way to do things, as if anybody outside of Birmingham, Alabama, even cared. For Monica's thirteenth birthday, Aunt Mignon had actually sent her a big fat book about manners.

Not that the book hadn't been useful. Monica smiled as she remembered using it to prop her bedroom window open on the nights she snuck out in high school. One of the few things she had enjoyed on the Monticello tour was the triple-hung window setup on the first floor. Now *those* were windows designed for the young and restless. You could walk right through them, not that there was anywhere to go.

As the group took seats at several tables in Shields Tavern for lunch, Monica pointedly avoided her relatives and sat beside the girl guide, Roxanne. She was a tight one, Roxanne, not giving much away, not making a lot of irritating small talk. Monica appreciated that. The biddies all felt obligated to fill silences by prying, asking questions that Monica wouldn't have wanted to answer even if her parents *weren't* being such absolute pinheads about Nick.

Monica was also sick and tired of all the Colonial slop they kept being served. She ordered a croissant sandwich and looked longingly at the beverage menu. The Rummer sounded particularly appealing: Myers's rum with apricot and peach brandies served on crushed ice with a slice of lime. Of course, Mom would have a *fit* if she ordered one, particularly in front of Aunt Mignon and particularly in the middle of the day. Even though alcohol had never really been a problem for Monica, not like the coke. Mom refused to acknowledge the difference, didn't even seem to understand that there might *be* one.

It was easier just to skip the drinks.

"I'm glad to finally have a chance to talk to you," Roxanne told her as they waited for the food. "I've been so busy with the others that I've missed being able to talk to somebody nearer my own age."

Actually Monica, who'd just turned twenty-three, thought Roxanne seemed a *lot* older. Probably at least thirty. "I don't see how you can stand taking people on all these trips," she confided, glancing down the table to check that her parents weren't listening. She grimaced. "I'd go loony."

Roxanne grinned. "I'm fairly new to the business, actually, but I have to say that for me it's really a dream job. I'm getting paid to take a terrific trip, after all, and meet some really nice people. Yourself, for instance."

Monica wondered if Roxanne could possibly believe this b.s. "Yeah, right."

Roxanne let the sarcasm slide right off her. "What about *you*, Monica? What do you do back home?"

Monica sneaked another peek down the table at her parents,

who seemed to be in deep conversation with Larry and Josie Vanguard. Aunt Mignon was at a different table, definitely out of earshot, with Harriet and Edna. Monica thought of them as Harriet-and-Edna, a single entity, and had trouble remembering which was which. Not that it mattered.

"Not much of anything right now," Monica admitted. "I was going to MiraCosta College for a while, but it was pretty tedious, I've gotta say. That was even a compromise, actually. My Aunt Mignon *really* wanted me to go to Sweet Briar in Virginia. It's where the women in our family traditionally get 'finished.' Whatever *that* means. Aunt Mignon and my grandma and my mom all went there. But it just sounded *too* tedious and deadly."

"So you've been working then?" That Roxanne just wouldn't *quit*.

"Not for a while," Monica answered after a moment's hesitation. Somehow she didn't think Roxanne was talking about the chores in rehab. Though it crossed Monica's mind to mention it, just to see how she'd react. Pretty cool, probably. It was older people who got freaked by the idea.

The waiter, a cute guy in a Colonial outfit with a tan vest and a big white apron buttoned in a point to the vest, brought their food. Monica almost gagged as he carefully identified the weird-looking stuff on Roxanne's plate. She'd ordered the Shields Tavern sampler plate. He made a point of saying that some of it might seem unusual, so it must really be swill. Her wisely ordered croissant sandwich looked blessedly ordinary in contrast.

Once the waiter was gone, Roxanne poked dispiritedly at the eighteenth-century foods arranged on her plate. "I can't believe I ordered this," she said, "me, who's started fantasizing about Big Macs. I need to start paying more attention to my better judgment. I know he *said* this is onion soup, but it sure looks like that white paste we used in grade school." She took a tentative nibble. "Tastes like it, too."

Monica laughed and gestured at her sandwich. "You want some of this?"

"Naw," Roxanne told her, picking up a meat pasty and eyeing it cautiously. "I'll tough it out. So. You've just been hanging out?" Boy, was she persistent.

"Yeah," Monica told her. And why not tell her the whole bit? Roxanne was one of those pale redheads, the kind too prudent to ever spend much time at the beach. But she was still a potential customer, after all. And she just might think it was a cool idea. If so, that was another argument for Daddy. "I'm planning to open a swimsuit shop this summer."

"How exciting!" And Roxanne *did* look excited, at least until she took a forkful of the chicken fricassee, which was very dark and about as appealing as the doggie surprise in Monica's suitcase. Roxanne reached for her water glass in a hurry and took a gulp. "Can they mess up a carrot puff?" She picked up a yellowish, deep-fried thing and took a little nibble, then smiled. "Not half-bad. So, do you mean something like a surf shop?"

Well, she *had* said she was from Texas, as if you couldn't tell from that crazy accent. She probably just didn't know that surf shops were pretty macho territory. It was a forgivable, even logical, mistake.

"Not really," Monica explained seriously. "That's a whole 'nother thing, a guy thing. What *I'm* going to have is swimsuits for girls, with cute cover-ups and all kinds of hats and sunglasses and maybe some sandals, but not many 'cause I don't want a *shoe* store, after all. And I'll probably put in a tiny section of conservative swimwear for—" she swiveled her head slightly to indicate the Irish Eyes group and lowered her voice "—older ladies."

Roxanne ate the last of what had been identified as ham relish and pushed the remains of her sampler to the side. "Sounds like a great idea. Where's it going to be?"

Monica was pleased to have her plans taken seriously. "Pacific Beach, probably. My partner's researching sites, but we don't have a firm location yet. I don't think that will be a problem, though," she concluded with a smile. This had gone far enough. Time to change the subject. "So tell me, is this Williamsburg stuff going to be like the army, or can we do whatever we want?"

Roxanne laughed. "As far as I'm concerned, this is your last official tour obligation till we get back on the bus Saturday morning. I have a list of different tours and activities I can arrange for you, both here and nearby. Jamestown, Yorktown, Carter's Grove."

Monica was drawing a real blank. They all *sounded* like places she'd heard of, maybe even ought to know about. And they all sounded boring.

"Everything from here on out in Williamsburg is optional," Roxanne continued. "Of course, your family might have more specific ideas about what you should be doing, but I'm afraid that's out of my hands."

"I can handle them," Monica told her with the confidence of long experience and a fleeting thought of Nick. "I can handle them just fine."

❧

Botsforth Tavern was everything Heather had hoped for, and more. And they had the whole place to themselves, just the tour group.

It was *perfect*, sitting right on Duke of Gloucester Street so you could walk out the front door and just be there, right in the middle of history. Botsforth Tavern had been a small lodging house during the Colonial Era, and it was one of the first buildings restored in the 1930s. Just inside the front door was a sitting room filled with antiques, including several upholstered chairs grouped around a massive fireplace with a dark gleaming mantelpiece. A beautiful clock bonged softly on the mantel.

"We'll be having tea back here at four," Roxanne told her from the hallway as she set down a couple of suitcases.

Heather squealed in joy. Tea in a real Colonial parlor in Williamsburg! It was almost too incredible to believe. She would have to unpack Felicity immediately.

Botsforth Tavern had two stories. Downstairs, across from the parlor, Monica and her family had three rooms, and back in a corner beyond the soda and ice machines were Mr. and Mrs. Forrester, who had a really neat canopied four-poster bed.

Upstairs was smaller. Heather and Grandma had a room up here, with deeply cut eaves and two windows actually *overlooking* Duke of Gloucester Street. Roxanne was across the hall, facing toward the rear garden. And the Flanagans, the folks who'd won the lottery, were in two rooms at the end of the little hall. On the other side of the stairway were the Vanguards, that goofy couple who were always chewing on each other's ears.

Harriet Greene and Edna Stanton were up there with them, too. Their setup was kind of strange, two single rooms with a totally separate bathroom across the hall. "Very European," Mrs. Stanton told Heather, not seeming to mind in the slightest. "In Colonial days, of course, we all would have been sharing—"

"—the necessaries," Heather finished for her. She was not at all sorry to miss that particular element of historical authenticity.

The room she shared with Grandma was really wonderful, two single beds covered by plain white, lightly quilted coverlets. The dust ruffles and curtains were in an old-fashioned heavy fabric with large red and white checks, and the armchair was red. It was *exactly* what Heather would have chosen if Mom had consulted her before going out and redecorating her room in that horrible white lacquer and egg-yolk yellow, with millions of sharp angles. Heather *hated* her room, except for Felicity's corner.

Heather had decided not to wear a Colonial costume herself this afternoon but she unpacked Felicity and swiftly changed the doll into her school outfit. Already she had seen two other girls in town carrying their own Felicity dolls. A Samantha, too.

All in all, Williamsburg seemed to be absolutely *perfect*.

❦

Only the promise of a visit to the Milliner's had kept Merrily Flanagan from bailing out immediately after lunch.

Patrick had gone to see about renting a car and finding the ABC Store, two *número uno* priorities. They definitely needed wheels. It was horrible not being able to get up and leave when they wanted. Merrily thought wistfully of the brand new black his-and-hers Dodge pickups they had back home, shiny as a night in hell and loaded with lights. Buying those trucks had been too fabulous for words. Merrily had almost gotten hers in candy-apple red, but the black was just too cool.

As for the booze, Virginia was the *damnedest* place; you could only buy liquor in state-operated stores, and even then not all the time. This had resulted in a *serious* shortage on the second night in Charlottesville. Once burned, however, they had vowed not to run out again. On a trip like this, it definitely helped to have a buzz on.

So now Merrily was stuck with Bridget for the afternoon, and she hoped she'd have the fortitude not to say anything too snippy about this stupid trip, which Patrick said his mother had been talking about for as long as he could remember. Though as far as Merrily could tell, Mom Flanagan was not exactly having the time of her life. Merrily wished that Bridget would be a little more forthcoming about her mysterious past Southern employer, or that Patrick could explain it.

But most likely he *didn't* know; Patrick could be incredibly dense if something didn't have to do with cars or planes. He'd bought a little Cessna and was taking flying lessons, which scared the bejeepers out of Merrily. Roxanne had mentioned a flying tour of the James River area with a professional pilot, which sounded to Merrily like a dandy way to speed things up, without actually having to walk around and admire the ugly bric-a-brac and ratty old rugs in one run-down house after another. A fast fly-by and they'd be *done*.

Merrily brought herself back to the afternoon's reality: These people even managed to make clothes boring. The milliner was discussing ladies' underwear now, which sounded like instruments of torture.

"Your stays were critical, to give you the ideal posture you wanted," the woman explained. She was rather plain, in a drab blue dress and a simple ruffled cap. "Chest out, shoulders back and narrow. Thomas Jefferson was over six feet tall, but he measured only fifteen inches across the shoulders in back." In short, Merrily thought, built like a real geek.

Now the milliner pulled out a set of stays, a truly scary-looking whalebone and canvas apparatus that one apparently tightened to the point of extreme pain. "You would keep your stays nice and tight at all times," she went on, "because to loosen them was to risk being labeled a 'loose woman.' You wouldn't want to accentuate the bosom, either. The ideal figure was cone-shaped."

Cone-shaped? Merrily, justifiably proud of her own considerable cleavage, shuddered. Far better to be a loose woman anyway; they were usually more interesting than the stuffy old prunes who ran society.

The milliner went on, with a nod toward Heather. "Children were put into their first set of stays as soon as they began walking well, and sometimes as early as three months. Boys wore them, too, till they went into breeches between the ages of five and eight. Up until that age, all children wore dresses. In family photos, the only way we can tell the boys from the girls is by the hats they're holding."

Beside Merrily, Bridget giggled. She'd had a couple rum punches with lunch and seemed to be feeling more cheerful. "Can you picture putting one of today's little boys in a *dress?*"

Merrily felt the sickening lurch in her stomach that generally occurred when Bridget slithered toward the subject of grandchildren. She murmured something noncommittal and prayed for a distraction.

"Are you wearing pockets?" Heather piped up, an answer to prayer. The kid seemed to know a lot about history. As if it would ever do her any good.

"Why yes, I am," the milliner replied, sticking her hands into slits in the sides of her skirt. She picked up another set of two bags attached to a cord. "These are my plain pockets, and I can keep anything I might need in them." Now she displayed a larger pair with rounded rigid containers like lunch pails. "For a very fancy occasion, a lady might wear these hoops tied around her waist instead, giving the fashionable wide look and providing her a place to store an extra pair of dancing shoes, in case she danced her soles through."

Merrily sighed as she thought wistfully about dancing. It was probably too much to hope that there'd be any kind of night life in Williamsburg.

And if they *did* dance, it was probably the minuet.

❦

Heather had adored the Milliner's, but the Apothecary Shop, which they visited next, turned out to be almost as fascinating. It had hundreds of jars, drawers, and containers, all labeled with names like CARYOPHYLL and LITHARGYRUS and GUM TRAGAC and CORNU CERVI.

"Colonial subjects treated symptoms, not diseases," the young woman behind the counter told them. She didn't seem as friendly as the milliner. "Nobody knew about germs or the causes of illness." Heather had already heard some of this from a man dressed as a Colonial doctor she had talked to at Mount Vernon. He'd told her that they used twigs from dogwood trees for *toothbrushes.*

"What's that?" Edna Stanton pointed to a large contraption that looked like Paul Bunyan's sushi roller.

"That would be used to set a broken leg," the woman explained. "You'd need to stay in bed for at least six weeks while it healed."

Six weeks! Heather couldn't imagine staying in bed for six *days.* When her friend Brittany broke a leg skiing at Tahoe last winter, she never missed a day of school.

Bridget Flanagan pointed to a jar on the counter labeled LEECHES. "What would those be used for? And are they *really* leeches?"

"Absolutely," the woman replied. She held up the jar, which contained three small black wormlike creatures suspended in liquid.

Gross! Heather backed away instinctively.

"Leeches really weren't used that often in Colonial medicine, but we do keep a few specimens because many doctors did use them. Leeches fell out of medical regard for quite some time, but today they're often used after microsurgery, to prevent swelling when a finger or thumb has been reattached after being accidentally amputated, until all the tiny blood vessels heal and rejoin."

Which, in a way, was even grosser.

❧

When the group fragmented to explore independently, Roxanne took off on her own busman's holiday and cut through the herb garden behind the Apothecary Shop heading for the Public Gaol, the hoity-toity British spelling for hoosegow.

There was no line waiting to get in here.

The jailer's office and housing were unremarkable, but the cells themselves were ghastly, open on one iron-barred side to all the elements. There were lots of places to attach the leg irons welded onto each prisoner's legs, and each cell was furnished solely with a pile of straw and a massive wood and iron commode. Prisoners were issued one thin blanket and a daily meal of mush. When one of them got sick, so did all his cellmates.

As she toured the sturdy red brick compound, Roxanne felt a strong connection, as though multiple generations of her lawman forebears were applauding the visit. "Gotta git them bad guys," Granddaddy Prescott always used to say, only half joking. She'd have to find a postcard to send him at the nursing home, something about the jail or hanging. Even the stocks would do.

Of course, he was too far gone probably to understand it, she realized glumly. Roxanne wondered if Granddaddy Prescott ever had moments of lucidity when he knew exactly where he was and what had happened to him.

She hoped not.

❦ CHAPTER EIGHT ❦

WHEN SHE returned to her room at the Botsforth Tavern, Roxanne called a number in Austin that she wasn't sure she'd remember until the very moment that her fingers started flying across the phone's number pad.

"Homicide, Connally."

"Quickie! You're back in Homicide!"

There was a moment's silence, then a tentative chuckle. "Roxanne? Is that you?"

"Damn straight," she told him. "What happened, Quickie? Those bad guys in gold cuff links too much for you?"

Quickie Connally was a good friend and sometime partner of Roxanne's older brother Tom. He had been known as Jim until one Saturday evening when the couple the Connallys were going dancing with arrived early—in time to hear Jim's wife call down the stairs that since she was ready early they had time for a quickie. Everyone in Texas law enforcement had heard the story within twenty-four hours, and after an initial awkward period, Quickie Connally accepted his nickname with a certain grace. The moniker had, indeed, outlasted the marriage. On the rare occasions when he was called upon to explain it to outsiders, he claimed it referred to the speed with which he cleared cases.

Tom Prescott and Jim Connally had gone on the force at the same time, risen through the department together to eventually become detectives. Both had worked Homicide until Quickie left on a temporary assignment with a white-collar fraud unit.

"Couldn't stand the paperwork," Quickie growled. "Lord have mercy, I'd close my eyes, see mountains of computer paper covered with numbers. Give me a nice bloated body full of maggots any day over those damned spreadsheets."

Roxanne laughed. "Well, welcome back. You working with Tom?"

"Yeah, and he's around here somewhere, Roxanne. How's California treating you?"

"Okay, I guess. It's a mighty strange place, Quickie. Oz with surfboards. They oughta issue bullwhips to the cops. But actually, right now I'm in Virginia."

"As in carry me back?"

"Yes indeedy. I told you I was leaving to see the world, and here it is. My aunt isn't even along on this trip. I'm doing it solo."

"She need any more help out there?"

"Somehow I don't think you're cut out for this, Quickie. It takes a certain mellowness of temperament."

Quickie roared. "Like yours?"

Roxanne joined his laugh. "Oh, I've gotten pretty laid-back-California."

"Do me a favor," Quickie told her. "You have your aunt get in touch with me if she needs anybody to go to Tahiti. Or maybe Italy? I've always had a hankering to see Rome. Have Glock, will travel. Listen, here's Tom. You stay in touch, girl. We miss you."

Tom's deep drawl sent an aching wave of homesickness down Roxanne's spine. "Hey, Sis! How you doing?" He sounded upbeat, enthusiastic, cheerful. Odd qualities for a homicide detective, but Tom had always marched to his own drum.

"Not half-bad, Tommy. Not half-bad. I was just down at the old Colonial lockup. These people had crime deterrence *knocked*. You mess up, they throw you in a truly godawful jail till your trial, and the trial itself would last maybe half an hour. Then they'd lock the jury up without food or water or heat or a pot to piss in till they reached a verdict. Kind of speeds up deliberation."

"So far, so good," Tom said. "Sounds like my kind of place."

"Absolutely. Punishment was swift and harsh, too. They'd hang you for all sorts of shit. Bigamy, even."

"Hey, a society's gotta have its rules."

Roxanne chuckled. "You'd like the pardon system, too, Tommy. Joe Horsethief puts in his pardon request, but before the governor gives him an answer, he's gonna be standing on his coffin with a rope around his thieving little neck out at the town gallows."

Tom whistled. "ACLU wouldn't like that. Cruel and unusual."

"Not for this gang. They'd as soon whip you as say howdy. Nine tails on the whip. Women, too, only they'd get ten lashes less than the usual."

"It has real possibilities for gang control," Tom said thoughtfully. "Maybe you oughta tell Ben about this." Their brother Ben was a juvenile officer in Houston.

"I'll drop him a card," Roxanne promised. "You know what else they had, Tom? There was this reprieve possibility called 'benefit of clergy.' They'd have you hold up a hand and swear you'd never be naughty again, and then they'd brand the hand. Or put a nice nick in your ear, something like that. So you'd be carrying your rap sheet around with you."

"I *like* these people," Tom said. "They understood the finer nuances of criminology."

"That they did, Tommy. That they did. But listen. I was wondering if you might be able to do me a little favor?"

"Consider it done."

"I've got a list of names I'd like you to run through NCIC." The National Crime Information Center had a computerized record of criminal convictions, time served, and current warrants.

"How come?"

She explained briefly. "I'd just like a better idea of who I'm dealing with here. Even Aunt Maureen's starting to get nervous. And she really doesn't know about a lot of them, 'cause they aren't from San Diego."

"I'll give it a shot," Tom told her. "No problem. But aren't most of them granolas?"

"You mean Californians? About half."

"Then for those folks it'd probably be better to have somebody check them through the California system, too." He considered. "I think Sullivan's got a Marine Corps buddy in LAPD. I'll check with Sullie if you'd like. Course, if you were still on the force, you could do this yourself."

"I could," Roxanne agreed. "But then I wouldn't be on this fabulous trip, would I?" Tom had tried to talk her out of leaving the force. Had convinced her to take an indefinite leave rather than resign outright. Had come very close to calling her a quitter. Time to change the subject. "How're Lynette and the kids?"

"Fine and frisky," Tom answered, letting it go. Part of what made him such a good detective was knowing when to ease up. "Brenna's all jazzed about going up to Dallas for cheerleader camp this summer." Tom's oldest daughter, Brenna, was the quintessential Texas girl, a perpetually peppy teenager consumed with fashion, grooming, and football. Roxanne enjoyed her niece in small doses, acutely aware that Brenna represented everything she herself had always feared becoming.

"Give them all my best," Roxanne told him. She gave him the names of all the Irish Eyes travelers, with Jerry MacKinnon and the Freemans from Nicholson Plantation thrown in for good measure. She had him check Nick Winfield, Monica Dunwoody's unsuitable boyfriend, too. "Call me as soon as you find out anything. My nerves are getting a bit frayed here."

But she actually felt a whole lot better after she hung up.

❦

Evelyn Tichener felt a bit silly in her Colonial dress. At Christmas when she and Heather began planning this trip, she'd been nipping at the eggnog and recklessly agreed that it would be great fun for both of them to travel with authentic costumes. But even while she was sewing her own dress, she hadn't quite pictured a scene where she'd be wearing it.

Now she was stepping out the front door of the Botsforth Tavern with Heather and the rest of the group, in a voluminous floor-length skirt and snugly fitted bodice. The dress itself was quite attractive, a rich midnight blue with white ruffled trim, though it wasn't entirely authentic. She hadn't bothered with the overskirt, for one thing; her hips were quite wide enough already. But Heather adored the way they looked together, and Evelyn adored Heather, and that was that.

"This Lanthorn Tour is supposed to be quite wonderful," Roxanne told them as they walked down the street. *Lanthorn* was an eighteenth-century spelling of *lantern*. "Maureen said it's one of her favorite parts of this trip."

It wasn't easy for Evelyn to keep up with Roxanne while wearing these cumbersome skirts and fancy shoes. The guide was in her customary slacks and sneakers. Fortunately Heather, who'd normally be running circles around the both of them, was practicing mincing little lady-steps.

The evening was warm and balmy, with gentle fragrant breezes and an intensifying sense of historical atmosphere as daylight faded. Despite Evelyn's self-consciousness, nobody paid any particular attention to her. Heather got a few stares, but they were invariably pleasant. Various costumed Colonial Williamsburg guides—*real* guides—swung lanterns as they assembled tourists in groups of about twenty.

Heather was so excited she could barely hold still, and Evelyn could see that the others in their group were similarly enthused. The entire event had a dreamy quality to it, sufficient to obliterate the odd nastiness of some of the past days' experiences. Everybody was here except the Flanagans, who really should have gone to Las Vegas or Miami.

The Irish Eyes group and a handful of others set off with an African American guide named Desmond from William and Mary, a lively young man who took the Ticheners' costumes completely in stride and complimented Heather on her dress. Heather beamed and curtsied in response.

At the Wigmaker's Shop, Desmond explained that with a few notable exceptions—the unusually hirsute George Washington, for one—Colonial men of all classes shaved their heads in order to wear wigs held on only by the itchy stubble on their scalps. The main difference in classes was simply the quality of the hair used. Horsehair was obviously far more affordable than the long pelts harvested from English and Irish girls.

"But *why?*" Heather wanted to know. "Why not just wear their own hair?"

It seemed an entirely reasonable question to Evelyn. A lot of the hair concoctions shown in the shop seemed ridiculously ornate for a community mired in mud or beset by dust through much of its muggy year.

Desmond smiled. "It's just fashion, like short skirts or baggy pants or everybody wearing the same color of green. Now, a really fine wig might use several heads of hair mixed together, and you'd send it back to the shop to be restyled and washed. You could powder the wigs to match your clothing, and you could even cheat a little." He held up a ponytail braid attached to a tricornered hat. "Men might use one of these braids, and women could attach little curls over their ears for variety." He pointed to a pair of ringlets hanging on the wall. "They were called heartbreakers."

Barbara Dunwoody was looking at a massive curly white wig that sat on a stand in the window. Her husband leaned against the back wall and looked like he was mentally composing his next fax. Monica was sullen as usual. Evelyn prayed that Heather wouldn't grow into such an unpleasant young woman.

"How many women would wear this sort of fancy wig?" Barbara wondered.

"Very few," Desmond answered. "Wigs like that were strictly for the upper class. You know, about two thousand people lived in Colonial Williamsburg, and fifty-two percent of those were slaves. We use an analogy to an apple pie to give you a sense of how things were set up. Two percent of the people were plantation owners, and they formed the upper crust. The bottom crust was the five percent of whites who were extremely poor. The filling in the middle was the rest of the white community, known as the 'middling sort.' And the pie pan was the half of the population who were black."

They moved on then to the Carpenter's Shop, walking

through darkened yards and along quiet back paths. Evelyn had always loved fine wood, and here the air was rich with the scent of fresh, fluffy sawdust from mahogany and black walnut. She knew this was a place she would have to return for a much lengthier visit.

"You can get a very real sense of what life was like here by walking around at night," Desmond told them as they left the Carpenter's complex and headed back up to the Apothecary Shop. "And when you're walking around during the day, you should try to go through some of the backyards and down the side streets to get away from the crowds. It'll take you right back through time."

Evelyn couldn't help wondering how Desmond *really* felt about being carried back through time, to this corner of eighteenth-century Virginia.

Where he would have been part of the pie pan.

Larry Vanguard leaned over to whisper in his wife's ear as they walked up the steep slope from the Carpenter's Shop. He could not remember a time when he had been more colossally bored than over the past five days. How this could interest Josie so much totally escaped him, but he had reason to accommodate his new wife's wishes. Several million reasons, actually.

"I think I've had about enough history for today," he murmured softly. "How about you?"

Josie's eyes glowed in the soft light of the torch at the Carpenter's gate. She was a fine-looking woman for her age, with a remarkable libido, and that was just fine, too. "More than enough," she agreed. "But wasn't that beautiful furniture?"

"I'd rather take another look at the furniture in our room," he suggested. "Maybe play some cards?"

Josie cocked her head and passed her tongue along her lower lip, a motion that invariably excited him. "Strip poker," she told him. "And the Queen of Hearts is *wild.*"

Heather had hoped that Grandma would have more energy tonight, but only half an hour after the Lanthorn Tour ended, she announced that her feet hurt too badly to go another inch. As Grandma trudged back to Botsforth Tavern, Heather stopped for a moment by the stocks where she'd had her picture taken this afternoon in regular clothes. Sometime in the daylight, she wanted to get another picture in a Colonial dress. Maybe one with her head in the pillory, too. Mom could put it on her desk at work.

Behind the stocks in the darkness beyond the Courthouse, Heather was surprised to see Monica Dunwoody talking to a guy in Colonial clothing. As she watched, the guy leaned down and kissed Monica. *Kissed her!* Boy, that Monica sure didn't waste any time! Heather supposed it was just like Grandma had said, that Monica was boy-crazy, something Heather could not begin to comprehend. She looked for Grandma to point the couple out, but her grandmother was way up ahead of her now, limping along.

Heather looked wistfully at the Magazine. Tomorrow night they absolutely would have to act out the Gunpowder Incident.

Up ahead, Grandma turned around and called out irritably, "Heather!"

Heather hustled to catch up.

❦ CHAPTER NINE ❦

EDNA STANTON woke, as always, at 6:00 A.M.

The morning had always been her favorite time of day, when everything was bathed in fresh soft light, and the birds trilled excited greetings. Sometimes, if Edna closed her eyes for a moment before getting out of bed, she could even hear the old rooster on the Ohio farm where she had grown up.

Today promised to be perfectly splendid, with the Garden Tour in the morning—a guaranteed treat—and Carter's Grove Plantation in the afternoon. Before meeting the group for breakfast, she planned a brisk walk around town. Watching how a town woke up helped Edna define a location and understand the feel of a place.

She tucked her feet into her fold-up travel slippers and put on the heavy terrycloth robe the management had provided as compensation for not having direct access to a bathroom. Actually, Edna didn't mind in the slightest. Her tiny single room under the second-story eaves was delightful, and it was nice to have a little break from Harriet's allergies. In Charlottesville and Richmond, she'd been snoring like a chain saw.

She took the bathroom key and crossed the hall, unlocking the door and stepping inside the large tiled bathroom. Edna had left her toiletries here last night, after carefully removing her dentures and setting them in a glass of cleaning solution. She started to pick up the toiletry bag, then noticed, out of the corner of her eye, something odd in the denture glass.

She picked up the glass and stared for a horrified moment. It *couldn't* be. It wasn't possible. And yet—

She felt it slip from her fingers and heard the smash of glass against the hard white tile floor.

A loud, piercing noise seemed to surround her.

It took a moment before Edna realized it was her own high-pitched scream.

❦

The neighbor boys had been playing cowboys, and they wouldn't let Roxanne rope. She could only be the schoolteacher, they told her, a position she flatly refused. She could rope better than little Ray Hudson and nearly as well as Bobby Featherstone, who was a couple years older. It wasn't fair, them leaving her out.

She was sulking up in Ray's treehouse, waiting for her brothers to get home and avenge her, though she didn't really like being up so high. She swallowed her fears so the boys wouldn't find out she was a chicken.

Flat on her back, she stared out the rough-hewn open window into the leafy branches of the strong bois d'arc tree, fiddling with the heavy, wrinkled green surface of a horse-apple, thinking how satisfying it would be to gather a pile of the heavy fruits and pelt that rotten Bobby Featherstone until he hollered for mercy.

"Bobby, *no!*" came the wail from Ray. "I don't wanna." It sounded like Ray was crying, which happened a lot when he played with Bobby. Bobby was a bully.

"Don't be such a baby," Bobby taunted. "Now don't go away."

She could hear a slight metallic clang as Bobby picked up his bicycle.

"Hey, don't leave me!" Ray called. He was definitely crying now.

"I'll be back," came Bobby's voice, as the gate banged shut.

Something made a small thump directly under the tree, and there was a kind of funny, choking noise, then silence. Roxanne didn't want to embarrass Ray while he was crying, but it couldn't hurt to take a peek down. Before she could move, however, she heard her brother Tom scream from somewhere nearby as the gate banged again.

"*Help!*" Tom yelled frantically. "*Somebody help!*"

Startled by the urgency in Tom's voice, Roxanne bolted to the doorway of the treehouse and looked down in horror. Swinging from a noose strung far out on a limb of the massive tree was little Ray, his face purple, his eyes bulging. His hands were over his head, trying to ease the tension on the rope. His legs kicked frantically. A pile of bricks lay tumbled on the ground below him.

As Roxanne watched, Tom—still hollering for help at the top of his lungs—grabbed the boy's legs. Now he was holding Ray high enough to ease the tension while he scrabbled with one hand to loosen the noose.

Roxanne shinnied down the ladder in seconds, for once forgetting her fear of falling. She reached Tom just as Ray's mother came out the back door and began screaming.

And screaming.

And screaming.

❦

The screaming continued, high-pitched and nearby, as Roxanne opened her eyes. The sun's rays slanted through the dormer window of her room at the Botsforth Tavern.

She leapt from bed and threw open the door to the hall. The screaming was louder now, more hysterical. Just to the right down the hall, Edna Stanton stood in the doorway of the bathroom she shared with Harriet, screeching and trembling.

Harriet's door flew open and Edna collapsed into her friend's arms. As the two women backed into Harriet's room, Roxanne came face to face with Bridget Flanagan, a startling vision in zebra-striped satin pajamas, toilet paper wrapped around her hair.

"Please stay back," Roxanne told Bridget briskly, and Bridget backed away, sniffing loudly.

Barefoot, Roxanne peered into the long bathroom, blindingly white in the morning sun. Shards of glass glittered everywhere on the tile floor. Edna hadn't appeared to be hurt and there were no signs of blood in the bathroom.

But there *was* something else. Perched atop the largest collection of glass shards was a set of dentures. There was some kind of black squiggle on them. Roxanne leaned in the doorway to take a closer look. Surely this couldn't be what it appeared. But the longer she looked, the more certain she became that she had correctly identified the small black object on the dentures and two similar ones on the floor nearby.

They were leeches.

The mood at breakfast in the basement of Shields Tavern was an odd combination of somber and slaphappy. Candles provided the only light.

"If this is a practical joke," Roxanne told the Irish Eyes guests in her best move-along-now-fellows cop voice, "it's extremely unfunny and probably illegal as well."

Her charges, fully dressed and very nervous, watched and listened in the manner of a sixth-grade class being lectured by the principal after the discovery of vulgar drawings on a blackboard.

Everybody was secretly amused and nobody was giving up a thing.

"You can't be accusing *us* of anything," Dave Dunwoody shot back. So far he had exhibited behavioral poles of intense belligerence and unctuous charm. His attitude this morning vacillated back and forth between the two. "I don't think I could even find that damned Apothecary Shop again."

A quick check by Colonial Williamsburg Security had determined that the leeches from the Apothecary Shop were missing, though the building showed no obvious signs of forcible entry. Which meant either that somebody had boosted the leech jar during a group visit on last night's Lanthorn Tour, or that the lock had been picked by a pro.

"One leech looks pretty much like another," the security investigator had told Roxanne, deadpan, "and nobody took any ID photos or sucker-prints from these guys. But I think it's safe to say they're the same leeches."

And they wouldn't be telling any tales, either. The denture cleaner chemicals in the glass had killed all three.

There was no reason to doubt Dave Dunwoody's last assertion, Roxanne realized, that he'd have trouble locating the Apothecary Shop again. The businessman's general attitude on last night's Lanthorn Tour was of one embarking on the Bataan Death March.

Now he was getting warmed up. "Furthermore, I never even saw the damned second floor before this happened, and I certainly wasn't—if you'll pardon the pun—privy to the hygiene arrangements of these good ladies." He smiled, swinging the pendulum briefly back to Charm. "As I understand it, that bathroom was supposed to be locked, anyway."

"It *was* locked." Harriet Greene spoke forcefully. She had proven to be a real trouper, calming Edna, issuing concise and fact-specific statements. Now she wore a trim heathery-gray jumpsuit, a lightweight jacket with an all-over floral design, and sturdy walking shoes. Ready for the day. "Edna and I have traveled together for years and we are always *extremely* careful. Besides, that door locks automatically once it closes. You can't get it to stay unlocked unless you leave it wide open."

Which was only a slight exaggeration. Roxanne and the security investigator, Max Becker, had spent quite some time checking out the bathroom door. And both Harriet and Edna were adamant that they had never left it unlocked. Nor had either lady visited the bathroom during the night. However, there was no obvious evidence that the lock had been taped or otherwise fiddled with.

"Why couldn't somebody have climbed in the bathroom window?" Evelyn Tichener wondered. "There *is* that big tall tree outside."

Dick Forrester snorted in his annoyingly superior way. "Pretty obvious, I'd say, climbing a tree outside a hotel. That bathroom fronts on DOG Street."

Roxanne considered. She didn't have any specialized crime-scene training, but she'd taken a pretty thorough look at the tree in question and so had Becker, a no-nonsense fellow in his mid-fifties who'd retired out of a midsized force in South Carolina to take this position at Colonial Williamsburg. Neither one of them had spotted any obvious evidence to suggest that the tree had been climbed recently, and the grass below the tree, dusted with early-morning dewdrops, appeared undisturbed.

"It's possible, I suppose, but that isn't a very good climbing tree—" here Roxanne spoke from decades of personal experience "—and the window is pretty small." Though it *had* been open and was plenty big enough to admit most of the people seated in this room. "It could even have been somebody with a ladder. Duke of Gloucester Street really bustles during the day, but it's pretty deserted in the middle of the night."

"After Gambols, anyway." It was Dick Forrester again, the practical joker, figuring out how somebody else's caper had been pulled. Or, equally possibly, deflecting attention from himself by *pretending* to analyze the situation. Still, Dick Forrester just wasn't physically fit enough to have climbed that tree. And even if he could find a ladder—at one of the outdoor building trades exhibits, perhaps?—it'd be a real squeeze getting his bulk through the window.

"Right," Roxanne agreed. "Once Gambols ends at Chowning's, there probably aren't many people who come by. Now I know some of y'all went to Gambols last night. Who else was there besides Dick and Olive?"

Gambols, as nearly as Roxanne could tell, offered genteel carousing with Colonial minstrels, liquor, and old-fashioned games. Colonial Williamsburg's version of the wild life. Not that she knew firsthand. She herself had gone straight to bed after the Lanthorn Tour and slept like a rock.

"Barbara and I were," Dave Dunwoody announced, "with Dick and Olive. We didn't speak to any of the others there, though I know some of you were in another room." He paused expectantly.

Patrick Flanagan offered a beguiling grin. "You mean us, I believe. We saw you guys when we went in, but your room was full."

"How late did y'all stay?" Roxanne asked him, becoming

the interested tour guide again. Stern cop wasn't working very well this morning.

Patrick's grin widened as he sang a drinking song featured in the Colonial taverns: "I fathomed the bowl." Meaning he'd reached the bottom of the punch bowl.

His mother and wife both laughed riotously.

"Thought you'd be fathoming the *porcelain* bowl, the rate you were drinking," Merrily told him loudly.

"Merrily!" Bridget reproved. It was a phony-baloney kind of reprimand, though, the sort she probably thought a proper lady would give.

Mignon Chesterton, who actually *was* a proper lady, looked aghast.

Roxanne moved on hurriedly. "So you stayed till closing?"

"Then stumbled on down the street. Don't remember seeing them others, but by then I was seeing double or triple." Patrick appeared apologetic. "Didn't mean to tie one on like that, but I got me a bottle of Virginia Gentleman bourbon down at the ABC store and I'd already put a bit of a dent in it when I started on the mint juleps." He shook his head in wonder. "You know they got fifty-six different kinds of bourbon at that ABC Store? I counted. Moonshine, too. Genuine white lightning."

This was getting way off-track. "Bridget, Merrily, did y'all notice anything odd when you came back last night?" Roxanne asked. "That bathroom's at the top of the stairs. Did y'all happen to notice if the door was closed all the way?"

"We didn't see a thing," Bridget pronounced firmly. "We were minding our own business," she sniffed.

"How about y'all?" Roxanne asked, turning toward the Dunwoodys and Forresters.

Dave Dunwoody spoke up first. "I don't recall seeing these good folks on the way home, but by the time we left at midnight, Chowning's was essentially cleared out."

"That's right," Dick Forrester confirmed. "All four of us were bushed, by golly, but we just about closed the place down."

"I don't suppose you happened to notice that upstairs

bathroom window when you walked up the street from Chowning's?" Roxanne wondered.

Dick puffed himself up, indignant, and squinted at her. "I still don't even know exactly what window you're talking about. And we certainly weren't looking around for some cat burglar climbing a tree carrying leeches."

Roxanne had to laugh at the image. It *did* seem improbable.

Barbara Dunwoody, however, was not amused. "Well, *I* think somebody is trying to sabotage this trip," she put in. It was the first time she'd spoken since ordering breakfast. "It's been doomed from the very beginning, when that poor woman fell and broke her leg. And I don't like it one little bit. As far as I'm concerned, we can all go home right now."

"Go, Mom!" Monica announced with sudden vigor, thrusting her fist into the air.

A murmur punctuated by a couple of discreet chuckles passed through the group and Roxanne watched their faces carefully. You could almost watch the coffee reviving them, like time-lapse photography. At the hotel management's suggestion, they were the only guests in the Shields Tavern basement. The Irish Eyes group was rapidly becoming the modern-day equivalent of a plague ship.

Monica offered her mother a perky smile. "We could be out of here in an hour, Mom. I'll go start packing right now."

Across the table, Dave leaned back against the wall, arms crossed, like a passing thunderhead that might or might not suddenly produce a storm. "Nonsense," he told his daughter. "That's all it is, harmless nonsense, and we certainly aren't cutting this trip short. Your mother has been looking forward to it for far too long."

Barbara frowned slightly, but she pasted a little smile on her face as she looked at her husband. *My hero.* Across the table, Mignon Chesterton sat haughty and silent, stirring her coffee, pretending the Flanagans weren't on the same planet, much less in the same room.

Heather Tichener's eyes were still as wide as they'd been when she first scooted out of her room and saw the leeches on the bathroom floor. By gosh, this was an adventure even Felicity couldn't match.

"We came in at ten," Heather volunteered now. "I could hear the TV in Mrs. Chesterton's room and Monica was still out." She looked around. "Upstairs was all quiet, except, of course, that the stairs are so creaky. We kind of tiptoed around, figuring everyone was already asleep."

"I know I certainly was," Roxanne agreed. And she hadn't heard anybody going up or down the stairs.

"Us, too," Harriet Greene put in.

Edna sat beside her, silently pretending to be on a long elevator ride with strangers. Max Becker of Colonial Williamsburg Security had confiscated her teeth, with a promise to return the dentures after breakfast, once he had a chance to examine and clean them. So the poor old gal waited bravely for a breakfast she would have to gum. Very mortifying.

"Edna and I came back after the Lanthorn Tour and read a while," Harriet went on. "I found a wonderful book on plant archaeology in one of the shops. And of course, there's also *Plants of Colonial Williamsburg*. We were in Edna's bedroom, boning up for the Garden Tour today."

Edna nodded glumly.

"How about you two?" Roxanne smiled as she cocked her head at Josie and Larry Vanguard.

Josie flushed slightly. "We came straight back after the Lanthorn Tour and didn't leave our room until we heard Edna screaming this morning."

Of the second-floor residents, only the Vanguards had not immediately come out into the hall. It had probably taken them a while to find some clothing. Behind his bride, Larry Vanguard shrank back into his chair and stared down into his coffee cup. Never terribly chatty, Larry seemed decidedly taciturn this morning.

"That seems to account for everybody's evening," Roxanne said, as two young men in Colonial garb approached the table with trays full of eggs, grits, and Sally Lunn French toast. "If anybody thinks of anything else, please let me know."

As she cut into her French toast, Roxanne remembered the dream that had been interrupted by Edna's frantic screams. It was a dream she had several times a year. She had been seven when Bobby Featherstone accidentally hanged poor little Ray. Tommy had gotten there quickly enough to save the boy's life, but his brain had been deprived of oxygen too long. To this day he lived with his parents in Mecklenburg, a thirty-one-year-old toddler with lousy coordination and virtually no attention span.

Bobby Featherstone had landed in military school, but it didn't take. The last Roxanne heard, he was serving ten-to-fifteen in Huntsville.

She and Tommy had wound up as cops.

And she had never stopped wondering if she might have been able to make it different if she had looked out of the tree-house sooner, had climbed down and tried to stop Bobby, had done *something*.

She had vowed never to make the mistake of paying insufficient attention again. Until Frank Rodriguez died, she thought she'd kept that vow.

But now she was in a spot where something felt terribly wrong, and she couldn't even figure out where her attention should be paid.

🍎 CHAPTER TEN 🍎

ROXANNE CAUGHT up with Larry and Josie Vanguard as they left Shields Tavern.

"I'd like to try to pin down some times a little more precisely," she told them, "since your room is next to Edna's. I'm hoping maybe you saw or heard something without recognizing its importance."

"I can't imagine what," Josie replied nervously. She glanced at Larry, who turned away slightly, picking at imaginary lint on his sleeve.

"Well, let's just run over it again, then. After the Lanthorn Tour, did y'all come back to the hotel straightaway, or maybe stop off somewhere?" Roxanne looked at Larry expectantly, but he merely shrugged and continued fiddling with his sleeve. Was he acting squirrelly from some sort of guilt, or was this simply his personality?

"We came back directly," Josie answered after a moment's hesitation. "I was surprised how tired I'd gotten."

Around them, Roxanne could see and feel Colonial Williamsburg slowly coming alive. There were more tourists on Duke of Gloucester Street than there'd been when the group went to breakfast, though the pace was still leisurely and the school groups hadn't yet begun to arrive. Various Colonial characters moved purposefully about, opening shops, setting out clotheslines of beribboned straw ladies' hats and artful piles of baskets.

Roxanne noticed a man in Colonial garb sitting on the front

steps of Botsforth Tavern, up ahead. A guard, perhaps? She had suggested that Security lock the building and issue keys to her people.

"Let's stop here for a moment," Roxanne suggested, "so we won't be distracted once we get to Botsforth Tavern." She gestured toward a wooden bench on the sidewalk beside one of the many buildings not open to the public. Many Colonial Williamsburg employees lived in restored lodgings rented from the Foundation. Not a bad gig.

"I don't intend to *ever* be distracted in that place," Josie replied with a shudder, taking a seat on the bench. "No telling *what* might happen if you're not paying attention!"

Larry waited till Roxanne perched on a flight of stairs beside the bench before taking a seat on Josie's far side and staring diffidently across the street. He still hadn't uttered so much as a grunt.

"Does that worry you, too, Larry?" Roxanne asked pointedly.

He shook his head as he took Josie's hand in his. "Some kind of screwed-up joke, that's all." He glanced quickly at Roxanne, then looked away as he gave his bride's hand a light squeeze.

"Do you have any idea what might be behind it all?"

"Nope." Larry Vanguard leaned back and stretched his legs out in front of him, all talked out. He made a show of watching a young woman across the street prop open the front door of a general store.

"How about you, Josie?" Roxanne persisted.

The woman frowned. "All I know is, I don't like this one little bit. I wonder if maybe Barbara doesn't have the right idea, and we shouldn't just all go home."

Josie Vanguard looked tired this morning, and she seemed jittery. Was she worried because she suspected—or maybe even knew—that Larry was involved in the continuing sabotage of the Guns and Roses tour? Or was her reaction perfectly normal for a sixtyish honeymooner awakened abruptly after only six hours of sleep?

Roxanne smiled gently. "Which door did you come in last

night?" Botsforth Tavern had both front and rear entrances, the back door opening into a charming garden.

"The front," Josie answered, "off Duke of Gloucester. We went straight upstairs."

"And stayed there?"

Josie started to nod, then stopped abruptly. "Oh, wait. Larry went back down for ice right after we got back."

"Uh-huh," Roxanne murmured encouragingly. "Did you see or hear anything when you came down for the ice, Larry?"

"Granny was coming in," he answered. "You know. Mrs. Chesterton."

Something was still wrong here. Josie was clutching Larry's hand so tightly that it must have hurt him. He put his other hand over hers and began to gently massage her fingers. Either affection or self-defense.

"Was the hall light on upstairs?" Roxanne asked.

Josie nodded. Larry continued to stare across the street.

"Do you remember seeing the door to the bathroom when you passed by?"

"Not particularly," Josie answered after a moment's hesitation. "I know it wasn't open, and I think I would have noticed if it were ajar. I remember all the doors being closed. Though I didn't really look at the ones on the other end, where your room is."

"I see. After you went into your own room, did either of you hear anything from out in the hall?"

"Not a thing," Josie said.

"Your bathroom shares a wall with Harriet and Edna's bath," Roxanne noted. "They came back pretty directly, too, with me. Do you recall hearing anything when you were brushing your teeth or getting ready for bed?"

The question seemed futile. From what she'd previously inferred, the Vanguards' process of getting ready for bed mostly entailed ripping off each other's clothes. During which they weren't likely to hear anything but each other's fevered breathing.

Sure enough, neither one of them remembered hearing a thing. Larry seemed visibly relieved when Roxanne stood up.

"I won't keep y'all," she told them with an easy smile. How had it happened that she was doing interrogations at an historic site in Virginia, anyway? "I need to go find our Yorktown guide. Just don't go too far away, all right? The Yorktown tour's supposed to leave in another ten minutes."

"I just don't understand," Josie whined, as she let Larry pull her to her feet. "It never occurred to me that I wouldn't be totally safe on this tour. And here I am, a nervous wreck."

For the first time all morning, Larry Vanguard spoke without prompting. "Then let's just leave, sweetheart. We could go back to Atlantic City, or any place you want to go."

"But this *is* where I wanted to go," Josie told him, near tears. "I just want to feel *safe* again."

"We all do," Roxanne told her, putting one hand on the woman's shoulder, wondering what in the devil she was going to tell Maureen *this* time.

❦

Maureen O'Malley had long ago networked her home computer to the office so she could work at home evenings and weekends. She hadn't realized it would also be useful in the instance that one contracted a disfiguring disease common to four-year-olds.

She was feeling considerably better, finally. Her fever had broken and the worst of the pocks were going away. She had scratched a couple on her legs and would probably have scars, but she was too old to worry about that. She'd managed to avoid scratching the ones on her forehead, anyway. Though a couple little facial scars might have provided a nice excuse for the face lift she'd been considering.

But she still wasn't quite presentable enough to be out in public. So Maureen had spent the morning juggling minor crises for Irish Eyes Travel out of her home office. It was overcast in Del Mar today, which fit her mood just perfectly.

The events in Virginia were simply inexplicable, and *had* to be aimed at her and her business. For three days, her every spare moment had been spent dredging up instances where someone had or could have taken offense. There were ample cases of both, but nothing that should have prompted *this*.

She had screwed up reservations now and again, of course, had reserved folks onto airlines that went belly-up, refusing to make good on prepaid tickets. On occasion, she'd booked people into hotels with vermin problems, recommended restaurants replete with salmonella. A tour group had once been stranded for forty-eight hours by a Central American earthquake.

But Maureen always made good on those sorts of things, even comped customers in certain extreme situations. Her willingness to make things better, to go that extra mile, had brought her plenty of good will. Or so she'd always believed. Hers was a loyal clientele, some of whom had been with her for decades.

As she waited on hold trying to untangle yet another airline snafu, she again tried to think of anyone who might want to harm her.

After a while, she gave up and checked on flights from San Diego into Norfolk. The connections were pretty ghastly, which fit the situation just fine.

❦

Safety.

Throughout the day Roxanne reflected upon the concept.

Safety. So often it was defined by its absence.

And yet almost everything entailed risk, whether it was answering a police call, or apprehending an armed gang member, or crossing a busy street, or simply getting out of bed in the morning.

Perhaps all safety was simply a question of degrees of self-delusion.

That afternoon, Roxanne looked into the hidden cellars beneath the slave quarters at the nearby Carter's Grove Plantation, where people who didn't even own themselves had tucked away the small things that were precious to them. And she thought again about safety.

Maybe safety could never be more than relative.

And transitory.

Harriet Greene watched her friend closely through the afternoon. Edna's teeth had finally been returned. After retreating into the bathroom and scrubbing them for at least fifteen minutes, Edna had emerged with the dentures in position and a grim, closed-mouthed smile. Harriet had known better than to offer any comment whatsoever.

She rather admired Edna's pragmatism, actually. In her friend's position, Harriet would probably have thrown the dentures away and cashed in a C.D. to get a new set.

Harriet found the overall sense of order in Williamsburg very satisfying. From the very start they'd done things right: proper zoning, strict housing regulations, a very English sense that they were creating something that would last. Most of the gardens in town and at Carter's Grove reflected that discipline and sense of order as well.

Mignon Chesterton had seemed particularly at home at Carter's Grove Plantation. In the Refusal Room, Harriet had cocked her head toward Mignon and whispered to Edna, "All you'd need to do is put her in a Colonial dress and turn the clock back two hundred years."

Her friend had nodded. "I can practically hear her ordering the slaves about."

Edna gradually perked up, but only once did she smile. That was when the guide explained that the woman who'd restored Carter's Grove in the thirties used to serve refreshments incognito and meander around the grounds during Garden Week when the place was open to the public, listening to gossip and spreading a rumor or two herself.

Like the one about both Thomas Jefferson and George Washington proposing marriage and being turned down in the "Refusal Room." Or the one about the British colonel riding his horse up the large curved stairway, leaving slashes with his sword in the banister as he passed.

Neither story, it seemed, was actually true.

Harriet found it interesting how much of that sort of mythology was associated with this period, how little people actually *knew* about life only two hundred years ago. Daily life in Colonial Williamsburg had been pieced together from odd scraps of surviving information: journal fragments, receipts, newspaper accounts, inventories of Governor's Palace items.

In contrast to the present, when every single move that *any* person made was documented and noted in a hundred different places and computers. The difficulty for historians seeking information in centuries to come would be sifting through this surfeit of material to figure out what, if anything, was actually important.

❦

Mignon Chesterton thought that Heather Tichener looked truly precious.

The girl wore a long russet skirt with a little white flower-sprigged jacket that laced tightly up the front and featured white ruffles at collar and sleeves. With it she wore white tights, simple black pumps, and a lace-trimmed round-eared cap that tied beneath her chin. Only her hair was wrong, unruly shoulder-length curls instead of a properly restrained eighteenth-century mane.

Her grandmother wore too much makeup and too many fancy rings ever to pass for an authentic Colonial matron. Still, Evelyn's lovely dark blue gown might have been stitched up at the Milliner's and worn with pride by the Colonial Governor's wife.

"I swear," Harriet Greene noted fondly, "the two of you look like you ought to be on the payroll here."

Heather offered a demure curtsy. "Thank you, Mrs. Greene. That's ever so kind of you to say."

The Irish Eyes group had just finished a dinner delivered by room service to the parlor of Botsforth Tavern. When Roxanne suggested dining in, Mignon had gratefully seized the opportunity. Her family was going to a seafood restaurant on the James River, but Mignon was weary of Monica's continual complaints. Fortunately, that wretched Flanagan family had also gone out, to some steak house where you ordered your meat by having them hack off a chunk of raw flesh at your table. Just their trashy style.

Evelyn sat by the fireplace in a dark blue wing chair that nearly matched her dress. She smoothed her skirts and chuckled. "Last night when we passed Chowning's Tavern after the Lanthorn Tour, Heather climbed up on one of those benches out front to look in the window. And then inside, I could see that a couple of people had noticed her. They were truly startled."

"I haven't seen any children in costume here," Roxanne noted. She also seemed more relaxed tonight, though not much. You had to give her credit for trying, *really* trying, but her inexperience was glaringly obvious. "They probably thought they were seeing things. You know, the local equivalent of a pink elephant." She dropped her voice an octave, simulating a male voice: "Cut me off, Ethel. I just saw a Colonial child."

Mignon watched with interest as Edna Stanton gave an inadvertently broad smile. Mignon found the idea of wearing teeth that had cohabited with leeches profoundly unsettling.

"Well, you're just as pretty as a picture, Heather," Edna told the girl. Continuing to smile.

"Thank you, Mrs. Stanton." Heather smiled conspiratorially. "We're going to reenact the Gunpowder Incident tonight. Where Felicity overhears soldiers in the Magazine getting ready to remove the colonists' gunpowder. She spreads the alarm."

Something very strange was going on in this group, Mignon realized. She did not believe that the group was banding together out of solidarity, or even the notion of safety in numbers. The hidden agenda, as Dave might have put it, was that nobody really wanted to let anybody else out of sight. And rightfully so.

Still, the dinner conversation had been pleasant, a congenial rehash of the day. The group was small and exclusively female: Roxanne, Heather and Evelyn, Harriet and Edna, Mignon herself. At this point, Mignon was willing to settle for anything that didn't involve the Flanagans or active disruption.

The Ticheners left on their historical errand. Roxanne remained with Harriet, Edna, and Mignon in the parlor, looking

increasingly restless. Suddenly the conversation took an astonishing turn.

"I heard you talking to the security officers this morning,
Roxanne," Harriet announced, her sharp gray eyes focused on
the guide. "Did I understand correctly that you told them you
used to be a policewoman?"

Roxanne nodded slowly.

Harriet's eyebrows rose high and stayed there. "I never met
a girl policeman before. How did you happen to choose that
line of work?"

"I guess it kind of chose me," Roxanne answered. She
looked uncomfortable. "You might say that police work is our
family business. My daddy's the chief of police in my home
town and my granddaddy and great-granddaddy were both
Texas Rangers. I always wanted to be a cop. It just seemed like
such an obvious thing to do."

Mignon was shocked. "Too dangerous, it seems to me," she
pronounced firmly. The very notion was appalling. There were
some things that women simply were not meant to do.

"I suppose there's a certain amount of danger in any occupation," Roxanne replied carefully. "But for me the satisfaction
always made it worth the risk." She seemed to be somehow
editing her remarks. "I was a patrol officer, and a lot of my
work involved traffic violations. Speeding, drunk drivers,
that sort of thing. People who shouldn't be on the road in the
first place." As she spoke, there was increased animation in her
face.

It didn't quite make sense. "Well, if you like it so much, what
on earth are you doing here?" Mignon asked. These young girls
all seemed to be so flighty, though perhaps it was unfair to
lump Roxanne with Monica or that scatterbrained Merrily
Flanagan.

Roxanne sighed. "I'm on a leave of absence," she said simply.
"My partner was killed in the line of duty. I decided I needed
some time away from the job."

Mignon Chesterton felt a crimson wave of mortification
sweep over her. How *could* she have been so appallingly insen-

sitive, so desperately rude? The girl had all but begged her not to pursue the subject.

"My dear," Mignon told her, leaning forward, wringing her hands softly, "I'm so *terribly* sorry. Such a dreadful experience for someone so young. I didn't mean to pry. Please forgive me for adding to your pain with my thoughtlessness."

"You're not prying," Roxanne told her calmly. "It's all right. I was ready for a change anyway." She grinned. "And now I have one of the most exciting jobs imaginable."

Edna Stanton rolled her eyes. "I could do with a little less excitement," she told Roxanne.

Smiling again. Mignon had to admire her fortitude.

❦

Heather was giddy with excitement as she and Grandma moved down Duke of Gloucester toward the Magazine. *Finally* they were going to recreate the Gunpowder Incident! She skipped along, moving up ahead and then coming back. Grandma was old, of course, but did she have to be so ridiculously *slow?*

It was nice and dark now and there weren't very many people around. Earlier there had been large, rowdy school groups around the Magazine, doing some kind of program that involved a lot of shouting and some really neat bonfires. But now the kids were gone and the last fire was nearly out.

Perfect.

Heather really didn't want to do this in front of an audience, after all. And it would spoil the authenticity if folks were wandering around in blue jeans and sweatshirts.

They approached the green surrounding the Magazine, where gunpowder and weapons had been stored for safekeeping in Colonial times. Heather decided it would probably be a good idea to explain again just what they would be doing. Grandma could be very dense and forgetful.

"You'll stand guard," she told Grandma. "I'll sneak up to the side of the Magazine where I can overhear the soldiers planning to remove the colonists' gunpowder. Then I'll circle back to tell you and we'll head off to spread the alarm."

"Whatever you say, dear." Grandma didn't seem too enthusiastic, but Heather didn't care. It was an absolutely perfect night, with lots of stars but only a bitty little crescent moon over the Courthouse. Very dark.

"All right, then. See over there, where the market stalls are set up?"

Heather pointed across Market Square at a grouping of rough wooden frame structures where folks in Colonial clothes sold hats and lemonade and other stuff during the day. Grandma nodded. She looked wonderfully Colonial in her dress.

"Well, you go wait over there by the animal pens," Heather told her. "If both of us sneak up, we might make too much noise and alert them."

"Okay."

Grandma positioned herself as suggested. Heather waited a moment, then slipped into the shadows. There was very little light out here, just a couple electric lights positioned high in the trees. After this little bit of cover, it would be wide open the rest of the way to the Magazine. She looked carefully around her in all directions, then sprinted across the open space toward the imposing brick walls of the Magazine.

Once there, she slipped back around into the darker area at the rear of the wall, away from the gate. She closed her eyes and breathed deeply, taking in the scent of the night and carrying herself back through time. She was Felicity now, had snuck out of her window in darkness to waken Ben and get Isaac. She imagined Ben and Isaac at her sides, could almost feel their presence as she flattened herself against the brick wall and moved slowly around the building. They'd be lifting her to see over the wall. She closed her eyes and imagined that part, could almost feel her body rising.

Out in front would be the tricky part. The front gate to the Magazine was locked now, of course, but it would have been closed up then, too. She could sense the presence of the governor's soldiers inside. It was all so wonderfully real. She was a little chilly now. If she'd had a shawl, it would be perfect.

She slipped past the front gates of the Magazine, then raced back to where Grandma stood guard by the market stalls. In her haste, she nearly tripped over some kindling left scattered on the ground at a chopping block in front of the Magazine.

"They're moving the gunpowder," she whispered. "We have to spread the alarm."

"All right, Felicity," Grandma told her. Then she turned and gave Heather a big hug. "You're having fun, aren't you?"

"Oh, *yes!*" Heather answered. "Can we do it again?"

"Of course, darling." And bless her heart, Grandma slipped into the shadows of the empty market stalls and turned to peer down the street. "Go ahead, Felicity. The coast is clear on this side."

Heather joyfully slipped back into the shadows again and repeated the entire scene. This time she noticed a couple coming out the side gate from the Market Square Tavern next door, but they ignored her and crossed toward the Courthouse. There was also somebody back by the Guardhouse, a vaguely familiar figure. She went on alert—the governor's men!—but when she looked again, the figure was gone. She continued around the Magazine and back toward Grandma.

After meeting up with Grandma the second time, she decided to change the game slightly. This time she would listen longer on the far side of the Magazine.

She was concentrating on hearing the imaginary voices inside the Magazine when she heard real footsteps coming up behind her. Before she could turn around, a hand clamped her mouth and a dark bag fell over her face. She couldn't scream because of the hand on her mouth and she couldn't see because of the bag.

All she could do was wiggle and try to squirm away. But then something was pressing into her neck and she could feel herself losing consciousness.

The last thing she managed to do before everything went black was to kick off one black leather pump.

❦ CHAPTER ELEVEN ❦

THE FRONT door of Botsforth Tavern crashed open and Evelyn Tichener rushed into the sitting room, distraught. She waved a small black shoe and looked around frantically.

"Is Heather here?" she asked. Her tone verged on hysteria. "Did she come back?"

Roxanne stood abruptly, gaze riveted to the shoe. She'd been looking for a gracious exit opportunity, but this was not it. This sounded like very bad news.

"Why no, Evelyn," Roxanne answered quickly. "We haven't seen her since the two of you left, and nobody's been in or out of here since then."

Evelyn threw her hands out at her sides. "Oh, what am I going to do?" she wailed. "I can't find her *anywhere*. She's *disappeared!*" She collapsed into a chair, sobbing wildly. "*What* am I going to tell her parents?"

Roxanne dropped to her knees in front of the woman, took hold of her trembling wrists. Evelyn's hands desperately clutched the small shoe.

"What happened, Evelyn? Tell me what's going on so I can help," Roxanne urged.

Evelyn looked around the room blindly. "We were at the Magazine," she began, choking through sobs. "Acting out that silly gunpowder business. Heather had it all planned. She would sneak up on the Magazine and I'd wait in the shadows. Then after she 'overheard' what was happening, she'd come back and we'd spread the alarm."

Evelyn ripped the ruffled mobcap off her head and tossed it onto the floor. Harriet Greene, circling anxiously, discreetly picked the cap up and laid it on the table.

Roxanne took a fast look at her watch. It couldn't be much more than fifteen or twenty minutes since Evelyn and Heather had left this room. "She wasn't mad at you or anything?" Roxanne made the question offhand, but watched the woman carefully. If Heather had run off in a tiff and Evelyn was covering her own ass, better to find out up front. Easier to look for Heather, too.

Though it didn't explain the shoe.

"Good heavens, no!" Evelyn was so indignant she sat up straight. "She was absolutely ecstatic that we had all evening to prowl the streets. As far as I could tell, we were going to be reenacting the Gunpowder Incident until I dropped."

Roxanne nodded. Evelyn's reaction seemed genuine, and it fit with the way the pair had seemed when they left Botsforth Tavern. Excited. Enthusiastic. Energized. "Could she have decided to change the game and be hiding as part of some new scenario?"

Evelyn shook her head. "No. We'd already done it twice. She did it the same way both times."

"Could you see her as she went around the Magazine?"

Evelyn shook her head again. "No, that's the whole problem. She'd be circling so I couldn't see her on the back side. And I was supposed to be a lookout." She looked mildly embarrassed. "I was watching for the governor's minions coming from the other direction, to steal the gunpowder."

Actually playing along with Heather's game. Roxanne found the notion rather charming even if it made things tougher now. "So on the third time you played the same game, Heather went behind the Magazine and didn't come out again?"

"Exactly."

"How long was it before you started to look for her?"

Evelyn's eyes went blank. "You know, I can never tell about time, and without my glasses I can't even read my wristwatch.

But it really didn't seem very long. Not more than a couple of minutes."

"After which you...?"

"Started walking toward the Magazine, calling her. At first I thought she was playing some kind of silly hide-and-seek or something, that she was planning to jump out and scare the daylights out of me. But when I got all the way to the far side of the Magazine and she wasn't there, I didn't know what to think. I started calling her and calling her and looking everywhere, and then I saw her shoe just lying there and I totally panicked. I guess I was hoping that something had scared her and she'd run back here, but she's not here and I just don't know what I'm going to *do*." Evelyn leaned back, exhausted.

Roxanne gently removed the shoe from her grip, sliding two fingers inside and avoiding the smooth black leather surface. There weren't likely to be any prints on it anyway, except Heather's own and the ones Evelyn had put on handling it just now. Which probably didn't matter anyway. If it had fallen off in the course of an abduction, *nobody* would have touched it.

In the course of an abduction. Why was she assuming the worst?

Because, Roxanne realized, she was a cop at her core.

Roxanne stood up. Harriet Greene, hovering like a hummingbird, moved in to light on her haunches beside Evelyn's chair.

"We'll find her," Harriet soothed. "Now don't you worry, Evelyn."

"I'm calling Security," Roxanne announced, "and the Williamsburg cops. Then I'm going to the Magazine and look for her myself."

"I'm coming with you," Evelyn said, trying to stand up. She miscalculated, fell weakly back into the chair.

"You might be better off staying here," Roxanne suggested mildly. Evelyn would only be helpful if she didn't interrupt the search to have a heart attack.

"No," Evelyn insisted. "I *have* to go."

Mignon Chesterton had been sitting silently beside the fireplace, wearing an expression of mild horror. Now she rose and crossed to the doorway.

"Time is wasting," Mignon proclaimed. "You may telephone for assistance from my room, Roxanne. I'm directly across the hall here."

"And then we'll all go with you to the Magazine," Edna declared. "Do you want your jacket, Harriet?" She frowned. "Perhaps somebody should stay here, in case Heather comes back?"

"An excellent idea." Mignon Chesterton unlocked her door and stepped aside. "I'll remain in the parlor here while you girls go." She waved a dismissive hand as Roxanne followed her into the room. "Please forgive the mess."

"Of course," Roxanne told her, crossing to the phone. "And do you have some kind of plastic bag to put this shoe in?"

"Certainly." Mrs. Chesterton reached in the closet for a laundry bag.

The alleged mess, Roxanne realized as she waited for somebody to answer the phone at Security, consisted of one copy of *Colonial Williamsburg* magazine lying slightly askew on the bedside table. Beyond that, there were no clues to show that the room wasn't being occupied by Mrs. Peyton Randolph in 1779.

Though Mrs. Randolph would have been mystified by the telephone and television.

🍂

Two security officers met the Irish Eyes contingent at the Magazine. One was very old and one very young, arriving on a bicycle. Garrison, the older officer, came in an unmarked white Chevy and spoke reassuringly at first. Not dismissive, but almost.

"She'll turn up soon," Garrison promised Roxanne. "Kids wander off all the time, never realizing the fuss they set off. You say she was playing a game with her grandma, why I bet she'll pop out from behind a bush any second now."

Roxanne shook her head. "She dropped a shoe," she told him flatly. "On that oyster-shell area over there, which she certainly wouldn't walk through barefoot. I have the shoe bagged for evidence back at Botsforth Tavern."

Garrison looked much more concerned now. "I'll call my supervisor," he said. "Maybe we should get the Williamsburg Police over here."

"I already called them. What I'd suggest is that you get Max Becker out here if he's not already on his way."

"Yes, ma'am." The Colonial Williamsburg cops were nothing if not polite.

Evelyn had already shown Roxanne where she had been standing during the game and about where she'd found the shoe. Now Roxanne began a more systematic search. From her father she had learned early on the value of a first-class flashlight. The small one she'd brought on this trip—while no match for what she carried in uniform—had an exceptionally bright halogen beam.

The Magazine was a singular structure, dominating a wide grassy lawn on Market Square. Originally built in 1715 to house the Virginia Colony's weapons and gunpowder, the solid octagonal brick building was surrounded by an equally solid octagonal eight-foot brick wall. The wall's diameter was large enough, Roxanne could see immediately, so that Heather, circling the perimeter, would have been out of sight a while before she reappeared at the opposite side. The only entrance in the wall was the front gate and it seemed thoroughly locked and forbidding.

Evelyn was vague about the precise spot where she'd found the shoe, but the general location was certain. It was on the eastern side of the Magazine, on an area of crushed oyster shells where foot traffic had worn away the grass over time. Evelyn was quite sure she had found it within ten feet of the brick wall.

Edna and Harriet, meanwhile, had immediately begun to look for the missing girl, calling Heather's name in firm midwestern tones. They were quickly joined by half a dozen others who happened along, including a pair of Williamsburg employees in Colonial dress.

The calls were soft and insistent as the searchers fanned out. Most went in the direction Heather had last been seen moving, due east toward the Market Square Tavern. Others headed toward the Guardhouse and bus stop to the southeast, the Courthouse to the north, Chowning's Tavern to the northeast. A couple even went due west toward where Evelyn had been standing during the reenactment.

Roxanne had been thinking the situation through as she sprinted down Duke of Gloucester Street after calling Security. Now she stationed Edna to keep people out of the general area where the shoe had been found, on the off chance that a diligent crime scene tech might find further evidence there.

Time was the critical factor.

There really hadn't been very much of it.

Give Evelyn two minutes' standing and waiting—watching for imaginary British soldiers—before she noticed that Heather hadn't returned. Maybe another minute or two to meander to the far side of the Magazine after she did notice. She wouldn't be in a particular hurry, after all. Just mildly annoyed.

That would provide enough time for somebody to sweep a little girl soundlessly off into the shadows, leaving behind only a black leather pump.

Somebody.

Somebody who might be male or female, Heather being a relatively small child. And in two minutes that Somebody could easily reach a car in the lot behind the Market Square Tavern and be long gone. Duncan, the younger security guy on the bike, had already set off to check that area.

That Somebody might possibly have even taken Heather into the Market Square Tavern itself. It was the nearest public building, after all, though most people probably didn't realize its doors were open. Like Botsforth Tavern, the Market Square Tavern housed guests seeking an authentic Colonial experience.

Roxanne urged Garrison from Security to start banging on room doors inside the Tavern, and after calling in for reinforcements, he readily agreed to start rousing the Tavern guests. To raise the alarm, just as Felicity allegedly had in the Gunpowder

Incident. Even if Heather weren't inside somewhere, it was entirely possible that somebody had seen or heard something.

Roxanne began her own systematic search by checking the Guardhouse southeast of the Magazine. The building itself was locked and showed no obvious sign of recent entry. But it was partially surrounded in back by thick bushes, reached by a well-worn path between building and shrubbery. A perfect hiding place near the Magazine for somebody waiting to grab a little girl passing nearby.

There was nobody back there now, however, and only one entrance. Frustrated, Roxanne returned to the Square.

Next she moved systematically along the low white picket fence along the Market Square side of the Tavern. Here there were bushes, ivy-covered trees with many low branches, piles of oyster shells, and split wood to be used for fires. Plenty of places for brief concealment, but no sign of anybody now.

The grasses along the fence were taller than those out on the field, overdue for mowing—or scything, or being chewed by goats, however they handled lawn management here. But there was no indication of a recent struggle.

In any case, Roxanne realized glumly, the impromptu search parties that now dotted the area were probably destroying any possible evidence.

And what was taking the Williamsburg Police so long, anyway?

Two gates led from the grassy field into the Tavern yard, each entering a different section of the garden. Roxanne moved into the rear Tavern garden through the back gate. This section of garden was relatively open, showcasing large rectangular beds full of tulips. She made a speedy circuit, calling Heather's name softly and flashing her light systematically, then moved into the section of yard closest to the Tavern. Here the dependencies were clustered. Outbuildings like these—which had housed the colonists' kitchens, laundries, and slaves—were often rented out as hotel lodgings or staff apartments.

The dependencies at Market Square Tavern included a posh two-story guest house that had once been the kitchen and a smaller, windowless building closed by a large old-fashioned padlock. A smokehouse, probably. Roxanne banged on the door of the small building, called Heather's name, and listened carefully.

No answer.

No sound at all.

She next went to the kitchen guest house, compact, with dormer windows on its second story. The lights were out here and nobody answered door-banging, window-knocking, or shouting. Outside, firewood was stacked beneath a tree in an undisturbed pile that hid no small girls.

The Tavern building itself had a slanted storm door presumably leading into the basement, but that, too, was chained and padlocked. The little corridor between the two rear outdoor sections of the main building simply led into an interior hall, and the narrow path between the building and the fence on the Magazine side dead-ended.

This was not going well.

And where in the *hell* were the cops?

Roxanne flashed her light around an old well, tightly covered, with a bucket nailed down artistically. Four picnic-style benches sat around the well and the whole thing was covered with a pointed roof. Nothing seemed to be recently disturbed.

"Heather!"

"Heather?"

"Heather!"

All around her she could hear voices calling the missing girl. The search party had grown dramatically, with people pouring out of the Market Square Tavern and Chowning's Tavern, eager to help once they learned of the problem.

Roxanne was acutely aware of time slipping past. And loss of control. They'd been back at the Magazine for over five minutes now, with nothing to show for it other than a growing crowd of upset people, roving in all directions.

Then, finally, reinforcements came.

Max Becker, head of investigations for Colonial Williamsburg Security, arrived first. Becker had impressed Roxanne this morning—was it really just this morning?—after Edna's close encounter with the leeches. He'd assessed the situation, taken it seriously, and turned it over to Williamsburg PD, which sent out an evidence tech who gathered up the larger slivers of glass and dusted for fingerprints.

Becker looked around the crowded Magazine area now and softly cursed.

"It's out of control," Roxanne conceded, "but there wasn't any way I could keep people out and still look myself. Looking seemed more important, frankly. I did set up somebody to keep folks out of the area where Evelyn found Heather's shoe." She allowed herself a brief smile. "Your buddy from this morning. Edna Stanton."

Max Becker emitted a low growl. Under his breath, Roxanne thought she heard him mutter, "Have you people considered going to Gettysburg?"

No answer seemed required. "What I'd like to do," Roxanne told him, "is clear all these people out of the area around the Magazine and then try to reenact what happened with Evelyn. Get her sense of how long things took. See just how far somebody could get. Your guy Duncan went to check out the parking lot behind Market Square Tavern early on."

Max Becker swiveled his head sharply. "Duncan!"

The younger officer appeared almost instantly. "Sir?"

"You checked the parking lot behind the Tavern?"

Duncan nodded intently. "Yes, sir. There's a couple were waiting at the bus stop to go back to their room at Woodlands. They said they didn't see any cars come out of the lot there, or come out Queen Street, neither."

"And nobody could have gone out Duke of Gloucester, 'cause it doesn't open to vehicular traffic till ten." For reasons that Roxanne couldn't comprehend, the historic area was open to cars at night. The Colonial Williamsburg Foundation, which had thought of virtually everything else, had somehow failed to buy up the streets.

Becker looked mildly pleased. "Did these people seem reliable, Duncan? You kept them around, I presume?"

"Oh, you bet, sir. They're over by the Guardhouse."

"Bring them over, will you, son?"

Duncan scooted away and Becker turned to Garrison. "You get anything out of the guests in the Tavern?"

Garrison shook his head. "Watching TV, mostly. Nobody saw anything, nobody heard anything."

"What about the rooms where nobody was home?"

Garrison looked puzzled. "What about them?"

Becker inhaled. "Did you check them?"

"Uh, no."

"Well, take somebody inside and check *all* the rooms. Use a passkey. Get inside. Closets, baths, under beds. But before you start that, round up everybody you see around here who's in costume, all the employees, and send 'em to me."

Duncan returned with the couple who'd been waiting at the bus stop. They were in their late sixties, and it was clear once they began talking that they were excellent witnesses, the kind of fussy, nosy folks who thrive on other people's business.

Ruth and Martin Schindelbaum were from Chicago, newly retired to Fort Myers, Florida. They had arrived at the bus stop at eight fifty-seven. Ruth had looked at her watch. An elderly couple passed a minute or two later, walking down Queen Street and crossing Francis Street toward the Williamsburg Inn. The couple had nodded and exchanged "Good evenings" with the Schindelbaums. A young black man in Colonial dress had ridden past on a bicycle. A car passed on Francis Street playing music that was far too loud.

The Schindelbaums missed little and approved of less. The bus was late. Ruth had consulted her watch again and Martin had consulted his. Martin's was one minute faster and said nine-eleven. Ruth's said nine-ten. It was around then that they first heard a woman calling, "Heather."

Evelyn.

Which gave them the precise time of the abduction, if nothing else. And the Schindelbaums were absolutely convinced that nobody had passed them coming from either the Magazine or the Market Square Tavern.

Max Becker turned on the charm. "Mr. Schindelbaum, Mrs. Schindelbaum, I can't thank you enough for being so observant and cooperative." Ruth came close to blushing. Fussbudget Martin twitched his head to suggest that fulsome praise got ever so tiresome for a chap such as himself. "Do you suppose you could wait for me inside the Market Square Tavern here, in the sitting room?"

"Why, certainly—" Ruth Schindelbaum began, but her husband cut her off.

"We wouldn't want to miss the last bus," Martin Schindelbaum whined.

"I'll see that you get safely back to your hotel, sir, absolutely. Now Officer Duncan here will show you where to wait."

Seven or eight Williamsburg employees in varying styles of Colonial dress had arrived by now. Becker looked them over, then spoke directly to a fortyish man with a graying ponytail that was clearly no wig. "Hank, can you give us a hand?"

"You bet," Hank told him. "I've got a daughter of my own." The man looked vaguely familiar. Was he a waiter? One of the craftsmen? That was it. Roxanne had seen him working at the Silversmith's shop.

"Hank, if you'd go with Officer Garrison here, I'd like you two to check all the rooms in the Tavern. Start with the cellar."

Becker turned to the other "colonists" around him. "The rest of you, if you'd clear the square for me, please. I want everybody out of the area from Duke of Gloucester back to Francis and from Queen Street to the first buildings and fences on the west. Get their names and home addresses as you kick them out, and then when the area's emptied, spread yourselves out along the perimeters and keep people from coming in. You see any buddies come along, folks who work here, deputize them. Any questions?"

Four Williamsburg city patrol officers finally arrived as the costumed employees set off on their crowd control mission. The cops all knew Max Becker and deferred to him automatically on his own turf. They were apologetic, delayed by a nasty accident out near the James City County line that had sent three people to the hospital and one to the morgue.

The cops had arrived, Roxanne noticed, without sirens or flashing lights. A tacit agreement, no doubt, to avoid any unsettling commotion that might upset the tourism upon which the entire town was so dependent.

A minute or two later, Detective John Clemens of the Williamsburg Police arrived. Clemens, like Max Becker, exuded the easy authority of a truly professional lawman. He was in his mid-thirties, tall and lean. He wore a light sport coat over dark slacks, and his poorly tied necktie appeared to be an afterthought. He had dark penetrating eyes and dark hair thinning at the temples.

Clemens listened closely as Roxanne recapped the past half hour's madness.

"I met the people in this tour group earlier today," Max Becker put in, when she was done. "We had a little episode up at Botsforth Tavern where they're staying. Some leeches found their way into a glass holding a lady's dentures. Your man Sam Nash came out and checked for prints."

Clemens raised his eyebrows. "And?"

"And nothing," Becker answered. "Had all the earmarks of a mean-spirited prank. Ms. Prescott here was right helpful. She's a sworn officer in Austin, Texas. On leave. I checked her with Austin."

Oh had he, now? The action showed a thoroughness that Roxanne rather admired, even though it startled and vaguely offended her.

"Is that so?" Clemens considered a moment. "You called this in, Ms. Prescott?"

Roxanne nodded.

"You don't think the girl just wandered off?"

Roxanne shook her head firmly. "I'd consider it, except she seems extremely responsible. More to the point, she dropped a shoe out there on the oyster shells."

Clemens winced. "Ouch. Where are the parents?"

"She's here with her grandmother. Over there, in costume." Evelyn stood wringing her hands beside Harriet Greene, who had taken on the role of stalwart companion.

The detective looked mildly puzzled. "What's she dressed up for?"

"It was part of the game she was playing with Heather. Heather's in Colonial costume, too."

"Oh. And where *are* the parents?" Clemens asked.

"Back home in California," Roxanne answered.

"Any custody problems that you know of?"

Roxanne shook her head. "Nothing that anybody's mentioned. The parents are still married to each other. Heather told me quite a bit about her family life the other night. Nothing she said set off any warning bells." She had the feeling that John Clemens would be a useful person with whom to discuss the continuing series of bizarre problems that had plagued the Irish Eyes group. Once Heather was found.

"The family has money?"

Roxanne allowed herself a minor chuckle. "These people *all* have money, at least by *my* standards. If you mean, is this a ransom situation, I suppose it's possible. But listen, we were just about to try to reenact what happened." She explained briefly. "Could we go ahead with it?"

Clemens cocked his head. "Don't see what it could hurt."

And so they took their places, Evelyn standing with Harriet on the far side of the green and Roxanne playing the part of Heather.

"Just concentrate on what we're doing," Roxanne told Evelyn soothingly. "Don't think about the people around us. Close your eyes if it will help. Now. Detective Clemens here is going to time what happens. We can do it a couple times till you feel we have the time frame right."

"I won't be able to tell anything," Evelyn wailed helplessly.

"Of course you can, dear." Harriet Greene was softly reassuring. The lady was a real rock. "Just close your eyes and take a deep breath and then we'll start."

"All right," Evelyn answered doubtfully. She inhaled twice, then turned to Roxanne. "I'm ready."

Roxanne nodded to John Clemens, then sauntered off across

the green toward the Magazine, pretending to be ten years old. She tried to get inside Heather's head as she moved. Stealth would be paramount. She slunk across to the Magazine and then flattened herself against the wall. When she looked back, Evelyn was gazing off toward the Courthouse. John Clemens pointed his finger as a signal to keep going.

Heather would pretend to be listening, Roxanne realized, so she stayed close to the brick wall as she circled the Magazine. Once on the far side, she stopped and looked around. As long as she continued to concentrate on the building, anybody could creep up behind her. She allowed a moment more, then stopped. She counted to ten to simulate a minor struggle, then headed due east into the Market Square Tavern yard.

Roxanne stopped by the smokehouse and waited, watching the second hand sweep around her watch.

Now Evelyn appeared at the north end of the Magazine wall. The woman looked confused and anxious. She moved all the way around the wall until she was almost out of sight and began calling, "Heather, Heather." Then she returned to the lawn where she pretended to pick up Heather's shoe off the oyster shells.

John Clemens moved into the Market Square Tavern yard and joined Roxanne beside the well. "Two and a half minutes. Just barely."

Roxanne shook her head. Such a short period of time. She looked at the smokehouse again, at the heavy black padlock.

"Did you open this up?" she asked Officer Duncan from Security.

He shook his head. "No, ma'am."

"Did anybody?"

Duncan shrugged. "Don't rightly know."

John Clemens was at her side. "Well, then let's open it *now*," he told Duncan urgently. "You got a passkey'll work?"

Duncan fumbled with a couple of keys before finding the right one. He pulled off the padlock and opened the door.

Roxanne had her flashlight already moving as the door swung open. The smokehouse was nearly empty, a repository for small odds and ends: barrel hoops, coat hangers, crockery.

She stepped carefully across a battered wooden doorsill onto the dirt floor, John Clemens right behind her. A large rolling laundry cart sat in the middle of the tiny room, its wheels wedged in position.

But the cart was gently swaying.

In a flash Roxanne was at the cart, looking down at a little girl in a Colonial costume, lying on her side with hands tied behind her. Some kind of dark cloth bag was secured over her head by a tight gag that appeared to be pantyhose. Her chest rose and fell shallowly.

"Heather?" Roxanne told her softly. "It's Roxanne, honey. You're safe now."

John Clemens was at her side, pulling on latex gloves, opening a Swiss Army knife. "I'm a police officer, Heather. You're all right. Just hold still for a second and I'll get that gag off you."

Clemens used two fingers to pull the gag away from the bag and Heather's head, then slipped a knife blade underneath and sliced neatly upward. He lifted the dark cloth bag gently away from her face.

Slowly Heather opened her eyes, squinting against the flashlight. Then she began to silently sob.

❦ CHAPTER TWELVE ❦

ROXANNE SLEPT fitfully, and was awake at first light.

She lay in the monastic twin bed with its rock-hard mattress and tried to talk herself out of an overwhelming sense of despair. Things were totally out of control on her tour—on *her* watch, dammit—and she had no idea how to set them right again.

So much of the charm of Williamsburg was the suspension of disbelief that allowed people to fully immerse themselves in the eighteenth century. But Roxanne no longer felt comfortable with this immersion. Even if she'd yearned for the sort of game-playing that Heather embraced, she didn't dare let herself go enough to enjoy it.

Initially she had worried about making mistakes, getting historical facts wrong, making some silly tour-guide blunder. But the stakes were higher now.

Whoever was sabotaging this trip was doing a damn fine job of it.

After tossing for a while she accepted the fact that she wasn't going to get back to sleep. Slipping into shorts and a sweatshirt, she went for a run. The exercise she'd gotten in the past week or so was so sporadic that it barely counted, and she was surprised just how stiff she felt as she limbered up briefly before heading out.

The early-morning streets of Williamsburg were cloaked in fine mist, an alluring study in timelessness. She encountered a few other runners, young men and women who were probably students from William and Mary. But save for these few figures in running shoes and shorts, it could have been 1765, with the House of Burgesses in session, Pat Henry bunking down at Wetherburn's Tavern, and Tom Jefferson in student digs at Market Square Tavern.

Ah, yes. Market Square Tavern.

She detoured down Queen Street to pass by the place and saw police tape around the smokehouse where they'd found Heather. A guard from Colonial Williamsburg Security was on duty, sitting beside the well.

She didn't stop. What she really wanted to do was simply keep running till she got back to Texas. The hell with Guns and Roses. The hell with Irish Eyes Travel. The hell with California, and particularly the hell with people who had too much money.

She kept running, following no special course. She went down alleys and through back streets and along paths that seemed vaguely familiar, intentionally losing herself in the rhythm of her movement.

At one point she stopped to tie a shoelace and heard loud insistent chirping, which she traced to a sparrow's nest atop one of the old-fashioned streetlights. A pair of sparrows were feeding their babies in the nest, and not nearly fast enough to suit the kids.

Finally she returned to her room and found the message light on her phone blinking. It was all of seven A.M.

The message was to call John Clemens, and she found the detective at his desk and sounding almost chipper. Fairly impressive, since he almost certainly had been up all night.

"I'll buy you breakfast," he offered.

"So long as it's nothing Colonial," she answered immediately. "What I'd really love is some cop hangout with nice greasy doughnuts."

"Consider it done," he said. "I'll pick you up in fifteen minutes."

It wasn't quite Mackie's Donuts, one of her favorite Austin haunts, but the coffee shop that Clemens picked was wonderfully generic. The coffee was bitter, and the biscuits and gravy offered a splendid sense of saturated fat run amok.

"Now, where were we?" John Clemens asked, after the two of them had exchanged various pleasantries about early-morning running and turned-around cop hours and summer weather extremes in Tidewater Virginia and the Texas Hill Country.

"The last I heard," Roxanne answered thoughtfully, "was that Heather seemed physically fine and was being sent home from the hospital to a high-security room at the Williamsburg Inn. I was the one who packed their stuff up and moved it over."

For some reason, the most touching element of the hotel move had been gathering Felicity and her things. The doll seemed so pure, somehow, in the light of all that had happened. When Roxanne reached the Ticheners' new room, she made a point of dressing Felicity in her lace-trimmed nightie and putting her in Heather's turned-down bed.

John Clemens nodded. In daylight his eyes were a rich chocolate and his hair chestnut. Both had seemed darker last night. "The docs said there's nothing physically wrong with her. No signs of molestation of any kind, though given the time frame it would have been almost impossible. She says she doesn't remember anything, but I don't believe it."

Roxanne considered. "Me neither. She's very observant, John, and very bright. Of course she may actually be traumatized to the point where she *doesn't* remember, but it seems unlikely to me, just from what I've seen of her this week."

"You've got a pretty good relationship with her?"

"I don't know that I'd go that far. I've had some one-on-one conversations with her. In Richmond, I took her out to dinner, just the two of us, after the dog shit episode I told you about. But I don't have much close experience with kids, really."

"Never worked Juvie?"

Roxanne shook her head. "Never wanted to, either. One of my brothers does, though, in Houston."

It was easy to talk to John Clemens, she realized. This was the same kind of comfortable camaraderie she had always experienced hanging out with her brothers, and with other

cops. There was a form of shorthand involved, a shared aware-
ness and sensibility that she was surprised to realize she genuinely missed.

"How'd you like to talk to her this morning, see what you
can get? Or are you supposed to be running around with your
people?"

The request was no surprise, given the setup. And Roxanne
had every intention of spending time with Heather this morning, unless bodily prevented from doing so. Evelyn last night
had carried on about departing immediately for California,
though it seemed unlikely the police would let her leave the
tour so quickly.

If in fact the Guns and Roses tour still existed in any recog-
nizable shape or form. For all Roxanne knew, everyone would
choose to bail out now, and who could blame them?

The original itinerary called for leaving Williamsburg on
Saturday morning, winding along the back roads of Lee's re-
treat toward Appomattox, where they would spend Saturday
and Sunday nights at another plantation bed-and-breakfast.
Monday they would return to D.C. and disperse.

Those plans would almost certainly have to be changed. It
was now very early on Friday, though it took Roxanne a moment to figure the day and date.

"No group activities today," she answered first. "Even before all this crap started happening, today was scheduled as a
totally open day. Which translates to shop-till-you-drop for
most of these folks. The Forresters are going to Jamestown
with another group in the morning. And I think the Flanagans
are going to Busch Gardens. Which is probably where they
should have headed in the first place." She grinned at the detective. "They're this very nouveau riche midwestern family that
won the lottery. Highly entertaining, in their own way."

"And the rest of them will just be shopping?"

"*Just* doesn't quite do them justice," she told him. "They've
been accumulating a pretty amazing collection of souvenirs, my
little tour group. But back to your original question, of course
I'll talk to Heather. What did you have in mind?"

"You know her better than I do. What do you suggest?"

Roxanne thought for a moment. "Up front and honest. And if you'll get Evelyn out of the way, I think I'll have better luck."

Clemens grinned. "I'm hell on older women. But before we go—have you been able to think of *any* reason for somebody to snatch the kid?"

Roxanne shook her head slowly. "It doesn't seem to have anything to do with her family. Which is reinforced by not even a hint at ransom plans, aborted or otherwise. And in a real abduction, wouldn't they have gotten her out of here immediately?"

"One would think so," Clemens answered gloomily. "The two parts don't fit. The snatch itself was good, so good you'd almost *have* to have inside info on what the kid's plans were."

He smiled cordially at Roxanne, who grimaced in return. "I know, I know. Back to one of my people. Thank you *very* much."

"But the follow-up doesn't make sense," Clemens went on. "'Cause it was just as carefully planned. It's no accident she got dumped in that smokehouse. It was *prepared*, waiting for her. In that time frame, he'd've needed to have that lock open, and it didn't show any signs of being forced."

Roxanne shook her head. "If ransom wasn't part of it, they'd have to assume we'd find her quickly. So it seems more plausible to me that somebody was trying to scare the pee out of Heather. But I can't figure out *why*, unless it ties back to the dog shit and all."

"It could have been a diversion." Clemens rubbed his chin thoughtfully. "I've got somebody looking into anything else unusual might have been going on last night, starting with that wreck that killed the guy from New Jersey. But I'll tell you right now, this is a quiet little town. This sort of shit doesn't *happen* here."

"Maybe we don't know yet what the diversion was for," Roxanne suggested. "Maybe there was a burglary last night, say, that hasn't been discovered yet."

"Now *there's* a cheerful thought."

"Or this could be the machinations of an international spy ring," Roxanne added brightly, "trying to get something out of one of the naval installations around here."

Clemens grabbed the check and rose. "Like what? Mothballs?"

❦

Evelyn Tichener had not felt so thoroughly miserable since the final weeks of her husband's struggle with cancer.

She had sworn to her son and daughter-in-law, Gray and Karin, that this trip would be a special opportunity for her to spend time with Heather doing things that she and her granddaughter loved. Things that held little interest for Gray and Karin themselves.

The trip, she had argued, would be quiet, charming, and educational. Well, it had lived up to her billing on the latter two counts at least. As for *quiet*, however... She cringed as she recalled last night's phone call to Gray and Karin. Gray was furious, Karin stunned. Akin to Felicity, Heather saved the day. She got on the line and put on a masterful show of bravado.

"I'm just fine, Mommy," Heather had insisted. "And I don't *want* to come home. There's just a couple days left and tomorrow is the actual Felicity *tour*. With Miss Manderly's tea lesson and everything. Oh, *please!*... I'm sure it was a joke, Mommy.... You *promised* me I could take this trip, and I want to finish it."

Evelyn fully expected one or both of Heather's parents to show up today. They were a pair of Type As with little time for noncompetitive amusement, or for that matter, their daughter. But they were both control freaks, and Evelyn knew they considered her performance as Heather's traveling companion and protector to be woefully inadequate. Indeed, she had to agree with them, even though she'd tried her very hardest every step of the way.

Heather was unusually withdrawn this morning, hardly surprising. She'd picked a bit at breakfast and was dressing Felicity now. And she was sure to pitch a fit when Evelyn told her the police didn't want her taking *any* tours, not even with

Miss Manderly, the fictional tea tutor from the American Girls book. Evelyn no longer had any sense of where fantasy ended here and reality began.

Except that reality was turning out to be pretty dreadful.

❦

Heather was wearing blue jeans and holding Felicity tightly when Roxanne arrived at her hotel room at eight-thirty. The doll wore unfamiliar and elaborate clothing.

"Ooh, I like Felicity's outfit!" Roxanne said immediately, focusing on Heather, leaving Evelyn to John Clemens.

Heather nodded somberly. "It's her riding habit. Did you put her to bed for me last night?"

"Uh-huh." Roxanne examined the riding habit more closely. It was a truly ridiculous getup in which to attempt riding a horse, forest-green wool, with mildly militaristic gold trim and a dandy tricornered hat. "Do you ride horseback, Heather?"

Heather shook her head. "My friend Jenny has horses at her dad's, but I've never been there."

Roxanne moved farther into the room. "I bet you'd really like it. Maybe sometime after we're all back in California I could take you."

"You ride horses?" Heather sounded surprised, and she almost met Roxanne's eye.

"Since I was about three years old." Roxanne gestured casually toward Detective Clemens, who was meandering across the room, pretending to examine some botanical prints in elaborate frames. "You met John last night, didn't you, Heather?"

Heather glanced quickly at the detective, then looked away. "I didn't know his name was John."

Roxanne smiled. "They probably called him Detective Clemens, or Mr. Clemens. I guess they're more formal here than we are in California, huh? Listen, Heather, John needs to talk to your grandma for a minute, and he told me I could stay here with you while they go talk. Is that all right?"

Heather shrugged and looked over toward the window, where her grandmother had retreated once she admitted Roxanne and John. Evelyn had aged thirty years since yesterday.

"I guess," Heather said, looking down. "I don't care."

"You'll be very safe," Roxanne assured her. "There's a guard outside in the hall to keep folks away, and I...did you know that I used to work as a police officer?"

For the first time Heather looked straight at her. "Really?" The girl's eyes widened.

"Uh-huh."

"Were you a DARE officer?"

Roxanne shook her head. "I drove a patrol car, and sometimes I arrested bad guys and took them to jail."

"Wow!" Heather seemed truly impressed. "Do you want some breakfast? We've got some blueberry muffins left." She pointed to a room service tray.

"Oh, I might have one," Roxanne said. Her breakfast biscuits and gravy had formed a leaden lump in her stomach.

John Clemens had finally reached Evelyn. "Mrs. Tichener? Do you suppose you could possibly give me just a minute, ma'am? Roxanne will stay here with Heather."

Evelyn looked anguished, but agreed. After a few minutes of fussing, Roxanne and Heather were left alone in the spacious, expensively decorated room. The antiques here were all magnificent reproductions, the upholstery and draperies splendidly opulent. Since last night a very formal flower arrangement had appeared.

"Here's the muffins," Heather offered.

Roxanne helped herself to one from a little basket of assorted breads and checked out the rest of the room service table. There was a metal cover over a plate of virtually untouched pancakes, a used coffee cup, and a pot of stone-cold water with a selection of teabags. "Did you have tea with breakfast?"

Heather shook her head. "I ordered it, but I wasn't very hungry."

"Well, I've got an idea. Why don't you and I and Felicity have some morning tea together? I could order a fresh pot. This one's cold."

"I think I'd like that," Heather answered slowly. She turned to the doll. "Would you care for tea, Felicity?"

"Oh, yes," Heather answered for the doll, in a tiny voice. "That would be lovely."

Roxanne called room service, then stuck her head out into the hall to tell the guard. He sat on a fussy chair beside another enormous formal flower arrangement that stood in front of an antique mirror with very bad silvering.

John Clemens and Evelyn had disappeared. When Roxanne went back inside, she helped herself to a blueberry muffin.

"How are you feeling this morning, honey?"

Heather shrugged. "All right. I don't want to go home."

"I think your grandma does, though." And in a New York minute.

"But we were supposed to have a whole 'nother day here!" Heather protested. The girl was nothing if not resilient. "The Felicity tour is today. It's the whole reason we came!"

Colonial Williamsburg, initially cool to the Felicity phenomenon, had now come full circle and offered Felicity tours, complete with a costumed character, Miss Manderly, giving authentic lessons in dance, needlework, and the art of tea.

"I'll see what I can do," Roxanne promised. "But I think your grandma was badly frightened last night. I know I was, and I think you probably were, too."

Heather said nothing. She sat down and examined Felicity's hat.

"John told me that you don't remember what happened. Sometimes that happens when you have a bad experience. Or sometimes it's like that for a while and then it comes back to you and you remember later." Roxanne was watching Heather closely. The girl was uncomfortable, and growing more so by the moment. "Or, the other thing that happens sometimes is that the bad person makes a threat. Says something awful will happen if you tell anything."

This time Heather flinched.

Bingo.

There was a soft rap on the door, as room service delivered the tea tray in record time. Roxanne wondered if the service here at the posh Williamsburg Inn—the top of the line of Colonial

Williamsburg accommodations—was always so peppy. Or if they were on special alert for the latest Irish Eyes victims.

Roxanne traded trays with the waiter, hanging on to the muffins, then set out three cups. "Heather, would you like to pour?"

"Why certainly, Roxanne." Heather was the epitome of graciousness, would be the star of Miss Manderly's tea lesson. Surely they could sneak her in somehow.

They continued the tea ritual for a few minutes. Then Roxanne leaned back and spoke casually. "You know, Heather, speaking as your friend, I'd sure like to make sure that the person who bothered you last night won't bother you again. And as a police officer, I'd like to make sure he doesn't bother any other little girls either."

Heather listened, deadpan.

"I'm wondering if maybe there isn't something you've thought of this morning that could help us find him.... It *was* a him, wasn't it?" She made the question offhand.

Heather nodded slowly.

All right! She *did* remember.

"Help us find him and keep him from bothering anybody," Roxanne pleaded quietly. "I promise we'll keep you safe."

Heather looked troubled. When she spoke, it was to the doll. "He told me he'd hurt Grandma, Felicity."

"We won't let him do it," Roxanne promised. "I won't let him and the police here won't let him. All we need is to figure out who he is so we can stop him." She spoke to the doll herself now. Funny, she'd read and heard about kids talking through dolls and stuffed animals, but this was her first experience with it personally. Who'da thunk it would be in a Virginia hotel room that probably ran four hundred bucks a night? "Felicity, does Heather remember anything more about him?"

Long silence.

"Any little thing might help," Roxanne went on softly, still talking to the doll. "What he looked like, what he said, how he talked, what he wore. Anything."

"He was in Colonial costume," Heather said suddenly. "I

only caught a glimpse. He put some kind of bag or cloth or something over my head, so after that I couldn't see."

Roxanne waited, watching Heather closely. There was more, she could tell. Let the girl get it out her own way.

"But he wasn't for real," Heather said after a moment. "He doesn't work here."

"How could you tell?"

"'Cause the people who really work here, their costumes are perfect in all the little details. But this guy, he was wearing tennis shoes and a watch."

"What kind of watch? Could you tell?"

Heather thought a moment. "It was on his right wrist, the hand he put over my mouth. I just got a quick look at it, under his sleeve. But it was black and had a lot of stuff on it. You know, like extra dials and stuff."

A high-tech black wristwatch on his right arm. A lefty? "What about the shoes?"

Heather shrugged. "They were just some kind of big black sneakers. Not black leather with buckles, the kind the men who really work here wear. And certainly not single-lasted!"

"Is there anything else you can remember?"

Heather frowned. "Not when he actually grabbed me. He just came up behind me *real* quietly, and all I could see was his shoes and the watch, and them not for very long. But there was something...." The frown deepened.

"What, honey?"

"A little bit before it happened, over by the Guardhouse, I saw somebody, a guy in a Colonial costume. Not a militia uniform, like they usually wear at the Guardhouse." Heather hesitated.

"Yeah?"

"And he looked like the guy I saw with Monica Dunwoody the other night, after the Lanthorn Tour."

❦ CHAPTER THIRTEEN ❦

"SO WHERE'S Monica?" John Clemens asked irritably.

He and Roxanne were back at Botsforth Tavern. The back door was locked and the front guarded by a costumed security officer. But not a single Irish Eyes tour member was on the premises.

Not one. They'd scattered like dandelion fluff in a blue norther. And who could blame them?

"I don't have any idea," Roxanne told Clemens with equal irritation. She could hardly be held responsible for the whereabouts of all fifteen tour members on an open day. It was tough enough to keep track of them when the bus stopped for gas. "Let me check my room and see if anybody left any messages."

They went up together. Maid service hadn't gotten to her room yet, and Roxanne nonchalantly pulled the heavy white bedspread up over the rumpled sheets. With John Clemens she felt like a cop again, a feeling she was definitely enjoying. Still, there was something strange about entering her hotel room—a bedroom, essentially—with him. He was young and attractive, the kind of dark and mysterious guy she had always been attracted to. He wasn't wearing a wedding ring, either, not that that meant anything with a cop.

The light on the phone was blinking, and the message was to call her brother Tom in Austin.

"This may help," Roxanne told John as she dialed. "I asked my brother to run the people in the Irish Eyes group through NCIC. He's Homicide in Austin. Maybe he's come up with something."

"Then take notes," Clemens ordered, casually sprawling in a red wing chair. He had a chameleon quality that allowed him to melt as seamlessly into the antique-filled rooms of Botsforth Tavern and the Williamsburg Inn as he had into the diner.

Roxanne looked at him thoughtfully. She kept forgetting that all this crap was not somebody else's problem, that she wasn't the objective police observer/arbitrator/problem-solver. She and her Irish Eyes group were the problem.

Tom picked up on the first ring. "Hey, little sis," he greeted her cheerfully. "I'd've gotten back sooner, but we've got a kind of ugly homicide came in yesterday. Essentially a domestic, but one of the things holding us up is, it's kind of a toss-up whether the brain damage from the beating killed her before the heroin overdose had a chance to."

"And you wonder why I never wanted to work Homicide. You got the guy?"

"We got the boyfriend who beat the shit out of her for being on the junk," Tom answered. "Still working on the dealer angle. I'd like to figure a way to nail them both."

"Well, more power to you. Did you get a chance to run my Irish Eyes people?"

Tom chuckled. "Indeed I did. Quite a group of citizens you have there, Rox. Where'd you *find* these folks? Aunt Maureen set a booth up outside the probation office?"

"Oh come on, it can't be that bad."

"Well, no. And most of them seem just fine, actually. So let me give you the good news first. NCIC has nothing on—let's see, now—Evelyn Tichener or Harriet Greene or Edna Stanton or any of the Dunwoodys. The Chesterton lady from Alabama is clean. In fact, the only woman with any kind of problem is Bridget Flanagan, who likes to write checks whether or not she's got any money in the bank. There doesn't seem to be anything out of the ordinary with any of the other women, at least under the names you gave me. You might want to find out Mrs. Vanguard's maiden name, though."

Josie? Josie was one of the few people Irish Eyes had known before, as a longtime valued customer. "How come?" Roxanne asked cautiously.

"I'll get to that in a minute. Anyway, the ladies are pretty much clean, but the gentlemen are a different story. Richard Forrester was convicted on a DUI three years ago in Grand Rapids, Michigan. Ditto Patrick Flanagan, in St. Louis. His license is suspended, by the way."

And yet somehow Patrick had managed to rent a car and get to the ABC Store in Williamsburg. Interesting. Seventeen million bucks could probably purchase a lot of documentation.

"Nicholas Winfield did time twice at the California Youth Authority for burglary," Tom went on, "and was released eight months ago on parole."

"My, my, my," Roxanne murmured. No wonder the Dunwoodys found Nick Winfield such an unsuitable boyfriend for Monica. This also raised some interesting questions about where Nick intended to come up with the financial backing for Monica's cute little swimsuit shop.

"But I've saved the best for last," Tom told her. "Larry Vanguard, aka Larry Van, aka Lawrence Vale, aka Lance Vedder. The guy have a lot of monogrammed clothing?"

Roxanne felt the hairs stand up along her neck even as she laughed. So Larry Vanguard was a wrong'un, eh? It sure didn't feel like a surprise. "Not that I've noticed. Maybe his undies? I think I'm liking this, Tom. I *knew* there was something squirrelly about that guy. What'd he do?"

"Scammer," Tom said shortly. "Convictions in New Jersey and Florida, most recently two years ago. Sounded interesting, so I made a fast call to Florida and they remembered him real well. Pyramid sales was your boy's fave. The one they got him on was some kind of weight loss vitamins. There was also some question of being married to two rich ladies at the same time, though the guy in Florida said those charges were dropped."

"Bigamy?" Now that was a crime you didn't run into every day.

"Like I said, they thought he'd gotten divorced after the legal hassle. But it could be worth pursuing."

"It certainly could," Roxanne agreed. Poor Josie. Did she know? "Could you fax me this stuff? Whatever you've actually got on paper about these people?"

"Sure. You want me to send it to the hotel?"

Her laugh came from deep inside. Damn, she was actually *enjoying* this. "No way! I'm on shaky enough ground with management here. If I start getting faxes of my group's rap sheets, we'll be booted by lunchtime. I've got a better idea. Send them to John Clemens at the Williamsburg PD." She looked over at John, who'd been listening attentively and was now digging in a pocket. "Hold on while I get you the number." On cue, Clemens located and handed over a card.

As Roxanne read the number, she thought about Tom back in Austin. About his homicide, and how jazzed he was about it. Tom brought an enthusiasm to his work—to his *life*, for that matter—that was infectious. She thought, very briefly, about where she might be right now if she were back in Austin, on duty.

But she dismissed the thought quickly. The wondering raised too many questions she felt incapable of trying to answer today.

❦

Maureen O'Malley put her bedroom phone on the speaker and pulled her emergency travel bag out of the closet. She kept a carry-on suitcase partially packed at all times for sudden trips. She angrily opened the bag and added three outfits, working by rote. Some part of her mind was processing her destination and the time of year, but there was nothing conscious about it.

Maureen's conscious mind was far too busy right now to worry about minutiae like packing. Twenty-seven years of business were gurgling right down the tubes, like one of those dreadful drain-opener commercials on the daytime TV shows that she'd been half watching during the earlier, most miserable stages of her chicken pox.

She examined her face carefully in the mirror. The last visible pocks had healed. So long as she wore pants and long sleeves, she could get by anywhere. She didn't exactly feel great, but she felt sufficiently recovered to go and face her fate head-on.

If she couldn't stop her business from self-destructing, at least she could be there for the denouement. Like those folks who drank champagne in tuxedos on the deck of *Titanic*.

Another great moment in the annals of the travel industry.

❦

When Roxanne and John Clemens went back downstairs, the Forresters and Vanguards were just coming in the front door of Botsforth Tavern, laden with packages.

"How is dear little Heather?" Olive Forrester asked immediately, her sweet face radiating concern. She was, Roxanne suspected, a really crackerjack grandmother, the kind who would bake interesting cookies and give thoughtful little presents and even make a genuine effort to understand electronic games.

"She seems pretty good this morning," Roxanne answered. "I was over talking to her a while ago. Kids can be amazingly resilient." She didn't intend to let anybody know that Heather's resilience extended to a firm resolve to do further sight-seeing.

"Such a dreadful business," Josie Vanguard added. "Have you found the kidnappers yet?" The question was directed, rather pointedly, at John Clemens.

"We're working on it, ma'am," Clemens answered genially. "Did any of you people happen to see Monica Dunwoody this morning?"

Dick Forrester moved toward the back hall. "I'll put these things in our room, Olive." He shook his head and grinned. "You'd think they didn't have stores back home. You'll need to ship some of this stuff for us, Roxanne."

Pompous Dick Forrester would never forget that Roxanne was an employee.

"Of course," she answered agreeably. "No problem, Dick."

Olive, however, was barely listening. "The last time I saw Monica she was headed out with her mother. She had been thinking about going to Busch Gardens with the Flanagans, and there was some kind of little brouhaha about it. I believe it was left that Monica and her mother were going shopping."

John Clemens nodded thankfully, the gracious Southern

gentleman. "That'll be a big help, Mrs. Forrester. Do you have any idea where they might have been planning to shop? Here in the historic section?"

"Oh, I don't know." Olive shrugged. "Maybe. Barbara's really a pretty serious shopper, not that I'm in any position to be throwing stones on *that* account! She was talking about taking Dave's car to the outlet mall, wherever that might be."

Josie Vanguard shook her head. "Dave drove to Richmond this morning on business, so she couldn't be using his car. I'd bet she's somewhere right around here. She's been buying all sorts of Colonial accessories, you know. She told me she's decided to do over her kitchen when she gets back, in Early American."

Ah, the pastimes of the idle rich. When Roxanne did over *her* kitchen, it meant changing brands of frozen dinners.

"I'd been talking to her about how much I thought she'd like the furniture exhibits at the DeWitt Wallace Gallery," Olive said. "She may be there, or at the Folk Art Center."

"Not the Folk Art Center," Josie put in, sounding very positive. "Barbara specifically told me she didn't like primitive art at all. She's been to that museum before, said it was the kind of stuff any idiot could do, including herself. No, if Barbara stayed around the historic section to shop, I'd try Craft House first. She wanted to have some linens shipped, and possibly a set of dishes, too. Also there was a nice little chest of drawers she had her eye on." Josie smiled gently. "On sale, marked down to twenty-eight hundred."

Twenty-eight hundred dollars? Roxanne could only assume that the drawers were lined with gold leaf.

"We'll check on that," Clemens said. "Thanks. Now, while we're all here. Have any of you folks thought of anything else that might help us with Heather's abduction?"

"Not a thing," Josie answered regretfully. "It seems like such an utterly pointless and cruel thing to do."

"That poor child," Olive agreed. "Lying there helpless all that time, hearing us all around calling for her and not being able to answer."

True enough, Roxanne thought, but at least Heather had known that help was nearby. She could hear people calling her name, and would have figured that sooner or later, a searcher would open up the smokehouse. And that in the meantime, whoever put her in the smokehouse couldn't get at her again.

Larry Vanguard, Roxanne noticed, was sidling down the hall toward the stairs. Or was it Larry Van, or maybe Lance Vedder?

"Mr. Vanguard?" John Clemens's tone was suddenly crisp. He'd noticed, too. "Could I have a minute, please?"

"Just let me make a pit stop," Larry answered, continuing down the hall. "Josie, love, you have things to go upstairs?"

"Just this one bag, dear." She winked at Roxanne. "*I'm* keeping my purchases small. Jewelry is *so* portable!"

Roxanne watched the Vanguards go upstairs and turned to John Clemens. Her long-dormant cop juices were flowing again in anticipation of somehow nailing Larry Vanguard. And Clemens wore a look that overlaid a veneer of placidity upon what Roxanne knew was unadulterated glee.

❦

"I've made some mistakes," Larry Vanguard told them expansively. "But that's all behind me now and Josie knows all about it." He took one of his wife's trembling hands. "We're looking forward, not back. And I'm just grateful to have such a special and understanding wife."

They were in the parlor of Botsforth Tavern with the hall doors closed, seated around the central table. Not exactly an interrogation, but several steps removed from a friendly conversation.

Larry Vanguard was exhibiting a side that Roxanne had only glimpsed in the previous six days, charming and persuasive. In this guise it was easy to see why Josie was so smitten, easy to understand the hasty adjournments to their various bedrooms, easy to believe that Larry Vanguard was capable of any number of cons and swindles.

Josie herself was no longer winking, girl-to-girl. She was hideously embarrassed and fighting tears. "I don't understand how harassing poor Larry is going to help anything," she finally said. "I *know* he's made mistakes and I don't *care*. Isn't somebody entitled to turn over a new leaf?"

"Of course," Roxanne murmured sympathetically. Larry Vanguard had probably turned over enough new leaves to be nicknamed Quaking Aspen.

"Then why aren't you out there beating the bushes trying to find out who took poor little Heather last night?" Josie was gaining strength and now she seemed almost angry. "It certainly wasn't *Larry*, because I was with him every minute. Unless you think *I* did it? Is that it? You're planning to arrest me for putting that sweet little girl into that awful old shed?"

Larry Vanguard clasped Josie's hand between both of his own. "Of course not, darling. Anyone who's spent a minute with you would know you could never hurt a fly. These people are just doing their job."

Josie shot Roxanne a fiery look. "I was under the impression that *your* job was seeing to the comfort and needs of the tour group."

"And it is," Roxanne assured her. "But Heather wasn't very comfortable in that smokehouse last night, and we *need* to find out what happened."

"Then you ought to be out doing it, not sitting around trying to persecute innocent bystanders." She turned to her husband. "Larry, I want to get *out* of here. Right now, this very minute." She was turning into a real spitfire. "We can go back to Atlantic City, or fly to Bermuda. *Anywhere* but here."

"I'll take you wherever you want to go, sweetheart," Larry told her, his voice a gentle caress. "To the ends of the earth. But these good people may not want us leaving town just now." He looked at John Clemens with the world-weariness of one who's spent plenty of time cooling his heels in the back rooms of various cop shops.

John Clemens ignored Larry and smiled sweetly at Josie. "Your husband is right, Mrs. Vanguard. I realize that you're all being inconvenienced by poor Heather's terrible experience, and I do sympathize. But your tour was originally scheduled to remain in Williamsburg until tomorrow and your husband's correct. We'd definitely prefer to have you stay here for the time being. *Not* because either of you is under suspicion, but because we hope you can help." He stood up. "Thank you both for your cooperation. We appreciate it."

Roxanne stood as well and followed John Clemens out onto Duke of Gloucester Street. A gaggle of unruly fourth graders was being chewed out by a harried-looking teacher as a guide stood patiently by. A determined-looking woman navigated her wheelchair through the crowds. Video cameras whirred, horse-drawn carriages clip-clopped, wayward children shrieked.

John Clemens turned to Roxanne. "So. You've spent some time with Monica Dunwoody. Where would she go?"

Roxanne laughed. "Straight back to California if she could get away with it. It's funny about Monica, John. She's not all that much younger than I am, but she seems like such a kid. Always acting out, being rebellious. But not actually rebelling to the point of going on her own."

"A sense of entitlement?" he suggested.

"Exactly! Like, 'I'm rich and I know I'm special and some-times I have to be nice to Great-aunt Mignon and stuff, but I could really be *something* if they'd just let me do what I want.' Which in Monica's case means giving her a lot of money to open a swimsuit shop with the no-account boyfriend."

"I wonder if California has located Winfield," Clemens said, looking at his watch. "Time to call in and check."

"I don't think you're going to find him there," Roxanne told him. "A lot of things make more sense if he's here somewhere, if that's who Heather saw with Monica. She's been acting smug and much easier to get along with ever since we hit Williams-burg. He could have been dogging us ever since Washington, for that matter. There was a call that got re-routed to the desk during the business with the laughter in the middle of the night in Richmond. The operator said it was the voice of a young man." She shook her head. "But I still don't see what they think they'd accomplish by frightening *Heather.*"

"If the tour's called off, Monica could go home."

"The tour's practically over," Roxanne reminded him. "Why bother trying to screw it up now?"

"Except that somebody's been trying to screw it up all along. And if you weren't the guide, it would probably have happened a lot sooner and much more easily."

Roxanne smiled. "Thanks. I guess. But you obviously haven't met my Aunt Maureen. She's a pistol."

"If you say so." Clemens frowned. "I just wish Heather had gotten a better look at the guy."

"Once you get a mug shot from California," Roxanne told him, "I think she'll give you the ID we need."

"Then all we need to do is find the asshole and ask him why."

❦

Lillian Jackson pushed the linen cart up to the back porch of the Botsforth Tavern. She was way behind schedule today, all from the inconvenience of having to haul everything half of forever to do the rooms in Market Square Tavern. It was a damned nuisance, not being able to use the smokehouse that served as a linen shed over there.

And why? Some little rich white girl playing dress-up causing a ruckus, some nonsense about being kidnapped and tied up in the linen shed there—now who could believe a silly story like that, anyway? And in a place like Williamsburg, where everybody worked so hard at being just too perfect for words? Now, *really.*

The child was most likely playing games with a friend, and the game got out of hand somehow. That sort of thing was always happening to LaTorshia, Lillian's own youngest, who always had a convincing story and could weasel her way out of the most outrageous kinds of scrape. It was, Lillian believed, akin to a miracle that LaTorshia hadn't turned up pregnant just yet.

Lillian used her passkey to open the locked back door of the Botsforth Tavern, shaking her head. Such a lot of nonsense these people here were causing. Imagine having *leeches* in the bathroom! And then expecting her to clean up the mess—not just the leeches and all that broken glass, which would have been plenty bad enough, but fingerprint powder, too, all over everything.

The sooner this bunch of nutcases checked out, the better.

She set the door lock to stay open and carried an armload of linens up to the holding closet on the second floor. She repeated the trip twice, bringing additional sheets, towels, and toiletries. The little girl's room was in this building, with her grandma, but they'd moved them over to the Inn. So *that* room needed to be made up fresh.

Lillian glanced at her watch. Nearly one, much later than she'd normally be getting to Botsforth. Still, the place seemed deserted. She could at least catch part of the soaps.

She began upstairs, knocking and calling a cheerful "House-keeping" at the lovebirds' room on the second floor. The love-birds were always leaving the beds torn apart and underwear scattered everywhere you could imagine. Racy stuff, his as well as hers. She'd told May about that pair of silk boxer shorts with the lipstick prints and red arrows and directions: PRESS HERE FOR INSTANT PLEASURE. Seemed ridiculous to look at the scrawny pair of them, but that one day she saw them coming out of the room—the sheets still wet and all but steaming behind them—they both looked mighty satisfied.

Lillian turned on the TV softly and closed the door nearly all the way. It was right at the half-hour break, so she'd have a chance to square away the bathroom before the show came on. Humming, she turned the tub on full blast. Looked like they were sharing a bubble bath again, from the water puddled everywhere. She looked up with a grin at the shower curtain rod, where yesterday morning she'd found an odd purple doo-dad hanging. It had turned out to be a satin G-string, like *strippers* wore!

Lillian just hoped that when she got that old, there'd be some man hot for her and worth the trouble of having around.

❧

Barbara Dunwoody was tired.

Her temples pounded and her stomach was a little bit

queasy. That vegetable soup had seemed innocuous enough when she ordered it down at that cute little sidewalk café in Merchant's Square, but it didn't want to set right and she was too tired to eat anyway.

Once she'd taken a little nap, she'd feel better. Barbara was a firm believer in the restorative power of naps.

The Botsforth Tavern garden was innocent and peaceful as she walked into the backyard. The maid's cart was parked by the back porch, but when Barbara went inside and opened her own room door, it was obvious the woman hadn't been there yet.

The hell with it. She could make her own bed, later. Right now she just wanted to lie down.

Barbara stuck the DO NOT DISTURB sign on the door, kicked off her shoes, and dropped her bags by the dresser. Monica had seemed quite content to go off on her own this afternoon. Damn, that girl was up to something, no doubt about it. Thank God they'd all be out of here tomorrow. Then to Birmingham with Aunt Mignon for long enough to be polite, no more than a week, and finally home. Monica was pissed about that, too, going to Birmingham, but Barbara had had about all she could stand of Monica's temper tantrums.

Damn, she was tired! She pulled the white embroidered bedspread up over the rumpled sheets and collapsed on top of the bed, loosening the zipper on her slacks. Ought to take them off, they'd wrinkle, but never mind.

Why was she so sleepy, anyway? No reason, really...

❦

When the doorknob turned silently, twenty minutes later, Barbara Dunwoody lay on her back, her face away from the door, toward the window. Softly filtered light came through the curtains.

Barbara's eyes were closed, her exhalations deep and regular.

It was all over very quickly.

❦ CHAPTER FOURTEEN ❦

DAVE DUNWOODY strode up Duke of Gloucester Street, taking in the balmy afternoon breezes, the children clamoring outside the Milliner's Shop, the young man in tricornered hat and Colonial breeches standing nonchalantly outside the Botsforth Tavern. Dave turned toward the tavern.

"Good afternoon," he told the man at the head of the stairs, who had moved smoothly to intercept him. Some security bozo, probably. "Dave Dunwoody. I'm with the group staying here."

"Could I see some identification, Mr. Dunwoody?" the young man asked politely. Yeah, definitely Security.

"Sure thing," Dave responded cheerfully. He pulled out his driver's license and handed it to the man. "They find out anything more about Heather's kidnapping last night?"

"You'd have to check with Detective Clemens or Mr. Becker about that." The young man handed back Dave's license with a smile and swung the door open for him graciously.

"I'll do that," Dave promised, walking inside.

As always, it was much cooler and quieter inside the old building. Very quiet, in fact. He walked to the end of the hall, pulled out his room key, and unlocked the room. It was dark, but not so dark that he had any trouble making out the shape on the bed.

Something was very wrong with the shape.

"Barb?" he asked tentatively, in a half whisper.

No response.

He inhaled sharply, crossed to the bed in two strides, and stared down at the figure lying there.

Barbara.

Barbara, with the wooden shelf from above the bed lying across the upper part of her body, obscuring her face and chest. But after twenty-four years of marriage, Dave Dunwoody knew every contour of his wife's body. An open catalog from Craft House lay partly under the shelf.

He touched her right hand, which lay closest to him, pale and still against the white bedspread.

Cold.

By now his eyes had sufficiently adjusted to the darkness so that he could see the blood.

He gave a strangled cry, turned, and bolted down the hall toward the security guard.

❦

Roxanne had been at any number of death scenes in her years on the force: shootings, stabbings, car wrecks, heart attacks in inopportune locations. But this was the first time she'd seen anyone killed by a falling shelf.

She stared through the open doorway across the room at Barbara Dunwoody's body. The Dunwoodys' bedroom was one of the larger in the building, but it was still fairly small and certainly not intended to accommodate the activity bustling inside it now. The now-familiar Williamsburg PD evidence tech—who'd processed Edna Stanton's bathroom and been at the smokehouse after Heather was found there last night—was moving back and forth, taking photographs, humming something soft and tuneless. The medical examiner was fussing and clucking around the body. Colonial Williamsburg Security's Max Becker left the room and stepped outside onto the back porch, where he murmured inaudibly into a walkie-talkie.

What Roxanne wanted was a clearer view of the body. When John Clemens slowly backed out of the room, she finally had an unobstructed panorama.

The shelf-cum-reading lamp that was anchored over most of the beds in the building had apparently crashed down on Barbara.

Roxanne could see the shelf, noted that a heavy stoneware preserve jar was still securely bolted in place on the shelf.

But from what she'd been overhearing, it seemed that the blow that killed Barbara had come from a five-pound iron ball that had been sitting on top of the shelf.

So much for redecoration in Early Americana.

The instrument of death was one of the gate-closing balls that hung from chains to automatically shut all the picket fence gates in the various yards of the historical section. Roxanne had seen the balls for sale in several of the shops, usually displayed in a bushel basket on the floor because of their weight. She'd even picked one up out of curiosity, been surprised by its heft. Five pounds for the ball and another three for the chain, a saleswoman in Colonial garb had told her.

Like those she'd seen in the shops, the one now resting on Barbara Dunwoody's abdomen was unpainted, a dull metallic gray.

Except for the bright red bloodstains.

Roxanne followed John Clemens down the hall toward the front door. He had taken charge with quiet competence, sequestering Dave Dunwoody with an officer in the tavern parlor, making a fast survey of the building that had found the only occupant to be a maid making up the Ticheners' former room upstairs. The maid claimed to have seen and heard nothing.

Roxanne and Clemens had been at police headquarters when the call came in from Colonial Williamsburg Security. She had been horrified by the news, but had also felt a strange surge of energy as the two of them sped in silence the few blocks to the restored area and squealed into the small lot behind the Tavern, blocking half a dozen parked cars. The back door was open when they arrived, a uniformed officer on guard.

And Barbara Dunwoody was dead.

"Can we use your room?" Clemens asked Roxanne, heading up the stairs.

"*Mi casa es su casa,*" she replied, following him.

The room had been made up, the bedspread perfectly smoothed, fresh glasses positioned beside the ice bucket on the dresser. Roxanne closed the door and sat in the wing chair. Clemens paced.

"Harmless pranks, eh?" Clemens asked. "Is this supposed to be another harmless prank?" He moved over to the head of one of the twin beds and began examining the shelf-lamp there. "You use this thing?"

"Uh-huh." She got up and joined him. The shelf-lamp was an odd hybrid, a long narrow hanging box about two feet wide, five inches tall and five inches deep, suspended from the wall by miniature flying buttresses at its top. Its front was completely covered by a sort of drop-leaf panel hinged at the top. When the panel was opened and pushed up, a light bulb inside went on, providing a reading lamp for the bed below.

"It's kind of a pain," Roxanne explained, "because it's all or nothing. On full-bright or totally off. And it's kind of clunky, too. It's awkward to open and you have to really whack it to get it closed."

John Clemens was busily opening and closing the apparatus, as if to demonstrate. He looked carefully at the two screws holding the unit in place, then gave an exploratory tug. It stayed put, but looked shaky.

"There was a furniture catalog on her bed," he said, "so she could have been trying to turn on the reading light above her head. But the unit downstairs didn't look like it was yanked out of the wall. No plaster chunks or anything. I wonder what would happen if you unscrewed it partway."

Clemens dug in a pocket, pulled out his Swiss Army knife, and popped open a tiny screwdriver. He experimented for a moment, then carefully closed the drop leaf. He looked around the room, picked up Roxanne's flashlight from the bedside table, and set it atop the shelf.

He stepped back and gave a critical look. The unit appeared sturdy. Then he leaned forward and gave a reasonably hard upward jerk on the hinged front panel to open it and turn on the light.

The flashlight slid forward and bounced onto the center of the bed just before the lamp and shelf came crashing down on top of it.

"Very interesting," he said thoughtfully. "*Very* interesting. You probably couldn't see from out in the hall, but there was a screwdriver under her bed down there." He glanced around. "I don't suppose you have one of those iron bowling balls, do you?"

Roxanne stared at him, suppressing a grin. "Do I strike you as the sort of person who buys fence-closing equipment as a souvenir?"

Clemens laughed, lighting up his whole face. "No, I guess you don't, at that. We'll have to try this again once I get my hands on one. But before we do that, anything strike you as strange about what I just did?"

"I had the impression downstairs that the ball landed on her face." She pointed at the mess on the bed. "But the flashlight touched down first a good three feet from the top of the bed. A ball might roll differently, but I don't see how it could hit her head."

"Unless it bounced, which, being that it's six or seven pounds of solid iron, I find unlikely."

"Five actually, but who's counting? And that means it wasn't a prank. Or even an accident. It *couldn't* be."

"That's right," John Clemens said with a grim expression. "It appears to me that somebody smashed that ball right into her face, and from the looks of her, maybe more than once. Which, once again, would be difficult to explain in terms of bouncing, given what little I remember from high school physics."

"She wasn't the sort of woman who'd just lie there and let you smash an iron ball into her face," Roxanne said.

"Who is? But she wouldn't notice if she were asleep," Clemens replied, opening the door, "or drugged."

As he stepped out into the hall, a high-pitched scream rose from downstairs. Clemens was halfway down the steps by the time Roxanne got the door locked and followed.

Monica had finally returned.

She stood in the center of the downstairs hall, shrieking. *"Nooooooo! Not my mother!"*

Dave Dunwoody burst out of the parlor, brushing aside a

protesting young cop, someone Roxanne hadn't seen before. He shouldered his way past Max Becker and grabbed his daughter. "Baby, baby," Dave said to Monica, wrapping strong arms around the slender young woman.

Only now did Roxanne notice Mignon Chesterton, who had apparently arrived at the same time as her great-niece. The older woman sat in a hall chair with her head between her knees, being ministered to by the front door guard. After a moment, Mignon pushed the guard back and lifted her head, rising to her feet slowly. Roxanne had a fleeting image of a battleship emerging above the horizon.

Dave was beginning to bluster. He kept an arm wrapped around Monica, who showed no signs of settling down, though her hysterics weren't quite as loud as before. "Will somebody tell me," he bellowed, "just what in the *hell* is going on around here?"

"I'd like to know that myself," John Clemens told him, all mild-mannered geniality once again. He turned to Mignon Chesterton. "Ma'am, are you all right? Would you like me to call a doctor?"

Mignon Chesterton gave a brief shake of her head. Funny how somebody who'd just been a hair's breadth from a faint could suddenly look so imperious.

Clemens looked around the crowded hallway, then focused again on the older woman. "I'm terribly sorry about your niece, ma'am," he told her. "Perhaps Monica could wait with you in your room? We'll need to speak with both of you when it's convenient."

"Of course," she answered, moving tentatively toward Dave and Monica. "Come along, dear." She touched Monica's hand and the girl recoiled.

"Leave me *alone!*" Monica screamed.

Roxanne cocked her head toward Monica's door. Her room was between her parents' room, which faced on the back garden, and Mignon's, which fronted on Duke of Gloucester. "Maybe she could wait in her own room," she suggested quietly to Clemens. "It's right here."

He nodded. "Good idea." Behind him, Max Becker materialized with a passkey and opened Monica's door. "Would you like someone to stay with you, Miss Dunwoody? Perhaps Roxanne—"

But Monica's screams had subsided into dull sobs now. She shook her head violently as she disengaged herself from her father's grip. "I just want everybody to leave me *alone!*" She darted across the hallway through her open door, then slammed it violently behind her. Roxanne could hear the bolt fall into place. It was a scene that had probably been carried out a thousand times through Monica's adolescence. Screaming exits and slamming doors were such a staple of the female coming-of-age experience.

She realized, however, that never before had Monica had such a horrifying reason to seek her own solace. Roxanne felt a momentary ache for the girl, but her attention was almost immediately redirected toward Dave Dunwoody.

"Will somebody tell me," he brayed, "how this could happen? I've never seen such piss-poor security in my life!" He angrily turned on Max Becker. "I thought this building was under guard, that after last night somebody'd start paying a little attention. You clowns aren't fit to be guarding Kiddyland at the church carnival."

Now Dunwoody caught sight of Roxanne. "And as for *you*— This tour has been out of control from the very beginning. Obviously you're not competent to handle this sort of responsibility. There's some kind of psycho loose here and nobody gives a good goddamn about it. All through this whole godforsaken trip there's been trouble and it's always been the same. 'We'll see what we can do about it.' Well, *I'll* see what *I* can do about stopping Irish Eyes Travel from any more of this kind of reckless disregard for safety, you'd better believe it. By the time my lawyers are finished with you—" He shook his head in disgust and turned back to Max Becker.

Becker hadn't even blinked through the entire tirade. He'd make a fine international negotiator.

But Dave Dunwoody wasn't finished. "My wife is dead and

my daughter's been harassed into hysteria and what's going on here? A bunch of clowns shuffling around in the hall like the Three Stooges."

Roxanne was leaning against Monica's door. She appeared to allow the blistering tirade to slide right off her, but still felt the furious resentment of the falsely accused. What did some textile importer know about security, anyway? Now that Dave had turned his attention away from her, however, she was more aware of what was going on in Monica's room, just behind her.

Rather, what *wasn't* going on.

The screaming and sobbing had stopped, and it sounded very much like Monica was *talking*. Roxanne rested her ear against the door. Sure enough, it was a rhythmic murmur that might have been some kind of prayer or recitation, though she doubted it. Much more likely, Monica was on the phone. Now she heard a faint click and jingle, as if a receiver were being replaced.

Roxanne nonchalantly walked down the hallway, past Barbara's crowded bedroom and out the back door. She walked along the porch to the end and cautiously stuck her head around the corner.

Bingo!

There was a leg sticking out of Monica Dunwoody's window, followed shortly by another leg as the girl perched momentarily on the sill. As Monica twisted and dropped quietly to the ground, Roxanne quickly pulled her head back out of sight. When she checked again a moment later, the girl was already slipping out into the pedestrian traffic on Duke of Gloucester Street.

Roxanne hesitated a moment. She ought to let John Clemens know what was happening, but if she went back to explain, there was an excellent chance that Monica would evade her. Better to stay with the girl, she decided quickly. Clemens was a bright boy. He'd figure it out. Besides, somebody like Max Becker might want to stop Monica instead of following her, and following definitely seemed to have the best potential for wresting some sense out of this mess.

It was a long time since Roxanne had tailed anybody on foot. She and her brothers had played endless tailing and sneaking games as kids, but the skill wasn't called for often when you drove a patrol car. Rather than having to discreetly tail somebody, you'd more likely be hightailing it through overgrown shrubbery or a cactus patch, yelling at some fleet-footed punk to freeze. Which of course never happened. You always had to run the bastards down, unless they got away from you.

There seemed no danger, just now, that Monica Dunwoody would get away from Roxanne. Once across Duke of Gloucester, the girl didn't even look back. She moved forward quite purposefully.

Where was she headed?

Roxanne held back, keeping Monica in view but allowing various tourists to pass between them. This time of day the streets were crowded, and she almost lost sight of Monica when a group of kids dashed out to intercept a horse-drawn carriage.

Monica cut down Botetourt Street, which was less crowded. Instinctively Roxanne hugged the sides of buildings, used trees as cover, tried to make sure that the girl wouldn't see her. It was nice to know that she still had the skills, though she probably could have been following in a bulldozer and the girl wouldn't have noticed.

Now Monica turned down Nicholson Street, even less crowded because there were no public buildings open between the Cabinetmaker and the Gaol. Virtually no buildings at all, actually. Roxanne had to rely on the vegetation for cover.

Could Monica possibly be going to the Gaol? It seemed terrifically ironic, though she had showed no signs so far of any sense of irony.

Monica walked briskly past the Gaol, however, into a small triangular field. She looked around while Roxanne hovered behind a convenient tree. When she peeked out, Monica was pacing back and forth, crying, pulling at her hair distractedly. After a few minutes, the girl sank to the ground in apparent exhaustion.

Five minutes passed. Ten. Roxanne wished now that she *had* taken the time to let somebody know where she was going. A full-blown search could be on by now and nobody would have a clue where to look. But she didn't have a radio or a cell phone and God knew where the nearest public phone might be tucked away. Sure as fire ants in a Texas summer, the minute she left to find one, something would happen.

But wait!

A young man came loping across the field from behind the Capitol Building toward where Monica sat sobbing. He was dark-haired, slim, dressed in tight faded jeans and a T-shirt. As he approached, he called out and Monica rose. She faced him accusingly.

They were too far away for Roxanne to hear them. But Monica was past being discreet. Whenever the young man tried to touch her, she recoiled as if stung. She yelled at him, most of the words carried away by the wind.

Gradually, he soothed her. He took her hand and gently pulled her down to a sitting position, spoke earnestly to her. She looked puzzled, shook her head.

Then abruptly, she stood. He rose with her, reached a hand out. "Don't touch me, Nick!" she screamed.

Nick.

It was all the ID Roxanne needed. She approached the couple cautiously, realizing just how ill-equipped she was to apprehend a possible murderer. She had no gun, no baton, no radio to call for backup. No handcuffs, not even a fat rubber band. She'd have to do this one on charm.

But charm wasn't enough.

Monica saw her first. "What are *you* doing h—"

Roxanne ignored her.

"Nick Winfield?" She was close enough to see that his hands were empty, and the jeans and T-shirt were tight enough so that any weapons he might be concealing were small. Not that that mattered much. She'd seen a burglar on a society bedroom floor once, killed by a single shot from a derringer the size of a lipstick.

The boy started, looked at Monica. Looked at Roxanne. Looked at Monica again and said, "What the fuck?"

Then bolted.

He headed back toward the historical section, running at a speed possible only for the young or those who train regularly. But Roxanne was in shape herself. She called after him to stop, then started to run.

She'd run these streets herself, in the early morning haze. Now it was midday, the sun was bright, and the streets were jammed with tourists. Quite different.

Nick Winfield raced toward the heart of town, vaulting low picket fences, dashing through gateways and alleys and quaint backyards filled with historically correct herbs and flowers. He ran with the practiced ease of one who had previously eluded pursuing police officers, but Roxanne was damned if he would get away this time.

She tried fleetingly to remember the last time she'd made such a chase. It had to be at least a year ago. The kind of recreational fitness running she'd been doing lately was much too proper and urbane. This kid was fast and slick and had a lot to lose. It was not the same at all.

Still, she managed to keep pace with him. And now, as she had feared, they were on Duke of Gloucester Street, which had never seemed more crowded. Damn! She raced around couples consulting maps, accidentally jostled a man backing up while using his camcorder, nearly collided head-on with a heavy woman in Colonial dress who stepped into the street without looking.

Now, suddenly, she realized where they were headed. Botsforth Tavern. But why in God's name would Nick Winfield want to go there?

Winfield stopped his broken-field running just for a moment to check on his pursuer.

It was all the lead Roxanne needed. She'd been gaining steadily on him and now she pounced. They were maybe ten yards away from the front entrance of the Botsforth Tavern which right now—dammit *anyway!*—didn't even have a guard at the door.

Nick Winfield was wiry and he fought hard. She had him pinned for a moment and then he bucked and broke her grip. He fought with the strength of fear and adrenaline, which she matched with out-of-practice reflexes and a sense of righteous indignation.

After a moment, though, she thought she had him. They were on their feet again now. She was twisting his arm up between his shoulder blades, when she felt his entire body go suddenly rigid.

"Dave, *no!*" he yelled, fear reverberating in his cry.

Three shots rang out in rapid succession, and Roxanne instinctively dove to the ground. Nick Winfield went down with her. The silence was sudden and absolute.

Roxanne looked up and around, saw tourists scatter like a flock of frightened birds. Saw Dave Dunwoody standing at the side of Botsforth Tavern, slowly lowering a nine millimeter semi-automatic to point toward the ground.

"Drop it, Dave!" Roxanne ordered, not getting up, keeping the bulk and weight of Nick between herself and the man. Nick was limp and heavy and she saw now the spreading wet crimson stain on the front of his T-shirt.

Dave Dunwoody obediently let the pistol slip to the ground and slowly raised his hands, just as the front door of Botsforth Tavern burst open, letting out a flood of law enforcement officers.

John Clemens raced toward Roxanne as she began carefully extricating herself from beneath the flaccid body of Nick Winfield. She cocked her head toward the corner of the building where Dave Dunwoody stood.

"This one's a slam dunk," she told him. "I'm an eyeball witness."

Clemens turned toward Dave Dunwoody, who stood immobile, making no attempt to run or resist. Meanwhile, Max Becker crossed to Roxanne. She was busy with Nick Winfield, who had three neat holes in the left front pocket of his T-shirt, was losing a lot of blood, and had no apparent pulse. His open eyes stared unblinking into the Virginia sun.

On Nick's right wrist, just as Heather had noted on her abductor's, a large black digital watch was strapped. It changed from 3:32 to 3:33 to 3:34 to 3:35.

Time had stopped, however, for Nick Winfield.

❦ CHAPTER FIFTEEN ❦

MAUREEN O'MALLEY drove her rental car directly to Botsforth Tavern. She'd worry about registration later. She was tired and she was cranky and she was impossibly worried about her Guns and Roses tour. Damn! She'd actually picked up that smart-aleck phrase from Roxanne. Her History and Gardens of Virginia tour.

There were cop cars all over the place and she could see, as she slowed down, that there was some kind of commotion out in front of the hotel. She double-parked, blocking a couple of expensive American sedans, cut the engine, and scurried up the side walkway toward Duke of Gloucester Street.

The first thing she saw was Roxanne.

With blood all over the front of her green blazer.

❦

Heather Tichener and her grandmother were in the Milliner's Shop again, accompanied by a very nice guide who had taken them to Miss Manderly's tea lesson at Christiana Campbell's Tavern. Miss Manderly had been truly wonderful. The guide was probably a policeman, she suspected, but that was all right and actually made her feel safer. Also, Heather was dressed in jeans and had done up her hair in a neat little bun on top of her head, under a baseball cap. She looked like an entirely different person, which was what Roxanne and Detective Clemens had insisted on.

The Milliner's was Heather's favorite shop in all of Williamsburg, and this was her fourth visit. Each time she came, the ladies behind the counter always had something new to say. Today they were talking about that amazing dress-in-a-day in the corner cupboard. Ten ladies had worked for eleven hours on it, cutting up twenty-seven yards of purple silk, making every stitch and ruffle by hand. It was an *awesome* accomplishment. Heather hadn't even been able to manage the sampler in Felicity's needlework kit, and the pincushion she'd attempted just now with Miss Manderly was really pathetic.

When she heard the sharp cracking noises outside, Heather was standing near the window. She looked out and saw Roxanne in the middle of the street, holding somebody in her arms.

What on earth?

And what was all the commotion?

Before anyone realized what she was doing, Heather streaked out the door and raced outside. Roxanne was carefully setting down a man in the street. He had blood all over the front of his shirt and his eyes were wide open, with long hair falling down over them.

"That's him!" Heather blurted out. "The guy I saw talking to Monica that night!"

Roxanne turned her head around so quickly that Heather didn't even see the motion. "Heather! What are *you* doing here? Where's your guard?"

"I was at the Milliner's," she answered impatiently. By now the guide/guard and her grandma had caught up with her. Grandma was starting to make that whimpering sound again. Big trouble. "But that's not the point, is it?" She looked at the man and felt herself start to shake uncontrollably. There was so much *blood*. "Is he dead?"

"I'm afraid so," Roxanne said, standing slowly. "You say you recognize him? Is this the man who kidnapped you, Heather?"

But Heather had finally reached her limit. She burst into tears and collapsed into her grandmother's arms.

☙

Monica Dunwoody was spilling her guts.

They'd cautioned her, all right, given her that stupid Miranda warning from TV and told her she could have a lawyer. Told her that Daddy didn't want her talking to any cops until his lawyer got there from Richmond. As if she'd be likely to do *anything* Daddy wanted right now, after he *killed* Nick.

Especially after what Nick had told her, right before he died.

Monica knew that if she lived to be a thousand, she'd never forget the horror of watching Nick die. She couldn't run as fast as Nick or Roxanne, but she'd managed to keep them in sight and had been at the edge of the crowd when they were wrestling out in front of Botsforth Tavern. And she'd seen Daddy come around the corner of the building and raise that gun, just as cool as can be. Everybody seemed to find it amazing that he hadn't hurt Roxanne, too, but they didn't know how much Daddy loved to shoot. How *good* he was at it.

"Nobody was supposed to *die*," she whimpered.

That detective, John Clemens, sat across from her at a table in a little room. He'd gotten her a Coke, asked her again if she wanted a lawyer or her great-aunt or anybody else with her. Yeah, right. Send in Aunt Mignon, and maybe some of the other old bats, too. Tell them not to forget their knitting.

"When Nick first brought it up, it was all kind of a goof," she explained. "Mom had her heart set on taking this stupid trip, and Nick said, well, how about we get it cut short. And I said, yeah, right, as if they ever do anything *I* want. And he said, no, really, we can do it. Make it seem like a jinx on the trip, just for laughs."

How innocent their plotting had seemed at the time. How could everything have gone so wrong?

"Nick would never have killed my *mother*," she went on after a moment. "He wouldn't have killed *anybody*, and he *told* me he didn't know anything about what happened to Mom. Besides, he *liked* Mom."

In one tiny corner of her mind, Monica realized that she was discussing the death of her mother. *The death of her mother.* She couldn't allow herself to realize what had happened or she'd fall apart completely.

"What did he say?" John Clemens asked mildly. He was

soft-spoken, gentle. The way Nick could be, when it was just the two of them. The way Nick would never be again. Oh God, she couldn't let herself think about *that*, either.

"That he'd been in his room all along, watching TV. That he hadn't even left his motel today." Though why anybody would want to stay in that room one minute when they didn't have to was a mystery to Monica. It was a dive down by the College of William and Mary, a hot-pillow house with weekly rates and a lot of big, ugly bugs. The only reason she'd spent any time at all there was because it would have looked mighty funny if she brought Nick to her bedroom in the Botsforth Tavern.

"When you called him after your mother's body was found, he answered in that room?"

Monica nodded. "He sounded groggy, like he just woke up. He said he was watching TV and he dozed off."

"And you told him what happened?"

"Uh-huh."

"What was his reaction?"

"He said, 'You're kidding' or something like that, and I said that it was true and there were cops all over the place. I told him I had to see him right away and he said he'd meet me." She sipped the Coke. "He found this place when we first got to Williamsburg where we could meet each other, and there wasn't much chance of anybody seeing us together by mistake."

"Down behind the Capitol, over toward the Gaol?"

"Uh-huh."

John Clemens leaned forward, earnest and congenial. "I understand that there were some problems earlier in the trip, pranks and so on. Now I don't think that anybody's inclined to really make a fuss about it, but it sure would help if we could clear up exactly what was happening there."

He paused expectantly, leaned back in the chair.

Monica couldn't quite believe it.

Here she sat in this crummy little room in this crummy little police station in this crummy little town.

While her mother and Nick were both *dead*.

Monica turned defiantly toward the mirror that covered one

end wall of the room. "Hey, whoever's back there, listen up. My mother's *dead*. My lover's *dead*. What kind of shit-ass town you running here, anyway?" Then she burst into tears.

John Clemens waited her out, put a box of tissues on the table. He was still sitting patiently when she calmed down a few minutes later.

"You were going to tell me what you knew about the pranks on the trip," he said, as if there had been no pause.

He *hoped* she was going to. Monica knew she hadn't made any promises. And...and now would be the time to tell. The temptation to pour everything out was almost overwhelming. But she couldn't quite make herself do it yet.

Where was Daddy? They wouldn't tell her.

Monica spoke slowly, wondering what to do. "It was all just a joke, so I could get out of this stupid tour sooner. It was all harmless enough."

"Was Nick Winfield involved in these pranks with you?"

So. They really didn't know anything. "Well, of course he was. I couldn't do all that myself."

"But it was your idea?"

Monica stared at the detective. Now or never. "We talked about it together, back home. Nick was mad that I'd be gone so long and he started saying that if the tour seemed jinxed, I could just cut out and come home."

"It was Nick's idea?"

"Uh-huh." And as she looked back on things, she realized just how much Nick had really been egging her on. Which also fit with what he said just before Daddy killed him. Even though she couldn't quite make herself believe it yet.

The detective looked puzzled. "But he wasn't part of the tour group, and as I understand it, nobody with the group ever saw him."

"Except that little busybody Heather." The brat. Just thinking about Heather snapped Monica out of her melancholy and got her good and mad again. Heather sidling up to her with that little smirk on her face, asking who was the cute guy in the Colonial costume.

"Did Heather threaten him somehow? Is that why he kidnapped her?"

"He didn't *kidnap* her," Monica answered irritably. She was still furious with Nick for doing such a stupid thing. How *could* he? "I didn't know about it before it happened or I'd never have let him do it. I was a little girl once myself, after all." She took a deep breath. "He said he just wanted to teach her to mind her own business. It was really wrong and totally unforgivable to scare her that way. I *know* that. But at least she wasn't hurt, and she got found right away."

The detective didn't change his expression. "As I recall, you were at dinner with your parents when Heather was being taught to mind her own business. And you say you didn't know in advance what Nick was going to do?"

This was all getting really tedious. "Look, apart from it being wrong, if he'd told me, I'da told him not to bother. I could tell she was the kind of kid who'd never give up. Like I said, I didn't find out anything about it till it was all over, and there wasn't anything I could do about it then anyway. Except give him hell, which I did."

"All right, then. Was Nick along the whole time you were on the tour?"

Monica shook her head. "He didn't hook up with me till Richmond. The first part, it would've been too hard to hide him. I mean, we were out at this awful plantation in the middle of absolutely *nowhere.*"

"So you were responsible for the pranks up until Richmond?" John Clemens frowned as if trying to remember. "Would that be starting with the lady who broke her ankle in Washington?"

Monica felt her eyes widen involuntarily. This changed things. If he'd put it all together with *that*, God knows what else this detective knew. Or what Roxanne did. Monica had known instinctively all along that Roxanne was not to be trusted. Fine thing it was to learn only now that she was a cop.

"That was an accident," Monica answered carefully.

"I understand that where she fell, there was a spill of some kind of soap…shampoo, actually. It matched the complimentary bottles in the rooms."

Was he bluffing? Nobody had ever said a word to suggest they thought it was anything but an unfortunate accident when that fat lady went down on her ass. Better try to bluff this one out herself. "That's all news to me."

Fortunately the detective let it go. "Let's see, now. There was some business with the salt and pepper shakers in Charlottesville. Did you do that?"

This one was safe enough. A piece of cake, too. "It was the sugar bowls, and yes, I did. Is there some law against putting salt in a sugar bowl?" She'd brought the plastic bag of salt along with her, packed inside one of her rain boots. She and Mom were staying right above the dining room. It couldn't have been simpler.

Be flexible, Nick had told her, when they were planning it all.

And flexible she had been. The dog shit was totally spontaneous, for instance, once she realized the dog's dumping ground was totally hidden from view of the plantation buildings by bushes. A stroke of genius, Nick told her later. And that was almost as easy as the salt.

The only nasty part was gathering the dog shit in those little Monticello souvenir shop bags everyone had thrown away in the parlor. Her only real regret was that it hadn't been possible to put some into those outrageous suitcases with the pink lightning bolts on them that the Flanagans carried, but their bags were out in a separate building somewhere. And since she'd been clever enough to put a bag of poop—a very carefully sealed bag—in one of her own suitcases, nobody ever dreamed that she might be responsible.

"Malicious mischief, maybe," he answered, all seriousness. "But we're not interested in that sort of thing, Monica. I don't even care so much about the lady who broke her ankle. Accidents happen. I'm just trying to put together the big picture. So. After you got to Richmond, Nick met you?"

"I didn't actually *see* him, 'cause my dad had joined us by then and my room was connecting to my parents'. But he said he'd be there, and Nick never let me down."

"He was a guest at the hotel in Richmond?"

Monica nodded. Now was the time. But somehow she couldn't do it.

"Under what name?" Detective Clemens persisted.

What difference did it make? "I don't know. And yes, he made those calls to everybody, but *honestly*, it was no big deal. All he did was *laugh.*"

"The leeches in Mrs. Stanton's glass weren't very funny. How did that come about?"

Improvising again, though she wasn't going to tell the cop that. Nick was good at keys and locks, from his dad being a locksmith. Give him a little time and he could pick almost any lock. Once Monica learned that the old ladies had that separate bathroom, she and Nick had decided immediately to put the rubber tarantula he'd brought along in it and scare them. Of course, after Monica saw the leeches in the Apothecary Shop, she realized that they would be *much* better.

"That was Nick's idea," Monica explained. "He stole them out of the Apothecary Shop and then picked the lock on that bathroom."

"Did he pick the lock at the Apothecary Shop, too?"

Was this a trick question? "No. Anyway, he said he didn't. He figured the place would probably be alarmed 'cause folks would expect there to be real drugs in it." Like that jar labelled OPIUM, for instance. "So he tagged along on a Lanthorn Tour— not the same one I was on—and made off with them then."

"Didn't you worry that an elderly lady being frightened that way might have a heart attack?"

The elderly ladies in Monica's experience—starting with Aunt Mignon and working her way through the entire contingent of old bats on this trip—were remarkably sturdy and not easily scared. They seemed, indeed, to be virtually indestructible.

"Not really. And she didn't."

"No, she didn't. Fortunately. You know, Monica, it sounds

like Nick was pretty good at this sort of thing. Weren't you worried that it might get out of hand?"

"But it *didn't*," Monica protested. Whatever had happened to Mom had nothing to do with Nick or their silly plans and pranks. It *couldn't* have. Nick was so *gentle*. He'd even felt bad that the denture cleaner was probably going to kill those stupid leeches.

The detective shrugged slightly and shifted subjects again. "When was the last time you saw Nick before you met him behind the Capitol this afternoon?"

She hesitated. It was hard keeping up with these questions, the way he kept jumping around, trying to trick her. "I called his room at the motel last night when everybody was running around looking for Heather."

"Did you know he was planning to, uh, frighten her?"

She shook her head firmly. "No, sir. I *told* you I didn't. And I was *really* mad when I found out what he'd done. We had a huge argument about it."

"You called him from your room?"

She shook her head again. "No, from a pay phone down in Merchant's Square. I never called him from my room till today, on account of I didn't want my parents wondering about the charges."

Detective Clemens offered that soft smile again. He didn't really look like a cop, but neither did that snooty Roxanne, either. "Let's talk about today," he suggested. "You spent the morning with your mother?"

"Uh-huh. We all had breakfast together, me and Mom and Daddy and Aunt Mignon. Daddy had to go to Richmond on business and he was leaving kind of early."

"Early like when?" the detective asked.

"Eight-thirty. Then we came back to the hotel for a while and Mom and I went shopping."

"And you'd had breakfast over at the Cascades?"

Monica nodded. It had actually been rather nice, a big buffet in a room with floor-to-ceiling windows looking out into the woods. Like being in the woods, practically, but without all the bugs.

]178[

"Did anything unusual happen at breakfast?"

She shook her head slowly. She'd been tired, not paying attention too much. Aunt Mignon was upset about Heather, and Monica was too mad at Nick to say much.

"So then. Your father brought you all back to the hotel and left for his business meeting?"

She nodded again. It was easier than speaking, but sooner or later he was bound to ask a more complicated question.

Sooner. "And what happened then?"

"Aunt Mignon went to her room and Mom and I went shopping."

"Where did you go?"

As Monica outlined the various stops, she tried not to think about them as being part of her mother's last morning alive. It had all seemed so very *ordinary*. Mom really liked all this Colonial crap for some reason, and she had all these big ideas for redecorating the kitchen. If only she hadn't bought that horrible metal ball...

"And how did your mom seem while you were shopping?"

"She seemed tired. Or actually, she didn't seem tired, but she *said* she was and I guess she wasn't as peppy as she might have been."

"Did she talk about coming back to lie down?"

Monica thought a minute. "Not until after lunch. We ate in Merchant's Square at one of those places where you can sit outside. Only she wanted to eat inside, because she said the sun was too bright."

"What did she have for lunch?"

Monica thought again. "A chef's salad and a cup of some kind of soup, I don't remember what. I had a cheeseburger. What difference does it make?"

He ignored her question. "And what time was it when you finished lunch?"

"Around twelve-thirty."

"What happened then?"

"Mom said she was going to come back and lie down. I told her I'd see her at dinner time and that was that." Monica pictured her mother setting off down Duke of Gloucester. There had been nothing about the moment to suggest she would be dead within the hour.

"What did you do then?"

"I just sat and watched people going by for a while. There was some little girl banging a drum, and it got *really* tedious and annoying, so after a while I left. There wasn't anything *to* do."

Detective Clemens raised an eyebrow. "Seems like it might have been a good chance to slip off and see Nick."

"Well, I thought about it, but…"

"But what?"

But he hadn't answered the phone when she called his room. *He hadn't answered the phone.* Where had he been?

"But I didn't."

"You were right up there near his motel and you didn't go see him?"

"No. And it wasn't *that* close anyway."

He seemed not to have heard her. "Even though you hadn't spoken to him since your argument the night before?"

"No."

"Seems to me," the detective said, "that you must have been pretty frustrated. Here you and Nick had all these great plans for cutting short the trip and it was almost over. On schedule. I know *I'd* have been feeling mighty annoyed."

"We might have been, but we weren't. We'd had the fun of seeing everybody get all worked up over nothing, after all. And even if it didn't work the way we planned it, we were sort of together and had a lot of fun. Plus, we'd both be back home soon."

"But I thought you said your parents had forbidden you to see Nick at home."

Monica smiled. "That was only temporary."

"And that they didn't want him involved in your plans to open a swimsuit shop."

Now how did he know about *that?* Bigmouth Roxanne again, no doubt.

Suddenly Monica had had enough. "Am I under arrest?" she asked.

"Not at all," John Clemens assured her.

"In that case," Monica told him, standing up abruptly, "I'm outa here."

❧

Roxanne had watched the interrogation with mounting frustration through the one-way glass. About all she could say with certainty was that it had been interesting watching John Clemens at work.

Roxanne's mother had always maintained that the world could be divided into two camps: those inclined to roil life's waters and those inclined to oil them. Roxanne herself had a foot in each camp. And as she had watched John Clemens in action for the past twenty-four hours, it seemed clear to her that he was a born oiler, an asset in this kind of town.

A lot of cops, though, were definite roilers, folks for whom life might have gone either way, who might just as easily have landed on the wrong side of the law as pledged toward its enforcement. Even as cops, sworn to uphold the peace, they were forever testing boundaries, pushing the rules and regs, looking to see just how much they could get away with.

It was a single coin with two heads. The same adrenaline rush that coursed through Roxanne as she chased a suspicious Chevy through the bad part of town would have been there had she been behind the wheel of that Chevy, hoping and praying and maneuvering to elude the coppers once again. And just maybe succeeding. Roxanne felt quite confident that she would have made an abundantly successful crook. It was one of those areas of herself that she never really wanted to test or examine too carefully.

The wonder, she had long since decided, wasn't that cops went bad. The wonder was that so many of them didn't.

Now John Clemens looked exhausted and made no secret of his frustration. Dave Dunwoody's high-powered Richmond attorney had succeeded in cutting his client loose, and somebody from Colonial Williamsburg Security had taken Monica back to the Inn, where rooms had been readied for the remains of the Dunwoody-Chesterton entourage.

Roxanne and Clemens were sitting in his office at the station. The Williamsburg PD was a generic municipal building constructed some twenty years earlier, not precisely Colonial-style but red brick that fit right into its semi-residential part of town. Inside, it was vintage cop shop, with off-white walls, linoleum floors, and plenty of metal and Formica. In a rather charming concession to the town's principal industry, the interior trim was painted bright Colonial blue.

"I don't care what Dave Dunwoody says," Roxanne announced. "I was *not* in any kind of danger from that kid and if I had been you still couldn't tell from where Dunwoody was standing. This crap about protecting me is absurd. I saw him right after, and he looked totally calm and deliberate. Like he was on the shooting range."

"You're sure Nick called out his name?"

Roxanne nodded. "Absolutely."

"It doesn't follow," Clemens said. "Something's wrong. But we're stuck here."

"Monica says nobody else knew that Nick was in Virginia," Roxanne pointed out. "We'd *just* found Barbara's body, and we sure didn't know yet about Nick's prints on the screwdriver under her bed. In fact, we might not have known for days that the prints were his if my brother hadn't run the group for me."

"You sure Dunwoody didn't say anything before he fired?"

"Not at all. I was rolling around in the street with Nick and my concentration was focused on him. If Dave said anything, I missed it. I just heard Nick call out."

"Monica's holding something back," Clemens mused. "But what? Nothing fits."

"Isn't there some way to at least get Dave on the gun?" Roxanne asked wearily. "No teeny little loophole in some obscure law that never got taken off the books, like from 1752 or so?"

Clemens shook his head. "He's got a concealed weapon permit that's meticulously in order, and of course, there's no handgun registration in Virginia. No registration, period." He looked at her and smiled. "A situation I surely don't need to spell out for a Texan."

Roxanne laughed briefly, then scowled as she thought of Dave Dunwoody walking out the door. Scot-free and likely to remain so. "What's his reason for needing a concealed weapon, Clemens? The guy sells *fabric.*"

Clemens laced his hands behind his neck, leaned back and looked at the ceiling. "You don't need a reason, not anymore. Used to be, you had to show some kind of cause, but the law changed. It's a national trend, maybe you've noticed. So now if you make an application and you don't have any felonies, that's it. Permit's yours."

"Which doesn't answer the question of why the guy thinks he needs a gun."

Clemens raised his hands upward and extended them as he shrugged his shoulders. "My blood sugar's dropped off the charts," he announced, sitting upright once again. "I've *got* to eat something." He rubbed his eyes. "Join me?"

Roxanne herself felt a curious sense of emptiness, but she wasn't sure it had anything to do with food. She shrugged. "I guess."

Now Clemens cocked his head and sprang to life with a broad grin. "Have you had any barbecue since you've been here? *Real* barbecue, I mean?"

"Nope." As far as Roxanne was concerned, she hadn't had any real barbecue since she'd moved to California from Texas, and no meal she'd be offered in Virginia was likely to change that sorry situation.

"You're in for a treat then. Let's go."

Clemens drove in a hurry, heading west through town and then cutting up through dense forest toward the freeway. Ten minutes later they were at a barbecue joint in the woods, eating hush puppies and coleslaw and sweet minced pork, with white plastic forks. It was nothing like the tender slabs of Texas beef brisket on which Roxanne had been weaned, but it was still mighty good.

"I talked to your lieutenant," Clemens told her between bites. His spirits had improved considerably once he got some food into him. "He said you were a damned fine cop. And he told me about your partner." Clemens hesitated a moment. "I'm sorry."

"Thanks," she answered slowly. "I suppose you think I'm a coward for quitting."

He shook his head. "I'd never dare make that kind of judgment on somebody else. Who's to say what's right to do?" He smiled wryly. "To be perfectly honest, one of the reasons that I like working in a place like Williamsburg is that those sorts of things generally don't happen here."

She felt, as always, the need to explain. "I never would've thought I'd leave," she told him seriously. "I was always gonna be a cop. *Always.* My whole family's cops, going way back. And yet, after my partner got it, I felt almost as if I *had* to leave. Not so much that it might've been me. But that it was my signal somehow, that I didn't have to do it anymore."

He seemed to consider the statement for a moment before asking, "How long were you partners?"

"On and off for two years." Two years, in the context of a place like Williamsburg, seemed a nanosecond. And yet she and Frank Rodriguez had known each other well. Frank had never minded that she was female, the way some of the guys did, the ones who felt threatened by women on the force. He'd shared things with her that he'd never have discussed with a man, like his anguish over his wife's miscarriages and the joy in the pregnancy that was finally going to term. Frank Jr. was born two months after his father died.

John Clemens sat quietly, eating barbecue and drinking iced tea. Without realizing how or why it happened, Roxanne found herself telling him the whole story. Wanting to tell him the story.

When she had finished, Clemens was still silent. He understood the power of a shotgun at such close range. "Horrible," he said finally.

"Yeah," she answered, becoming Tough Cop again. "It was.

Still is. And the pisser is, I decided to take this job working for my aunt because it was a chance to do something nice and orderly and have a little fun at the same time. So what happens? I wind up in a homicide investigation with the Tour Group from Hell."

❦ CHAPTER SIXTEEN ❦

WHEN THEY reached Nick Winfield's motel room, the Williamsburg PD evidence tech, Sam Nash, had just about finished dusting for prints. Clemens had sent Nash back to the motel with instructions to check everything.

"Not much," Nash told Clemens, "but there never is. I heard the other day about a cop clearing a case on prints. It was reported in Ripley's."

"We could break ground here," Clemens answered mildly.

"The one advantage we have," Nash went on, continuing to work as he spoke, "is that maid service at this dump seems to be pretty cursory. Nobody'd been in here today even before we sealed the room this afternoon. There's dust bunnies under the bed would scare my cat."

Roxanne looked carefully around the pathetic motel room that had been the last residence of Nick Winfield.

It was furnished in faux antiques, and bad faux at that, cheap imitations of the finely crafted pieces found throughout Colonial Williamsburg. There was a double bed, unmade, with vaguely gray sheets and a chenille bedspread that had lost a lot of its tufting over the years. A dresser, a TV, a rickety desk with an even more rickety chair.

Certain evidence, she knew, had already been removed during Nash's first visit that afternoon. Nick Winfield's Colonial outfit was down at the police station, and Heather had been correct: it was a shoddy imitation, all polyester and vinyl. More significantly, Nash had also booked into evidence a first-class set of picklocks and some generic clothesline with cut ends that at first glance seemed to match those on the rope used to tie up Heather.

"I guess we might as well gather up everything else," Clemens said now, "and release the room. What've we got, Sam?"

"Jeans, T-shirts, Jockeys. Basic toiletries that all seem to be exactly what they're labeled. A black rubber tarantula and some rubber cockroaches. A bunch of electronic toys. Little bitty battery-operated TV, Game Boy with a lot of cartridges, Walkman, that kind of stuff. And that electronic gizmo over there on the dresser." He pointed to a small black box the size of a remote control unit. "You can go ahead and pick it up. I've already printed it."

As Clemens picked up the box, Roxanne moved in for a closer look.

"Hey!" she said. "I know what that is. My brother Tom got one for Christmas. It's a kind of calendar–address book thing. An electronic datebook. Tom got it to keep track of court dates, mostly."

Clemens laughed. "Probably the same reason Nick Winfield needed one. You know how to work it?" He offered the black box.

Roxanne took it and gingerly turned it over in her hand. "Tom's is voice-activated. He says, 'John Clemens' and the thing prints out your phone number. Or he says, 'Martinez homicide' and it brings up a mini-file, hearing date, whatever."

Clemens pulled up the chenille cover and sat on the bed. "Hmm. This might actually be worth something, then. Nash, you know anything about these things?"

Nash cocked an eyebrow. "I know enough not to mess with it without getting some specs first." He reached for the mechanism and Roxanne handed it over quickly. "Let me make some phone calls in the morning before I start fooling with it. There's probably a password of some sort, and it might even have some kind of built-in booby traps. Any indication that this guy's a hacker?"

"No idea," Clemens told him. "We'll have more from California tomorrow. I hope. So far all I know for sure is, he's a damn fine lock-picker and a semi-skilled burglar. I say semi 'cause he got caught at least twice."

"This is distributed by Sharper Image," Nash said thoughtfully, "so it's probably pretty basic. But unless somebody tells me it's *real* simple to operate—like your pet hamster can do it drunk—I say we send it to Richmond. Or the FBI. It'll take longer, but they're set up for this kind of thing better."

Clemens nodded. "Then send it out. Definitely. Drive it over yourself, first thing tomorrow." He looked around the room. "Lovely though this may be, Nash, I think we'll shove off now. Call me if you come up with anything else."

Nash shook his head. "Ain't gonna happen."

❧

Bridget Flanagan stifled a little belch and gazed around contentedly. *Finally* they were having the sort of meal she had envisioned eating several times a day on a trip as expensive as this one, aimed at the wealthy such as herself.

The Irish Eyes group sat at a long table in the dining room's center, a stone's throw from the groaning buffet tables of the Chesapeake Bay Feast at the Williamsburg Lodge. Bridget had always had a soft spot for all-you-can-eat dining, dating back to the parish potlucks of her Boston girlhood, and her affinity for seafood had survived the obligatory Friday cod of that same period. This was really quite a lovely spread and she had unhesitantly ordered Dom Perignon when the waitress asked what she'd like for her beverage.

Patrick and Merrily also seemed to be enjoying themselves, which was a relief, since Bridget was beginning to feel mildly guilty about having dragged them along on this wild goose chase. Not that either of them had complained, of course.

Tonight Merrily had plunged into the crab legs gleefully, filling a small soup bowl with drawn butter and bringing back two plates at a time to the table, which made perfect sense since crab legs were so *bulky*, given the small amount of meat each held. Her daughter-in-law now had a little film of melted butter all around her mouth. And Patrick, a meat-and-potatoes man like his father before him, had simply headed straight for the prime rib carving table.

Bridget stopped listening to Maureen O'Malley, blathering away across the table about how special Williamsburg was at Christmas. Special, indeed. The heating probably didn't work any better than the air-conditioning, and those snobby Williamsburg people probably didn't even string up any colored lights because they weren't *authentic.*

Bridget had pictured Maureen O'Malley as something of a kindred spirit when she first learned about Irish Eyes Travel. Instead, the woman was an incredible busybody, with the same mannerisms and snotty attitude as all those officious tour guides the group had encountered everywhere on this trip.

But never mind Maureen O'Malley, whose slipshod operation would *certainly* never get any of Bridget Flanagan's business again and might just hear from Bridget's attorney. There'd been a lot of emotional distress on this trip, after all, even before anybody got *murdered.* It was a miracle one of her own party hadn't been brutally slain.

Thank heavens that Merrily had insisted they all spend the day at Busch Gardens! And tomorrow they'd be away from the group as well, taking that private Tidewater air tour that Patrick was so excited about. Maybe the pilot would even point out a mansion belonging to the Virginia Masons.

And Bridget would shoot the place a cheerful bird.

Maureen O'Malley downed the martini she had mixed out of a compact traveling bar kit, mixed another, and chugged that one, too. It had not been quite as easy as she'd envisioned to play returning mother hen with the tattered remnants of her Irish Eyes group.

Maureen never drank with or in front of her clients, but it was 9:30 P.M. and she was as off-duty as she was ever likely to be on *this* doomed excursion. She had exercised great restraint in not joining the others in getting mildly plastered at dinner, particularly when that wretched Flanagan woman—whose preferred tipple was probably Bud Lite before the lottery came in—began ordering French champagne that she couldn't even pronounce properly. It sounded like she was asking for "paregoric."

The Flanagans seemed always to be first in line for anything that sounded free. Maureen was willing to bet that Bridget had a suitcase full of complimentary soaps and shampoos and had probably filched extras off the maids' carts.

Only the Vanguards and Mignon Chesterton had declined Maureen's dinner invitation. Dave and Monica Dunwoody, of course, were busy with the police. Roxanne had been out somewhere, too, presumably with the cops, and Maureen had felt quite confident that her niece was not interested in group dining this particular evening.

"Now let me see if I've got this straight." Maureen watched Roxanne feign an exaggerated cringe as she began ticking items off on her fingers. She was seated on the matching twin bed in Roxanne's tiny room under the eaves. She was trying to forget that she now sat *directly* above the spot where Barbara Dunwoody had died barely eight hours ago. Had died in her own bed in the room that was now sealed with ghastly yellow tape.

Roxanne's cringe, Maureen realized, probably wasn't all that exaggerated, either. The girl had been through a rough few days. And of course, it wasn't fair to lay this all on her niece.

Still, who else was there? Maureen *had* to vent some of this now before she blew a gasket. You could only ask so much of an antihypertensive drug, after all.

"Barbara Dunwoody has been bludgeoned to death," Maureen began deliberately. "Dave Dunwoody is in police custody because he was observed by a hundred witnesses—five minutes earlier and I'd've been one myself, dammit!—fatally shooting Nick Winfield, who's believed to be responsible for killing Barbara and for systematically sabotaging my tour. The late Mr. Winfield—whom I never had the opportunity to meet, alas—had a history of drug abuse, as well as some kind of criminal record, but none of that stopped him from being Monica Dunwoody's boyfriend. Monica Dunwoody, who's *also* a recovering drug addict and currently in police custody."

"Actually, they've both been released," Roxanne told Maureen mildly, "Dave and Monica. Dave went off with his lawyer, God knows where. And by the time he left, Monica was gone, too. When she pulled the plug on her questioning, they stashed her over in the Williamsburg Inn, with her great-aunt. For her own protection, they told her."

"Well, there's plenty to protect her from," Maureen snapped. "Not even counting me." She continued ticking off her fingers. "Larry Vanguard, for instance. A confidence artist with convictions in various states. I don't suppose she has much to fear from Dick Forrester, as long as she doesn't get into a car he's driving tonight. He could barely walk by the end of dinner. Or have I missed something else about Dick? Are he and Olive jewel thieves, perhaps?"

"Anything's possible," Roxanne answered serenely. She took her Big Bend T-shirt out of a drawer in the antique dresser and stepped into the bathroom. "Keep going, I can hear you."

"I'm *so* glad," Maureen told her irritably. "I was just getting to the kidnapping of a ten-year-old child, or aren't we supposed to count that, since poor little Heather was released unharmed?"

"That's Monica's line." Roxanne stepped out of the bathroom in the T-shirt and sidestepped past the fireplace to hang her slacks and blazer in the closet. The room was really quite minuscule for a putative double, but of course the best accommodations always went to the clients.

Roxanne gave the clothing a sniff and grimaced. "I had to throw away that other jacket and I think I may have to burn this outfit, too. I don't know *what* to make of Monica's story, to be perfectly honest."

She sat in the red wing chair in front of the box labeled FIRE LADDER. "Shit!" she said suddenly. "We never even *considered* a fire ladder when we were trying to figure out how the leeches got in with Edna's teeth." She shrugged. "Maybe because using the ladder would have necessitated an inside job with a confederate, which seemed ridiculous. And which was *exactly* what it turned out to be."

"You're getting ahead of me," Maureen complained. "You should always let your boss follow a serious complaint through to the end. Now. Edna Stanton had leeches put in with her false teeth. Fresh dog shit was packed in the luggage of Evelyn Tichener and Monica Dunwoody. And would have been in Bridget Flanagan's bag if there were a God. I do *not* like that woman, Rox. Do you know, she told me I have a low-class clientele?"

Roxanne laughed. "We have a saying down home that covers old Bridget. Spam-sucking trailer trash. Maybe you should have another drink, Maureen. To calm yourself."

"I don't dare," Maureen replied. "If I did that, I might feel the need to go show Bridget Flanagan just *exactly* how low-class I am." She looked around, leaned back on the bed, sat up again. "Now, where was I?"

"Chewing my ass," Roxanne reminded. "If you're not gonna drink that, pass it here." She poured a shot into the glass beside her and sipped. "Nice stuff, Maureen."

"Vodka's vodka. Don't try to sweet-talk me." Maureen glared ferociously. "I've been bullshitted by pros in my day. So. I believe we'd gotten to the crank calls in the middle of the night in Richmond. And that's it, unless I missed something?"

Roxanne hesitated. "Well, yes, though I don't really see much point in rehashing the salt in the sugar bowls at Nicholson Plantation. And the flat tire on the bus. Both those incidents really *did* seem prankish," she added. "On that I pretty much agree with Monica. Who *swears* she had nothing to do with the flat tire." Roxanne lay flat on her bed and stared at the ceiling. "You know, I guess it's actually possible that the flat tire just happened, that it wasn't planned or anything. The bus driver said it was a defect in the rubber and Patrick Flanagan agreed with him. Back when he was working, he was an auto mechanic."

"Nobody was looking for deliberate damage," Maureen pointed out.

"And nobody found any. But I'm surprised you aren't chewing me out about Blanche Weddington's broken ankle. I *did* notice the shampoo on the tile, after she went to the hospital. And I let it go."

Maureen sighed. "Anybody would have thought that was an accident. And it probably *was* an accident that somebody got seriously hurt."

"You can't start greasing the sidewalks when the AARP comes to town," Roxanne told her grimly, "and then act surprised when somebody busts a hip. To be charitable, I'll concede that she probably didn't intend to send anybody to the hospital. And as far as I'm concerned, there's no reason to do anything more about it unless the Weddingtons file some nasty lawsuit against the hotel. Or you."

"They won't, or at least I don't think they will. They've been nice as can be so far, and he used to be corporate counsel for GM, defending against frivolous lawsuits."

"How fortunate for us. Or rather, for you."

Maureen laughed and raised her empty glass. "It's *us*, Rox. This may be an unmitigated disaster as a trip, but you've been getting rave reviews from most of the clients."

"Perhaps you *do* have a low-class clientele."

Maureen started to pour another drink, then changed her mind and set down the silver flask. She was already jet-lagged. If she got drunk tonight, she'd be a zombie in the morning. "How in God's name did all this *happen?*"

"I wish I knew," Roxanne told her fervently.

Roxanne stood up now and began examining the shelf that still hung on the wall over the bed. Its partner sat on the floor nearby, a forlorn casualty of earlier tests. Maureen had arrived in time for some disturbing demonstrations of the trajectory of a five-pound iron ball onto a single bed. The sample ball was still sitting on the bedside table. Holes in the plaster showed where the fallen shelf had begun its last tumble. Maureen was very much afraid that Roxanne was going to begin another demo.

Blessedly, her niece sat down instead.

"There's an old saying in law enforcement, 'Always blame the dead guy,'" Roxanne began deliberately. "That seems to be what's happening here. And you know, Maureen, some of this may *never* get straightened out. Everybody's blaming every-thing on Nick Winfield, and Nick Winfield has no comment, on account of Dave Dunwoody shot him stone-cold dead be-fore he could say anything to anybody."

Maureen frowned. "Rather precipitous, wasn't he?" She shook her head in bafflement.

"Rather." Roxanne went back into the bathroom and a moment later Maureen heard the thunder of water pouring into the tub. The one amenity the Botsforth Tavern had in spades was strong water pressure.

Roxanne returned and continued. "Dave had no reason to assume that Nick had killed Barbara, or even that he was in town. There's no record of any threats from Nick Winfield at all, other than the obvious one of marrying their precious daughter, even though Dave says now that Nick threatened him a few weeks ago in San Diego. And violence wasn't involved at all in any of Nick's past crimes. He was strictly a sneak thief and he didn't even hot-prowl. He specialized in places where nobody was home."

She sighed, a sound that nicely matched her pale, exhausted appearance. "Maybe after I soak for an hour or so, I'll think of something. But somehow I doubt it, Maureen. There are just too many questions that don't have good answers."

"Like?" Did she really want to know? Too late now.

"Like, what really would be the point of trying to cut the trip short? Even with going to New York first and stopping in Birmingham at the end, Monica was only going to be gone a bit more than two weeks. So why bother?"

"For the hell of it?"

"That's Monica's answer, basically. But you know, there's no evidence that Nick Winfield was a prankster in the normal course of events. From everything I understand, he was a lot more direct. Like, if he went to the trouble of picking your lock, he'd be more likely to steal your jewelry than put some leeches in your denture glass."

"Where did he learn to pick locks, for heaven's sake?" Maureen asked irritably. "Prison? Public school?"

Roxanne laughed. "You won't like this, Auntie dear, but it's *his* family business. It turns out that Nick Winfield's father is a locksmith and Nick worked with him a lot in the shop as a kid. As I understand it, by the time the old man realized that Nick was using his special expertise to break into places, it was too late to do anything but feel guilty about it. They found a really fine set of picklocks in Nick's motel room. Along with the Colonial costume and the clothesline that I told you about. And a kind of interesting little electronic datebook."

"A young thug with an electronic datebook? What on earth for?"

"That's another big question. And I don't think he was precisely a thug, either. There's nothing says a criminal can't be organized—hell, the successful ones generally are." Roxanne grinned and stuck her head into the bathroom to see how her tub was filling. "Except Nick can't have been that successful, or he wouldn't have been busted so much."

Maureen was beginning to notice a throbbing in her temples. "Anything else I ought to be worrying about?"

"Sure," her niece told her cheerfully. "Try this. Monica says her mom was kind of drowsy and sluggish all morning. Now, I never met Barbara Dunwoody before this trip, but the whole time I observed her, she struck me as being extremely hyper and manic. I'm inclined to think somebody drugged her."

"Who? How?"

Roxanne threw her hands up. "Beats me. I can't quite see Barbara running into Nick Winfield, saying, 'Hey, fancy meeting you here, you slug we've deemed unworthy of our daughter'— and then taking some pill that he offered her."

"Monica could have slipped something into her mother's food at breakfast or lunch."

"She certainly could have," Roxanne agreed. "Breakfast is more likely, actually. They ate over at the Cascades, some kind of buffet, so they'd all be up and down, back and forth. Making it real easy to put something in somebody's food or drink while they're off getting more grits."

"So far it sounds plausible," Maureen acknowledged.

"And Monica could have slipped into the back door of Botsforth Tavern, too," Roxanne went on. "It was supposed to be locked, but one of the maids left it open while she was working in the building." She stuck her head into the bathroom again and turned off the taps.

"I hate this," Maureen said flatly. With the advent of what was bound to be a whopper headache, she was starting to get really mad.

"Me, too," Roxanne agreed wearily. "Listen, my tub is ready, and when I get out of it, I plan to sleep for about ten hours. But if you want something to think about while I bathe, try this: Why would somebody smart enough to pull off all the crap that Nick Winfield did on this trip be dumb enough to leave behind a screwdriver with his fingerprints on it in Barbara Dunwoody's room?"

"Well—"

Roxanne held up a hand. "I'm not done. And how come Dave Dunwoody—that mild-mannered importer of textiles— just happened to have a gun on his person and just happened to be outside waiting when Nick and I got back? And even given that the guy is a damned fine shot—he hit Nick three times and didn't get me once—why would he risk firing onto a street full of schoolchildren and tourists?"

They were questions, Maureen decided wearily, that called for at least one more martini.

❦

Roxanne reclined in her tub, watching steam rise around her body and wishing she had enough energy to go find the health club that was supposed to be over in the Williamsburg Lodge somewhere. A Jacuzzi would be wonderful right now.

So many questions. So much confusion. So many loose ends.

And yet this entire package was supposedly all wrapped up in Colonial newsprint and tied with a neat string bow, like the souvenir parcels purchased in shops all over town.

When she closed her eyes, Roxanne found herself back on Duke of Gloucester Street, holding Nick Winfield's lifeless body, watching the cold expression on Dave Dunwoody's face.

Had Dunwoody really gone to Richmond? John Clemens had people checking on Dave's business appointments over there this morning, but she was sure they'd hold up.

The back door of Botsforth Tavern had been left unlocked by a careless room maid, but nobody could have counted on that. Much more significant, the Dunwoodys' double-hung windows on the back porch were found unlocked and slightly open.

Coincidence? Yeah, right.

So, look at how it might work.

Dave finishes up in Richmond, speeds back to Williamsburg, and alters his appearance. A touristy hat and nice L.L. Bean jacket would do the trick neatly, render him all but invisible. Then when there are no witnesses, he could slip in that window he left open earlier. Finding the back door open would be an unexpected bonus.

Once in the bedroom, it wouldn't take more than a minute or two to bash Barbara's sleeping head and body, which Roxanne was certain the pathologist would find loaded with some kind of barbiturate. Then Dave could simply slip back out again and drive around town long enough to ditch the tourist costume in a Dumpster somewhere before returning to Botsforth Tavern.

Making a *very* visible entrance. An entrance that was clearly on record.

It would require nerve, but there seemed to be no shortage of nerve in the man who had taken out Nick Winfield in front of a hundred witnesses this afternoon.

❦ CHAPTER SEVENTEEN ❦

EDNA STANTON tapped lightly on Mignon Chesterton's door inside the Williamsburg Inn. At this rate, Edna reflected grimly, they'd all end up either dead or at the Inn.

She had reached the room after making several wrong turns down the Inn's long corridors. The woodwork was all painted an atrocious battleship gray, as if the Inn had attempted to economize by picking up a few surplus truckloads of paint from some nearby navy shipyard, following the mothballing of the *Missouri*.

Edna felt *summoned*. Mignon had rung her room not twenty minutes ago, asking if she might possibly be able to come by for a moment. Mignon was one of those women so accustomed to getting her own way that probably nobody ever questioned her.

Certainly Edna hadn't.

It was barely 6:30 A.M., an hour that suited both women. Edna and Mignon had shared a long chat, way back on the first night at the Nicholson Plantation. Hard to believe that was less than a week ago. And sitting in that lush and lovely garden watching the sun glide gently behind a stand of towering pines, the two women had agreed that—lovely though this particular afternoon was—sunrises in general were vastly superior to sunsets. They had also discovered a certain shared regret: neither of their late husbands had ever properly appreciated the cool calm beneficence of the day's earliest hours.

Mignon had not apologized for calling so early. She'd known that Edna would be awake.

Edna tapped again. "Mignon? It's Edna Stanton," she called softly. What if she had the room number wrong?

This time she heard a rustling inside the room.

"Edna?" Mignon sounded very tentative. "Is that you?"

"Yes."

"Are you alone?"

"Yes."

The door opened cautiously. Mignon Chesterton wore a severe navy dress, stockings, and proper low-heeled dress shoes. Despite her obvious effort to present an appropriate public face, her hair was slightly askew and her face looked ravaged. She hurriedly closed the door behind Edna.

"Thank you for coming," Mignon said simply.

Edna glanced around the room with a fleeting sense of envy. It was a dozen times the size of her own cubicle back at Botsforth Tavern. This room was spacious and magnificently furnished, in spanking-fresh period reproductions. None of the charmingly battered antiques featured at the Tavern were in evidence here. And the floral arrangement by the window was massive. Appropriately funereal, actually, though that probably hadn't been the intent.

A tea tray was set up on a table beside the window. Mignon gestured toward the table, then briefly looked into an adjoining room and carefully closed the door. Then she crossed to the table, took a seat, and without asking, poured two cups of tea.

Edna settled tentatively into the chair beside her hostess. She had never been very good at comforting, not even her own children when they scraped their knees and knocked their noggins. For the thousandth time in her life, she longed to be the sort of person who could unselfconsciously sweep a suffering child or friend into her arms. Even Harriet, snippy curmudgeon though she might be, managed to provide adequate solace on necessary occasions. Though perhaps that was just another aspect of Harriet's perfectionism.

Edna had practiced a statement of condolence on the short walk from Botsforth Tavern to the Inn, but now that she was here, the words eluded her. "I'm so terribly sorry," she began tentatively. "I don't know exactly what to say.... Barbara was such a lovely woman."

Mignon Chesterton stared out the window onto the early-morning golf course, lightly shrouded in mist. "That she was," she agreed quietly, her accent thick and rich. "She was always lovely. A pretty baby, an exquisite little girl, a beautiful young woman. So many girls have a gawky stage, you know. Barbara never did. She was always just...perfect."

Edna personally felt she had never exited her own gawky stage. Unsure what to do or say next, she busied herself with her teacup. Southerners were notoriously indirect, and Edna had noticed that Mignon often took a long time to get around to what she really wanted to say. This might take a while. Or, as Mignon would say, a "good long while." Edna could feel her stomach on the verge of a rumble.

Mignon sighed. "I've scarcely slept," she went on. "After Monica came back from the police station, I was frankly at a loss for what to do with her. I had some supper sent up, but neither of us had any appetite. Monica refused to speak to her father when he came back, so he left. Monica remained fairly distraught, but finally the poor child fell asleep."

This was a moment that Edna had been dreading. Yes, Monica had lost her mother and her young man in the space of a single hour, a shattering and overwhelming loss. Nevertheless, the "poor child" had apparently been *directly* responsible for one of the most unsettling and humiliating episodes of Edna's entire life.

Fortunately, Mignon had not forgotten. She was not the type who would forget, of course.

Anything.

"I must apologize, and beg your forgiveness for Monica's role in your dreadful experience the other morning." Only now did Mignon turn to meet Edna's steady gaze. "Of course there is no excuse for what she did, but I do hope that you can some-day find it in your heart to forgive her."

"It doesn't matter," Edna answered, somewhat shortly. It did, of course, and she was uncertain where she stood on the forgiveness issue at the moment. Unready, at the very least.

"Oh, it matters," Mignon went on smoothly. "Youth is no excuse. But that isn't why I asked you to visit me this morning. You strike me as a woman of great common sense, Edna. I feel suddenly very alone here, and I was hoping I might share with you the dilemma that kept me awake when I would have much preferred to sleep. There are expressions that cover the situation I find myself in. Things like 'let sleeping dogs lie' and 'leave well enough alone.' And yet…" Her voice trailed off uncertainly.

"Sometimes doing nothing can mean doing something very wrong," Edna suggested quietly.

Mignon nodded. "I knew that you would understand."

Edna listened intently as Mignon spoke, hesitantly at first and then with increasing conviction and strength. Edna nodded and murmured at appropriate intervals. Occasionally she asked a brief question. When the story was finished, she looked directly at the woman across from her.

"You need to tell all this to the police," Edna said firmly.

Mignon Chesterton sighed. "I was afraid that was what you would tell me. And you're right, of course. I just felt so alone, so *exposed*, somehow. I know I have no right to make such a request, but…could I possibly impose on you to make the call for me? And Edna, would you ask Roxanne to join us as well? This is quite difficult, and I believe I might feel more comfortable with her present."

❦

Roxanne stole a sideways look at John Clemens as she matched his stride on the carpeted hallway to Mrs. Chesterton's suite. Maybe they could move Heather and Evelyn Tichener up here and rename it the Irish Eyes Memorial Refugee Wing.

She had a sense that things were moving now, that there was a chance. By now, Sam Nash, the Williamsburg PD evidence tech, was on his way to Richmond with Nick Winfield's electronic datebook. Maybe they'd get lucky.

But first there was this bizarre call to see Mignon Chesterton. Placed by, of all people, Edna Stanton. Things were getting curiouser and curiouser.

John Clemens was beginning to show the physical toll of the last couple of days. This was the second night in a row that Clemens had been up most of the night—courtesy of Irish Eyes Travel, y'all come back real soon—and the lack of sleep showed. His grooming was fine, except for a smudge on his collar, but his eyes were tired and slightly puffy. He seemed spacy and jumpy, too, the inevitable result of too much coffee over too long a time.

Clemens knocked on Mignon Chesterton's door, which was opened a moment later by Edna Stanton. Mrs. Chesterton sat across the room beside the window, and as they entered and exchanged subdued greetings with the two women, Roxanne could feel tension radiating from the Southern matriarch.

At the same time, Roxanne herself felt a distinct adrenaline surge. Whatever Mignon had on her mind was clearly important to the older woman.

Roxanne quickly brought two more chairs over to the window. A brief awkward moment followed as Edna offered Roxanne the chair she'd been using. Roxanne took it without hesitation. That particular chair offered the best direct view of Mignon's face in the early-morning sunlight.

When they were all finally settled, Roxanne smiled sympathetically at Mrs. Chesterton. "This has all been terribly difficult, I know," she said, "and we appreciate your asking us to come by." She glanced at Edna, who gazed at Mignon with a sort of sorrowful compassion. "I understood from Edna's call that you have something you'd like to share with Detective Clemens."

Mignon Chesterton looked from Roxanne to John Clemens and back. "This is nothing that I would *desire* to share with anyone," she began, and Roxanne marveled that she maintained her imperious, matriarchal tone even now. "However, I feel there is no alternative. Detective Clemens, can you tell me precisely what criminal charges have been lodged against my nephew-in-law, David Dunwoody?"

Roxanne caught a fleeting flicker in Clemens's eyes, before he turned all polite business. "Ma'am, at the moment I'm not aware that the district attorney intends to bring any charges whatsoever against Mr. Dunwoody. He has been released, as you know." Clemens did a good job of keeping his tone level and cordial.

"What explanation does he offer for having shot this unfortunate young man?" Mignon asked.

Roxanne watched Clemens out of the corner of her eye. This would be entirely his call. There was no obligation to tell this woman anything.

"He claims to have shot Nicholas Winfield to protect Roxanne from grave personal danger, Mrs. Chesterton," Clemens answered. "He was unaware that she had police training and could take care of herself. He told us that Mr. Winfield had threatened him on numerous past occasions, most recently a week before this tour began, in the parking lot outside his California office."

Mignon Chesterton frowned. "Did he mention meeting up with the Winfield boy on this trip?"

Roxanne felt a tremor of excitement and she carefully smoothed her cop face to composed neutrality. The old lady was leading up to something, no doubt about it. The atmosphere in the room seemed to be building an almost electrical charge.

John Clemens shook his head. "No, ma'am. Mr. Dunwoody indicated that he hadn't seen Mr. Winfield since a week before the trip, the episode I just mentioned in California."

"I see." Mignon Chesterton closed her eyes for a moment. When she opened them, she looked directly at the detective. "I find myself in a fairly untenable position, young man. My niece Barbara, whom I loved dearly, is dead. My niece's husband has killed the boy who apparently murdered Barbara. As dreadful as all of this is, it is a tidy solution to an ugly and scandalous situation."

John Clemens listened sympathetically, nodding with genuine understanding. Clemens was a Southerner. He understood the social dynamics of scandal.

Mignon continued. "I take no particular pride in saying that

I have never been terribly taken with Dave Dunwoody, dating all the way back to the very first time that Barbara brought him home. But he's provided well for her, and Monica, and of course they live quite far away." She offered a tentative smile. "Absence has never made my heart grow much fonder of Dave, I'm afraid. But I'm tiptoeing around this, and I shouldn't. You say that Dave told you that he hadn't seen Nick Winfield in Virginia." She paused and took a deep breath. "I know that to be untrue."

John Clemens murmured, "I see."

Mignon Chesterton closed her eyes as she delivered the next sentence, the one she knew would cause all hell to break loose. "I saw Dave Dunwoody talking to Nick Winfield in the lobby of the Harrison Hotel in Richmond."

Oooh. Roxanne liked the sound of this.

"Are you certain?" John Clemens asked very quietly.

"Absolutely. My hearing perhaps is not what it used to be, but my eyesight remains excellent. Of course, I had never seen Nick Winfield before that and I didn't have any idea who he was at the time. I was aware of an uproar surrounding a young man's relationship with Monica, but the family lives an entire continent away, and under the circumstances, nobody was sending me any photographs."

"So the first time you saw Nick Winfield was in the lobby of the Harrison Hotel in Richmond?"

She nodded grimly. "Yes. And there was something...I hesitate to describe it as *furtive*, precisely, but...let me just explain what happened. Perhaps that would be easiest. I had gone down to the lobby to get a magazine at that little shop they had." She turned to Roxanne, seeking confirmation. "Do you recall the hotel gift shop near the entrance to the cocktail lounge and restaurant?"

Roxanne nodded. "I do indeed."

"I was in the shop selecting a magazine when I saw Dave come out of the men's room next to the cocktail lounge. He was deep in conversation with a young man and seemed rather annoyed with the fellow. Which wouldn't have made any impression on me, I suppose, except that Dave looked around rather nervously when they entered the lobby. He is not a man given to anxiety, and I found his behavior rather puzzling. It was almost as if he were fearful of being seen with this young man, though of course I couldn't imagine why."

"Did you speak to him?" John Clemens wondered.

Mignon shook her head. "No. I was well aware that Dave was meeting us in Richmond, but I hadn't seen him yet, and to be perfectly honest, I'd been enjoying the time alone with just Barbara and Monica. In any event, I sensed that he wouldn't want me to bother him at that time." She looked over at Roxanne. "You know how men can be when they're all involved in some kind of business thing. So I let him go his own way and shortly afterward, I went back upstairs. That night when we all met for dinner, Dave was terribly incensed about the dog mess Monica had found in her suitcase. And then later that night there was the nonsense with those dreadful phone calls. What with one thing and another, I never did mention to Dave that I'd seen him."

Roxanne nodded thoughtfully, gently. She felt like turning a fast cartwheel. "You had an absolutely clear view of both of them?"

"Oh my, yes. There was excellent lighting in that lobby. And if either of them had happened to glance my way, of course they would have seen me, too."

"But they didn't?" Roxanne asked.

"No, dear, and to be honest, I forgot all about the episode. Until I saw you holding that same boy out on Duke of Gloucester Street, with blood all over the both of you, yesterday afternoon."

Roxanne frowned. "I don't remember seeing you on the street, Mrs. Chesterton."

"Oh no, dear, I wasn't. I was inside when the shots were fired, but my room fronted on Duke of Gloucester Street and I looked out my window immediately afterward. You were holding the boy and I could see his face clearly. As for Dave, I could see him even more clearly." Her tone turned as tart as an unripe grapefruit. "He was just outside my window and he didn't seem the least bit upset. I had the distinct impression he was gloating."

"It sounds to me," Roxanne said carefully, "as if you think that Dave *intended* to kill Nick Winfield."

"I suppose I do, at that," Mignon answered slowly. "It's a fairly dreadful accusation to make, I know."

"Murder is fairly dreadful, Mrs. Chesterton," John Clemens interjected mildly. "And please forgive me, ma'am, but I don't really know any delicate way to ask this next question. Were your niece and her husband happy in their marriage?"

"I had believed them to be," she said slowly. "I saw them usually once or twice a year, less often since my sister passed away. In my presence, Dave has always been very solicitous to Barbara. But Barbara seemed worried this last week, Mr. Clemens. The second night in Charlottesville at Nicholson Plantation, she drank rather a lot of wine with dinner. She began unburdening herself to me. It was fairly awkward. Barbara said that Dave seemed to be having a lot of business problems lately, and had asked to use some of her holdings as collateral for business loans. She was very uncertain about that request."

"Your niece had money independent of her husband?" Clemens asked.

Mignon Chesterton fidgeted almost imperceptibly. How she must be hating this! "The money was *all* Barbara's before they married. Dave is extremely industrious, but he comes from a very poor background. He is a self-made man, which of course is very commendable. You'll have to forgive me for having trouble with this. I was raised never to discuss finance in any regard."

"I do understand that, and again I apologize," Clemens apologized. "Did Barbara tell you specifically that she was unwilling to put up her—what was it? Property? Stocks?"

"Both," Mignon Chesterton answered shortly. "As well as some more liquid holdings."

Which sounded like cold hard cash to fiscally unsophisticated Roxanne.

"And she was unwilling to support him in that way?" Clemens asked.

"She said she felt pressured, and that she believed her parents would not have approved." The tone grew imperious again. "About that she was absolutely correct."

"And this was money that Barbara controlled?"

Mignon nodded. "I hadn't discussed this with Barbara for some time, but I do know that she had a sizable inheritance from my father—her grandfather—and that when my sister passed away two years ago, she left everything to Barbara, her only child. My sister was the widow of a very successful businessman, and her estate was significant."

"Had Barbara supported her husband financially before?" Clemens kept his tone warmly conversational. They might have been discussing the day's activities at the Williamsburg Inn: lawn bowling, a round of golf, nature hiking on the Bassett Trace Trail, a spot of premeditated murder.

"Barbara told me that she thought Dave was in serious financial trouble," Mignon went on. Having taken the plunge, she was becoming slightly more at ease with what she clearly regarded as a family betrayal. She did, however, keep her eyes trained mostly on the arthritic hands clenched in her lap. "Barbara said it was more than what she called his 'usual two-step with the IRS,' though apparently *they* were after him for something as well. She told me that Dave had seemed worried for months."

Roxanne thought back over her admittedly limited contacts with Dave Dunwoody. He had not, on any occasion, projected an image of anxiety. Indeed, he had seemed spectacularly sure of himself, a controlling jerk when he wanted his own way but otherwise a cheerful and gregarious guy who made a point of being particularly charming to his wife.

"Did Dave strike *you* as seeming worried, Mrs. Chesterton?" Clemens asked.

"Not at all," she answered immediately. "Although of course, he was irritated by the odd things that kept happening to this tour, the phone calls in Richmond and that wretched business with the dog excrement. Overall, though, I'd have to say he seemed happy as a clam. God's own cheerful gift to us all."

Ouch. Roxanne would not want to get on this woman's bad side.

"Will he inherit from Barbara?" John Clemens wondered mildly.

"Handsomely," Mignon sniffed. "And at a time when he particularly needs money."

Roxanne glanced at John Clemens, who gave her an imperceptible nod. She took over. "This entire trip," she began, "has been plagued by what initially seemed to be relatively harmless pranks. Monica claims that it was Nick who engineered most of those pranks, with the intention of cutting the trip short."

Mignon was listening intently, sitting utterly still.

Roxanne went on carefully. "That didn't happen. But those pranks laid the groundwork for killing Barbara in a way that suggested another prank gone awry. What happened to Barbara *would*—at least at first glance, and maybe forever if the killer got lucky—appear to be a related prank."

Mignon Chesterton nodded, almost imperceptibly.

"We all had those shelf lights over our beds at the Tavern," Roxanne went on, "except the folks with double beds, and that was just the Vanguards and the Forresters and the Flanagans. You had shelf lights in your own room, I know. Now. If one of those shelves toppled down for any reason, well, it undoubtedly would startle and probably also hurt anybody who happened to be in the bed at the time. But it wouldn't be likely to cause a fatal injury. So under *those* circumstances, it might still be regarded as a prank."

Roxanne leaned toward the elderly woman. "What's so disturbing to me, Mrs. Chesterton, is the iron ball, which she bought the day before she died. Because regardless of how the shelf light came off the wall, nobody remembers seeing Barbara put that ball up there. And why *would* she? She lives in California. That's earthquake country. I recently moved to southern California, and one of the first things I learned is that you *never* put anything heavy over your bed. Nothing that could fall and injure you in an earthquake.

"Barbara had lived in California for years, long enough so that it would be automatic, instinctive probably, not to put anything heavy over her bed. And a little narrow shelf above your pillow is a ridiculous place to store something heavy that *rolls!*"

"Are you saying that Barbara's death was not an accident?" Mignon Chesterton asked carefully.

"Definitely not. She was murdered in her sleep. We know that from the nature of her injuries."

"By Monica's young man?"

Roxanne cocked her head. "If, as Monica says, Nick was the instigator of the pranks, then that would be a distinct possibility. But there isn't any obvious motive that we know of, and Monica is adamant that Nick told her he had nothing to do with Barbara's death. Furthermore, Nick headed straight for Botsforth Tavern when I tried to apprehend him. Why would he go there, of all places, if he were responsible for the murder?"

"Monica's parents had forbidden her to see him," Mignon noted quietly.

"True enough," Roxanne agreed. "But Monica and Nick obviously managed to get around that with no trouble at all." She shook her head. "There are a hundred other directions Nick could have gone in, and he knew his way around town. He also knew exactly where Botsforth Tavern was, because he'd been inside the place at least once, putting leeches in Edna's bathroom."

Edna wiggled uncomfortably and Mignon shot her a quick glance.

"You're certain he was heading to the Tavern?" Mignon asked.

"Well, we can't very well ask him now, can we? And I find it fascinating that immediately after he denied being involved in Barbara's death, to Monica, he made a beeline for the place where she had died. A place that was *certain* to be crawling with cops. Why did he come?" Roxanne paused a moment, watched Mignon Chesterton reflect. "Perhaps he was coming here to set something straight. Or to set *somebody* straight."

"The only other person he knew was Dave," Mignon said.

"That's right," Roxanne agreed. "Dave, who shot him as he arrived, before Nick had a chance to say a word to anyone about anything. Dave, who told us—contrary to what you saw in Richmond—that he had no idea Nick Winfield was even in the state of Virginia."

At this Mignon frowned. "Are you suggesting that Dave Dunwoody instructed that boy to kill Barbara?"

"It's a possibility," Roxanne answered, "but it's a possibility that I personally consider pretty remote. We don't know of any reason that Dave would have sufficient power over Nick Winfield to tell him to kill somebody."

Which didn't mean there *wasn't* some reason, God knows, and it could be as simple as cash. John Clemens had people on both coasts checking for a possible money trail right now. Nick Winfield wouldn't be a sophisticated financial whiz who'd use a windfall to diversify his investment portfolio. He'd either stick it in his checking account or put it under his mattress.

Or up his nose, but somebody would know about that. It would also show up in an autopsy tox screen.

"Then what you're saying is even worse, isn't it?" Mrs. Chesterton noted.

"I'm afraid so." Roxanne spoke slowly now. How far could she push this woman? "Mrs. Chesterton, Dave Dunwoody may very well have killed your niece himself."

"You really believe there's a possibility that Dave killed Barbara?" Mignon spoke haltingly, as if in pain.

"I'm very much afraid that may be true, Mrs. Chesterton," Roxanne answered. "We'll never be able to talk to Nick Winfield about what he did or didn't do. Just when it looked like we were about to have that opportunity, Dave Dunwoody shot him stone-cold dead."

"The young man did have a criminal record," Mignon pointed out, an edge of desperation in her tone.

"True enough," Roxanne agreed. "Nick had served some time in the California Youth Authority. But his crimes were never violent ones. He was a burglar, a sneak thief. He broke into places, picked locks and stole things. Which doesn't mean that he wasn't *capable* of violence or murder, certainly, but it makes him a less obvious suspect."

"Monica doesn't believe that he killed Barbara," Mignon noted.

John Clemens leaned forward slightly now, and Roxanne eased back. Damn, she realized, this was actually *fun*—being partnered with somebody again, reading the other person, taking cues. Acting, in short, like a cop.

"Mrs. Chesterton," Clemens asked, "you seem to be aware of your niece's financial situation to some extent. Do you happen to know if Monica will inherit anything from her mother?"

Mignon frowned and shook her head, as if to change mental directions. "Yes, from her mother and also through a family trust that will pass to Barbara's offspring, which is only Monica. Are you suggesting that *Monica* killed her mother? Because I really must say that—"

John Clemens held up a placating hand. "On the contrary, ma'am, I'm suggesting that Monica herself may be in danger."

Mignon Chesterton gasped and clasped a hand to her throat.

"That as of the moment," Clemens went on, "we can't charge Dave Dunwoody with anything. Certainly it was irresponsible to discharge a firearm in that environment, but he claims that Roxanne's life was in danger and that Nick Winfield had threatened him personally. What concerns me greatly right now is that if Dave Dunwoody deliberately murdered his wife and was clever enough to set up Nick Winfield, he may not be finished yet. Your great-niece Monica may be going back to California with a man who has already killed twice in cold blood."

"Monica? Dave would never hurt *Monica*. He dotes on

Monica, always has." Mignon's face blanched beneath the heavy powder. Clearly such a notion had never occurred to her.

"Monica was never rich before, Mrs. Chesterton," John Clemens said softly.

But loud enough.

❦ CHAPTER EIGHTEEN ❦

MIGNON CHESTERTON would never have believed that one day she might find herself engaged in such an outrageous cloak-and-dagger operation. For seventy-four years, her life had been clothed in propriety and dignity, as befit her station and her breeding.

And yet here she was, walking through the early-morning streets of Colonial Williamsburg toward a furtive assignation that would—if it met with success—further rend asunder the tattered remnants of her family.

Family had always been paramount to Mignon, family solidarity a given. She begged silent forgiveness of her mother, whose life had never been touched by even the breath of scandal, and she offered silent explanations to her dear sister Louise, Barbara's mother. Louise, she felt certain, would have understood. Louise's maternal instincts had been fierce and unyielding, her devotion to Barbara absolute.

Louise would want vengeance at any cost. The thought was oddly cheering. Louise would not have hesitated for a moment to undertake Mignon's mission this morning.

As she continued her reflections, Mignon moved purposefully along North England Street past the Rural Trades center, heading for the back entrance to the Governor's Palace Gardens. Edna Stanton had discovered, in her early-morning peripatetic strolls about town, that behind the Palace was a concealed but readily accessible pathway used as an employee entrance. Edna had known the Palace gardens would be deserted in the early hours, the perfect spot for an assignation. Edna had even offered to accompany her, but of course that would have defeated the entire purpose.

Mignon sighed as she entered the Palace gardens, barely conscious of the perfectly kept flower beds and geometrically trimmed hedges. There was a terrible itching on her back where that young woman from Richmond had positioned the little tape recorder, holding it in place with some sort of adhesive bandages. Making possible what would have once seemed utterly impossible.

Mignon Alberta Brownwood Chesterton was wearing a wire.

❦

Roxanne nursed a cold cup of coffee as she sat uneasily in the chilly kitchen of the Governor's Palace.

She was unnecessary here.

The electronic surveillance equipment from the state crime lab in Richmond had arrived with a couple of spectacularly competent technicians, and one of them had even been female, short-circuiting the modesty issues that might have torpedoed the entire operation.

Mignon Chesterton had proven to be far more formidable than Roxanne would ever have guessed, but it was impossible to conceive of the dowager permitting any man alive to tuck a tape recorder into her undies. In the hands of a female tech, however, she had endured the indignity with poignant silence and closed eyes.

Now Roxanne sat with Amos and Meredith, both in their early thirties and obviously accustomed to working together. They exhibited extraordinary calm, but of course they didn't have Roxanne's personal stake in this operation. It was all in a day's work for them, she supposed, wiring a septuagenarian lady and then monitoring the results.

Just as it was all in a day's work for Colonial Williamsburg Security's Max Becker, who sat sipping coffee and eating a Danish with absolute equanimity.

Why, Roxanne wondered, was she the only one who appeared to be experiencing such high-voltage adrenaline surges?

❦

John Clemens might have been a Colonial statue atop the remains of the old icehouse at the rear of the Palace gardens, so utterly still was he.

Of course, a statue would have been more prominently displayed. Clemens had arranged to have some recently cut shrubbery left atop the icehouse mound last night, the better to provide early-morning cover. Accessible by various stairways, the viewpoint was the easiest and best way to keep track of a wide range of locations until they knew just which way the old lady and her quarry would be heading.

Directly below him was the Palace maze. He hoped to Christ that the old lady wouldn't somehow let herself get talked into going into the maze.

No, he reassured himself, she wouldn't. She was one tough cookie.

❦

Dave Dunwoody had tossed and turned through the night in the hauntingly empty queen-sized bed. Something was seriously amiss here and he was not at all sure what it might be.

He had arranged yesterday to have Barbara's remains shipped to Alabama for interment in the family plot, and had spoken with the Birmingham funeral director. There was still the question of when her body would be released, but his Richmond attorney had promised to expedite matters. The sooner Dave got the hell out of Williamsburg, the better he would feel.

Monica remained distant and sullen, refusing to speak to him directly. She had sat with him and Mignon yesterday afternoon in the determinedly neutral little parlor at the Inn as he outlined his plans for funeral services in Birmingham and a simple memorial service at home in La Jolla. It would take time to regain his daughter's trust, he realized, but Dave knew she would come around. And he was a patient man.

It was Mignon who troubled him more, Mignon who had initially informed him on Monica's behalf that his daughter wanted her father nowhere near her. Dave had subsequently arranged to take his own accommodations far from the main building of the Inn, overlooking the duck pond in the east wing of Providence Hall. There was an anonymity here that he rather liked.

What he hadn't expected and couldn't understand was the call he had received from Mignon yesterday afternoon. She was brief and precise.

"Barbara spoke to me in confidence," Mignon had said, "and I am troubled by the implications of what she had to say. I must remain with Monica through the evening, but as we both know, she is rather a late riser. Therefore, I would prefer to speak with you tomorrow morning. There's a lovely garden behind the Governor's Palace. Governor Dunmore favored early-morning walks through those gardens and I discovered on one of my own morning walks that one can gain entrée from an employee parking lot on North England Street. I will be waiting for you there promptly at six A.M."

And before he could say a word, she had broken the connection.

Dave had attempted to call her back, and had been told by the hotel operator that Mrs. Chesterton was taking no calls. He had left a message, then gone directly to the Governor's Palace for a spot of reconnaissance.

Now it was almost five A.M. He swiftly dressed and slipped out of his room.

❦

A voice crackling in John Clemens's ear told him that Dave Dunwoody had left Providence Hall by car. The detective assigned to Clemens had almost missed the departure, expecting the textile importer to leave on foot. Clemens's man followed Dunwoody to an employee lot off Lafayette Street, where he nonchalantly parked, then emerged and sauntered off into the Palace gardens with easy familiarity.

The Palace gardens had been designed for elegant eighteenth-century vistas and private liaisons, not efficient twentieth-century surveillance. Even so, by the time Clemens's man had ditched his own car to follow Dunwoody inside, Clemens had sighted him.

He watched through binoculars with a combination of fascination and apprehension as Dunwoody passed through the northeastern part of the grounds and moved directly to a long tunnel-like arbor. He was dressed casually in a light gray sweatsuit and tennis shoes, with a khaki windbreaker that made it difficult to tell precisely how he might be armed. There was, however, unquestionably something heavy in the right pocket of the windbreaker.

Dunwoody had entered the Palace grounds at 5:15. Half an hour later, he remained hidden in the arbor.

Clemens opened his coffee Thermos and settled back contentedly to wait him out.

❦

In the kitchen command post, Roxanne felt her nerves jangling beyond belief. While on the department, she'd never been called on to do much in the line of surveillance and she realized now she would have been an abysmal flop at it. She had no patience.

She had followed on the radio as Dave Dunwoody drove to the Palace parking lot, and now as she listened to the mumbled comments of the man trailing him, she was glad she had insisted on coming over so early.

"Rags," they were calling Dave Dunwoody in these transmissions.

❦

"'Riches' has entered the garden."

Clemens had been following cross-town progress reports from Roddy Temple, a young detective clad in Colonial breeches who was discreetly trailing Mignon Chesterton through the streets of Williamsburg.

Everything was on schedule so far. Mrs. Chesterton had left the Williamsburg Inn promptly at 5:40 and now, at 5:55, she was walking into the gardens.

Now he could see her in the distance through the trees, a small figure with an erect spine and a brisk, firm stride that belied her years. Clemens murmured into his lapel mike and heard Max Becker's calm reply.

Maybe they'd pull this off after all.

❦

"Good morning, David." Mignon Chesterton's cultured drawl seemed to fairly boom through the Palace kitchen.

Roxanne reflexively raised a fist as the others snapped to attention, big smiles on their faces. The transmission was all they could have hoped for, wonderfully clear. "Yes!" hissed Meredith, as she fiddled with the volume control.

"Morning, Aunt Mignon." Dave Dunwoody's voice was calm and gracious. "You were right. This is a lovely place in the morning."

"I find it quite restorative," Mignon agreed.

"I was admiring the waterfowl over here on the pond," Dave said. "Do you suppose this was a natural lake?"

Mignon's laugh was brief. "It's not a lake at all. They call it the Palace Canal, but what it really is, is a fish pond and as I understand, it was rather controversial in its time."

"I can't imagine why." Dave's voice was somewhat more faint now. Had he turned away? Would they continue to have trouble hearing him?

"I believe it was considered somewhat excessive by the early Virginians," Mignon said. "At one point, Governor Spotswood actually offered to pay for its upkeep himself to ease the furor."

Don't go down there, Roxanne willed Mignon and Dave. *Stay away from the lake.* She was sure that up on the mound above the icehouse, Clemens was thinking similar thoughts.

"As you see," Mignon continued after a moment or two of silence, "there's a path all the way around it."

Dammit! They were down there.

Silence again. Roxanne didn't doubt that Mignon knew how best to play Dave Dunwoody, whom she'd known for a quarter of a century, but she wished the woman would get to it.

She also wished she knew just which way they were headed. The Palace Canal covered the entire north-south length of the Governor's Palace grounds, shaped roughly like a keyhole with the narrow end at the southern point, by the kitchen where Roxanne waited now. With luck, Dave and Mignon would

] 218 [

walk toward the kitchen, right into the warmly waiting arms of the law. But if they went in the opposite direction and Mignon got into trouble on the far end, it would be damned hard to reach her in time.

Roxanne shook herself. John Clemens was on the mound at the far end, had it covered beautifully. And as they had arrived with their subjects, she had heard Clemens re-station his other two men at appropriate locations through the garden.

"I feel somewhat uncomfortable mentioning this to you." Mignon's voice once again was clear and strong. "But Barbara spoke to me on more than one occasion before your arrival about some of her concerns over your joint finances."

Dave Dunwoody laughed softly. "She sure could be a worry-wart," he replied assuagingly. "But I can't imagine why. As you well know, Aunt Mignon, my businesses continue to do extremely well."

"That wasn't what Barbara told me. She spoke of loans you were taking out, using her holdings as collateral."

Roxanne could practically see Dunwoody's easygoing shrug. "Nothing out of the ordinary there. You don't spend your own money when there's somebody else's available. That's what business loans are all about."

"She said this was different, Dave. She was worried." There was worry in Mignon's tone, too.

Clemens's voice came through on the radio. "They're at the northernmost end of the pond. You getting anything?"

Becker pressed a button to respond. "Loud and clear," he answered.

"Outstanding," Clemens said.

Their exchange had obscured part of what Mignon and Dave were saying, though Roxanne knew it was all being caught on tape.

"...no reason for concern," Dave was saying. "Aunt Mignon, are you suggesting something that I'm not understanding here?"

"I'm not suggesting anything. But I know you lied to the police about that Winfield boy, and I can't help but wonder why."

"I told the police he was a social-climbing criminal," Dave answered. "Totally unworthy of my daughter. And that's the God's own truth."

"I mean, what you said about not knowing he was in Virginia."

"But I didn't! I was *stunned* to see him there out in front of the Tavern! But I knew he was dangerous, and he'd threatened me before. I could tell that girl guide was in serious danger and I had a sudden realization that he must have killed Barbara. Which, as we now know, turned out to be true. Perhaps I should have let him kill the girl guide, too? Would that have convinced you he was dangerous?"

Roxanne rolled her eyes and Max Becker shot her a grin, stifling a chuckle. *Girl guide*, indeed!

Becker spoke quietly into the transmitter. "Clemens? Where are they now?"

"Far side of the pond," came the answer.

Becker's grin turned to a grimace as he broke the connection. "Move faster, lady," he muttered. "Get closer to us. *Now!*"

"...at the hotel in Richmond," Mignon was saying. "It was quite apparent to me that you knew each other very well and that you were extremely unhappy with him for some reason."

"Oh, come on," Dave laughed dismissively. "I was probably talking to a bellboy."

"This young man wore no uniform," Mignon told him tartly, "and I was barely six feet away from the two of you. It was Nicholas Winfield, though I didn't know it at the time. I only made the connection later, after you shot him outside the Tavern."

Dave Dunwoody's laugh this time sounded a little nervous. "And I suppose you've been telling everybody that you saw him with me there."

"No," she replied hesitantly. "I wanted to discuss it first with you, before I see that policeman later this morning. I was certain that you would have some sort of explanation. But I was unprepared for a *denial.*" Her voice rose sharply. "Just what do you think you're..."

"I'm taking matters into my own hands." Dave Dunwoody's voice now was louder.

"He's holding her shoulders," Clemens's voice boomed.

Mignon sounded curiously unafraid. "Why, you're planning to kill me, aren't you? Just like you killed Barbara, and that boy."

"No," Dunwoody answered, "I'll kill you a different way. *You're* going to drown. I distinctly recall that you never learned how to swim, dear Aunt Mignon."

Becker and Roxanne were both on their feet, even as Clemens's voice crackled through the radio. "All units *now!*"

As they burst out the kitchen door, Roxanne could see the two figures on the far side of the pond. Becker was already racing across a painted Chinese bridge toward the other side and John Clemens was loping down the stairs from his watching post atop the icehouse.

"*Freeze!*" Clemens bellowed, echoed a moment later by Becker.

❦

Mignon watched Dave's face flush deeply and angrily as he told his terrible truths. He had pushed her off the path already, almost to the water's edge.

She was a fool to have allowed him to lead her all the way over here, she knew that now. There was no way anyone could reach her in time, not unless some policeman was hidden in a tree overhead.

She heard voices yelling, saw Roxanne on the far end of the pond. Dave had his hands on her shoulders when the shouting began, and he swung her body so quickly she didn't even realize it was happening. Now he held her from behind, with his left arm across her chest, using her as a shield.

Suddenly, across six decades, Mignon heard her mother's voice discussing an attempted assault on a distant cousin in Mobile. Mignon's mother had been both a proper lady and a practical woman. "She screamed her lungs out," Mama had reported with mingled horror and jubilation, "and she kicked him in the family jewels." Mama had exhorted her daughters to do likewise should the need ever arise.

In seventy-four years, the need had never previously arisen.

Now, out of a reservoir of strength she didn't even know she possessed, Mignon let out a mighty cry and flung her right foot backward just as high and as far and as hard as she could.

She connected with something and heard Dave grunt with astonishment even as he abruptly let go of her. Already off-balance from the backward kick, she tumbled forward into the pond.

❦

Roxanne saw Mignon fall into the water and took only a moment to determine that the shortest distance between herself and the elderly woman was a straight line directly across the Palace Canal. Without hesitation, she ripped off her sneakers and jacket and plunged into the water.

It was warm and muddy and she couldn't tell how deep it might be, but it hardly seemed to matter. Keeping her face clear as much as possible, she pulled herself forward through the water with a bastardized crawl. Barton Springs this wasn't. Fortunately Dave and Mignon had reached the narrower portion of the pond before the final confrontation.

She could see Mignon struggling in the muck at the edge of the pond. "Don't panic," she called as she neared the woman. A few more strokes ought to do it. "I'm almost there."

Whereupon Mignon Chesterton stood up in the muddy shallows, looked around herself in surprise, and toppled face-forward in a faint.

Roxanne reached her just in time to keep her face from entering the water, and by the time she had dragged the elderly woman ashore, a detective in Colonial costume was there to help her.

Mignon rapidly regained consciousness. Squatting on her haunches beside the woman, Roxanne watched with satisfaction as Max Becker handcuffed Dave Dunwoody, about ten yards farther down the path toward the kitchen.

Dave was protesting with great indignation. "What's *with* you folks? Aunt Mignon slipped and I tried to catch her. The poor dear can't swim."

The poor dear was struggling to sit up now and Roxanne decided not to fight her. Instead, she offered an arm as support.

"Did it work?" Mignon asked quietly.

"It sure did," Roxanne replied. "We got every word. You were *great.*"

Mignon looked over toward Dave. "Could they bring him a little closer?" she wondered. "I dislike shouting."

John Clemens had reached their side now and he beckoned to Max Becker, who obligingly brought the prisoner closer.

"David," Mignon began sweetly, "I neglected to mention something when we were on our walk just now. You see this little brooch here? It's a microphone. Every wretched word you said was tape-recorded."

❦ EPILOGUE ❦

ROXANNE HAD breakfast with John Clemens on the morning of her flight to San Diego. On the heels of her father's arrest, Monica had volunteered a piece of information that was absolutely unverifiable, but if true, put a new perspective on everything. Immediately before he had bolted back toward Botsforth Tavern and his own death, Monica claimed, Nick had told her that Dave Dunwoody was the real mastermind behind the tour pranks. That Dave had promised funding for the swimsuit shop and had suggested the pranks as a way to make the trip more interesting for Monica. And that Dave had visited Nick's motel room in Williamsburg, which would explain how he'd gotten hold of the screwdriver with Nick's prints. What's more, Nick's electronic calendar, decoded in Richmond, showed three appointments with "DD" in the month before the trip.

Monica and her Great-aunt Mignon had left for Alabama yesterday afternoon. Maureen and the others had been gone two days now. And now it was time for Roxanne to go home, too.

Clemens took her to the same greasy spoon where they'd eaten the morning after Heather's abduction. It was a congenial enough meal, and Roxanne sensed that had she given any encouragement whatsoever, she could begin something with the detective. *What* she wasn't sure, but...

It wasn't going to happen, though. Not now, anyway. And he seemed to realize and accept that, too.

"You're good, you know," he told her with a gentle smile.

He was looking better, more rested. Pleased by his success in so quickly clearing such a messy case. "You might want to give some thought to going back. You've got good detective instincts. Good instincts, period."

Roxanne shook her head. "Thanks. But I'm not ready."

Clemens smiled. "I've been watching you for days now. And I keep wondering, Hey, what's wrong with this picture? It thinks like a cop and talks like a cop and acts like a cop, but it's a tour director. You may not *think* you're ready now. But you are."

All the way back to California, Roxanne wondered if perhaps John Clemens had been right.

Even as she looked out the airplane window and thought about all the places she wanted to go next.

ABOUT THE AUTHOR

Taffy Cannon is the author of five previous novels, including *Convictions: A Novel of the Sixties* and three mysteries featuring attorney Nan Robinson: *A Pocketful of Karma, Tangled Roots,* and *Class Reunions Are Murder.* She has also written an Academy Award–nominated short film, *Doubletalk,* and a young adult mystery, *Mississippi Treasure Hunt.*

She has worked a multitude of odd jobs from carnival barker to professional feminist, but intends her epitaph to read: SHE NEVER WAITRESSED. She once correctly wagered everything on a Women Writers Daily Double as a *Jeopardy!* contestant.

Taffy Cannon is a Chicago native and graduate of Duke University. Since 1990, she has lived in southern California with her husband, daughter, and various highly indulged cats. She can be e-mailed at tcannon@nctimes.net.